PEYTON

PEYTON

A Western Duo

Max Brand

Skyhorse Publishing

First Skyhorse Publishing edition published 2015 by arrangement with Golden West Literary Agency

Skyhorse Publishing books may be purchased in bulk at special discounts for sales promotion, corporate gifts, fund-raising, or educational purposes. Special editions can also be created to specifications. For details, contact the Special Sales Department, Skyhorse Publishing, 307 West 36th Street, 11th Floor, New York, NY 10018 or info@skyhorsepublishing.com.

Visit our website at www.skyhorsepublishing.com.

10 9 8 7 6 5 4 3 2 1

Library of Congress Cataloging-in-Publication Data is available on file.

Cover design by Brian Peterson

Print ISBN: 978-1-62914-372-9
Ebook ISBN: 978-1-63220-089-1

Printed in the United States of America

Table of Contents

The Man from the Sky

"The Man from the Sky" is the second short story in the four-part saga of Paul Torridon. The first story, "Torridon", appeared in *Gunman's Rendezvous* (Skyhorse Publishing, 2015).

I

When Torridon wakened, the sun was not five minutes below the horizon, and he jumped from his blankets and reproached himself in silent gloom. For many days, now, he had been striving to imitate the habits of Roger Lincoln. That great hunter had observed that life on the plains was best begun with the first grayness of dawn, and best ended with the total dark. Or, he would say, a little more morning, a little more evening, made one day into two. Even the Indians might be gained upon in this manner, and as for the ordinary whites who trekked across the plains, they worked like moles, a step at a time, blindly.

But here was another day stolen almost upon Torridon before he was on his feet.

He was surprised that the fire was not burning, but, as a matter of fact, Roger Lincoln was nowhere around. The gray mare grazed close to the camp, near tall Ashur. But Roger Lincoln apparently had gone off to hunt; his rifle was missing with him.

This was not extraordinary. Between the dark and the dawn always was the best hunting, he used to observe—when the plains animals were least aware of the world, their senses yet unsharpened, and before they were aware that the sheltering blanket of the night had been withdrawn from them they might be stolen upon and dispatched.

The sun had a dazzling eye out over the plain before Torridon had finished these observations. In a moment more it was above the edge of the sky. It was time to prepare breakfast. As a matter of fact, Roger Lincoln did not like to make fires in the day; the thin arms of smoke that rose waved signals to a great distance and attracted unknown eyes.

"Everything you don't know is dangerous," Lincoln was apt to say.

Therefore, in the preparation of the fire, Torridon was extra careful. In a small patch of brush nearby he found some dead branches, and these he broke up small, and lighted and maintained the smallest of fires. He had learned from Lincoln, too, that a great flare of fire is not necessary for cookery. A small tongue of flame playing constantly right on the bottom of a pan will accomplish great results. And it is a fine art to extend gradually a bed of coals that casts off no smoke at all.

By great efforts and perfect concentration, he was assured when he had breakfast prepared that there had not been more than one or two puffs of smoke large enough to be worth noticing. The rest was a fume that hardly could have been visible two hundred yards away.

When he had finished the cookery, he sat down to wait. It might be that Lincoln had found an attractive shot, wounded the game, and been drawn far afield to track it.

So he waited a full hour, ate a cold meal, and settled himself again.

The sun was high, walking slowly through the heavens, and the heat became momently greater. The air was delicate with the scent of the May bloom of the prairie. And he began to drowse.

Since they began their long march for Fort Kendry, and had voyaged beyond the settlements into the emptiness of the plains, Lincoln had insisted on hard journeys every day, and Torridon, in consequence, had been put through a severe grilling. He had grown thinner and more brown in the open air. His muscles were taking on a tough fiber such as they never had possessed before, but nevertheless it had often been torture. He was just beginning to be inured to the labor and the constant racking in the saddle. If it had not been for the silken gaits of the great black stallion, he knew that he never could have kept up his end. But now he saw a chance to rest.

Roger Lincoln, no doubt, never would have dreamed of drowsing in the uncovered nakedness of the prairie during the day, but that was because he was almost more panther than man. And young Torridon felt that he was gathered into a deep security by the very fact that, no matter what enemy the prairie might hold, it also held Roger Lincoln. To the wisdom, the skill, the courage of that famous man he implicitly bowed.

So he fell sound asleep, with his head in the shadow of a small bush. There would be a quiet lecture from Lincoln when that hunter returned to the camp, but the joy of relaxing in the sun that drew the soreness from his muscles was more than the youngster could forego.

He wakened at last with a start, feeling that he had been hearing whispering voices. His heart was beating wildly, and he got to his knees and looked cautiously about him.

Lincoln's gray mare and Ashur still were grazing nearby; nothing stirred on the plain except the shining footprints of the wind upon the grass, now and again.

He was reassured by this sense of peace until, glancing down, he saw that his shadow lay small at his feet. The sun was straight overhead, and he had slept away the entire morning. Half a day had gone by, and there was no trace of Roger Lincoln's return.

In seven hours he could have gone afoot nearly twenty miles out and twenty miles back. But it might be that, starting back with a heavy load of newly shot game, he had stepped in a hole and wrenched an ankle. Even Roger Lincoln could not be entirely impervious to accident.

Torridon made up two packs, carefully, like a schoolboy working to please a master, for Lincoln was a shrewd and keen critic of everything that his pupil did. He knew how to make silence thunder with his displeasure.

When that work seemed fairly well done, then he mounted Ashur, and, taking the gray on the lead, he began to ride through the prairie. Lincoln had showed him how to go about such a thing, using a starting point as the center of widening circles, and so tracing a larger and a larger web, covering every inch of the ground.

For two hours he kept Ashur in brisk motion. At the end of that time he paused at the verge of a riverbed and began to arrange his thoughts. There had been no sight and there had been no sign of his companion. Though, from the back of a horse, half a dozen times he had been on low hillocks from which the plain was visible for many miles around, nothing had moved into his ken.

He freshened his grip on the heavy rifle that he had learned to balance across the pommel of his saddle, and fought back the panic that leaped up in his breast. Something had happened to Roger Lincoln! He swallowed hard when he thought what that meant.

Fort Kendry, where he hoped to find Nancy Brett, still was eight days' march away from them, Lincoln had said, and, as for its direction, he had only the slightest idea. He could see, now, that he had been following the great scout with half of his brain asleep, trusting blindly to the guidance of his companion and never trying to think out the trail problems for himself.

He was lost, then. He was totally lost.

Across his mind went grim memories of tales he had heard from Lincoln about the plains—men who wandered for weary weeks, with no game in sight, with no glimpse of a human being, until chance saved them—saved one out of a hundred who passed through such a time.

And he, Paul Torridon, ignorant totally of all that a lonely man should do, ignorant of the way to return, ignorant of the trail that lay ahead, what would become of him? Dreadful panic gripped him, shook him. He was lost!

He got down off his horse and took out paper and pencil. He wrote swiftly:

To whoever finds my body. If my gun and my horse are near, you are welcome to them. Treat the horse well. It is the best I ever have seen. Only—if you wish to ride him, don't wear spurs. They drive him mad. Whatever I have you are welcome to.

But for heaven's sake take the enclosed note to Nancy Brett, at Fort Kendry. She is living there with her cousin, Samuel Brett, and his wife.

He signed that *Paul Torridon*, and then he went on to write, more slowly:

Dear Nancy:

I write this knowing that I am hopelessly lost on the plains and that I haven't one chance in a hundred of coming out alive. This will reach you only if white men and not red find my body.

Dear Nancy, you will have heard terrible things about the way we broke out from John Brett's house. They kept me locked in the cellar for ten days. They did what they could to torment me, and on the eleventh morning they were to finish me off. That night Roger Lincoln came. He managed to slip past the guards and get to me. They surprised us as we were trying to get out. In the fight, I know that we shot down four men. I hope that all of them lived. If not,

I want you to know that we only fired because we were fighting for our lives.

Then Roger Lincoln started to take me west to Fort Kendry, because he had heard from Jack that you were to be taken there. We got to this point, then Roger disappeared one morning from the camp.

Whether some animal killed him, or Indians surprised him, I don't know. I only know that he didn't come back. If he is dead, heaven be good to him. He was the bravest and the best man in the world!

Oh, Nancy, if I had known that our ride down the valley was to be the last time that I should ever see you, I never would have left. But that chance is gone. I'd think that my life was thrown away—because I've never done anything worth living for—but I know that for one day, at least, you loved me, dearest Nan, and that is more than the world to me. And when I think of you now, it makes my heart ache more than death can do.

Beautiful, beautiful Nan,
good bye. Remember me.
Paul

When he had written this he put it away in his wallet, and then he gave himself up to sad thoughts until tears came into his eyes, and even trickled down his cheeks.

Something stirred on the inner side of the riverbank. He caught up his rifle from the ground beside him and listened, hair on end. It was a stealthy rustling, a stealing noise that seemed to his straining senses to come straight toward him.

And then, above the bank, came the proud head of a stag, and a beautiful young deer stood outlined against the sky just above him.

II

His heartbreaking sorrow he forgot with desperate speed. Here was food for a month, if only he could catch it. At the shift of his rifle to his shoulder, the deer saw him and leaped not back, but straight ahead. It was a blurred streak at which he fired. The racing animal gave three tremendous bounds, the last high in the air, and fell dead.

Torridon stood up and looked to the white-hot sky in mute thankfulness. Certainly this was a gift from heaven to him, the novice hunter.

Feverishly, paying no heed to the future, but all for the sake of the future, he worked during the rest of that day. He had been shown by Lincoln the proper way to strip off a pelt, but he rather hacked the good hide away. The meat was what he wanted, and that meat he cut into long strips. Out of the willows along the riverbed he prepared many slender sticks, and these he used to hang the venison upon.

How long would the sun take to dry the meat thoroughly?

Then night came on him as his labors neared an end. He was tired with excitement and with work. He lay down and slept like a child. Once, before morning, Ashur neighed softly, and stamped. Torridon was on his feet at once, and found the great black stallion beside him, almost trampling on him, while the pricked ears and the glistening eyes of the horse were turned toward the north. Yonder in the darkness some danger was moving—coyote, wolf, bear, Indian, renegade white. He knew that the two fine horses would be enough to enlarge the heart of any trapper with fierce greed, and, as for the Indians, Roger Lincoln had assured him that any Indian on the plains would pay all but life for the possession even of the famous gray mare, to say nothing of that matchless king of runners, Ashur.

Still lay Torridon, one ear close to the ground, his attention directed by the stallion, as Ashur veered a little, and pointed now more to the east. Yet Torridon heard nothing whatever. A long half hour—and then Ashur put down his head and began to graze once more. The danger had ended.

And Torridon, though he told himself that he could not sleep again after such a shock, was almost instantly in slumber once more. After all, there was Ashur, more keenly alive and alert, more dependable than any human sentinel.

The morning was only past him while his brain still was befogged. His first thought was: *I have lived one day in the desert, and the finish of me is not yet. No, there's the meat that will keep me alive for a long time, if I use patience.*

It was a day of burning heat. It ate through the coat of Torridon, stout homespun though it was, and fairly singed his shoulders. It covered the prairie with shimmering lines of heat as with a veil, and it wrought wonders upon the meat, as though a slow fire were playing on the wet venison.

All that day and the next Torridon watched the curing of the meat. But by that time he began to feel that the prairie, after all, was not so totally dangerous. Running down the edge of the narrow rivulet that wound back and forth through the pebbles and the boulders of the stream bottom, there seemed to be a constant procession of rabbits. He did not need to shoot them. The simplest little traps, constructed as Lincoln had showed him how to do, were sufficient to snare the jacks. Torridon lived well and watched his venison cure to strips withered and black-looking, hard as boards, but promising much nutriment. He had a pack of that food prepared before the thing was ended, and then he asked himself where he should go.

What would Roger Lincoln do if he were not dead and ever managed to escape from the troubles that now held him? It seemed obvious to Torridon. In the first place, the hunter would inquire at Fort Kendry to learn if the traveler had come. In the second place, Lincoln would go to the spot of that last camp and there strive to take up the trail.

So Torridon went back, and, where the fire had been built, he drove down a strong stake. The stake he split, and in the split he fixed firmly a bit of paper that simply said:

Dear Roger:

I've decided to go south to the first river, and then follow that river toward the right—west. I'll keep on it to its source. I don't know what else to do, and I'd go mad if I stayed here in the loneliness without a move of some kind.

Paul Torridon

He added as a postscript:

If I turn to the left from the river, I'll put two blazes on a big tree. If I turn to the right, I'll put one.

That might, eventually, be the means for bringing Roger Lincoln to the trail of him.

Then he went back to the river to the south, by the banks of which he had killed the deer and cured its venison. He turned to the right and journeyed slowly up its banks. He had no reason to journey fast; rather he dreaded leaving the stream by coming to the end of it. For a day he went up it, and then came to a fork. A mere trickle of water descended each big gorge. Apparently later in the summer the bed would be entirely dry, and only in the winter the water roared down in floods. He hesitated for a long time at that division of the trail. Both forks seemed of an equal size. Neither carried more water than the other, and as for their direction, one pointed a little northwest, the other a little south of west. There was not a whit to choose between them.

He chose the northern one, therefore, because this made it unnecessary for him to cross either of the beds of the streams.

Up the northern fork he continued for two days, and all that time he had no cause to use up his precious stock of dried venison. Rabbit meat was plentiful, and rabbit was not yet a weary diet to him.

The third day he found the stream diminishing rapidly in size. And before noon he came to another forking. Once more he paused to consider his course. At the junction of the two streams high water had carved off the point of land and left there a little triangular island, with one of two trees supported on it, a willow, and an oak, half of whose roots had been washed bare, so that the trunk sagged perceptibly to the north and seemed in danger of being carried away in the floods of the next winter.

The northern branch of the stream here swung off sharply to the right; the southern branch pointed almost due west, and this was the one that Torridon determined to take as his guide in these blind wanderings. So he rode down the steep bank of the gulley and crossed both streams above the fork.

He regarded the upstream face of the island with curiosity. It was cracked across and written upon with long indentations. The soil of which it was composed seemed falling slowly apart and waiting for only one more thrust of winter to tumble it into a complete ruin.

Drawn by his curiosity, he climbed to the top of the bank and there he clutched his rifle to his shoulder. For he saw a man dressed in the full regalia of an Indian of the warpath stretched on his side beneath the shadow of the two trees. Beside him stood a water bottle, a bow, and a sheath of arrows. His head was pillowed on a small bank of earth, apparently heaped up by him to serve for that particular purpose.

Torridon moved nearer, paused, and again examined the prostrate man with care.

There was no movement, he thought at first, and he had come to the determination that the fellow must be dead, when, observing narrowly, it seemed to Torridon that the elbow of the man moved a little. He looked again, and made sure that the Indian was only sleeping, and that the elbow was raised or lowered a trifle by his breathing.

Through this time he heard from behind him, to the north and west, a rumbling as of thunder, but thunder in the great distance, and now it seemed to Torridon that he was afraid to look behind him, as though friends of this sleeper were rushing upon him with many horses, ready to overwhelm him. This thunder was the beating of the hoofs.

It was a foolish fancy. But Torridon did not know what to do. A man armed and well dressed could not be in any great need, although it appeared that this warrior was extremely pinched of face—which might have been a mere characteristic of an unhealthy Indian. However, he was a native of the plains, and therefore he safely could be left to them.

Torridon gave up all thought of waking the sleeper or of offering him any succor. What concerned him was only to retreat as softly as possible by the way in which he had come. Yet a silent retreat would not be easy. There were sticks and stones that might stir under his foot. Once wakened, the Indian would be sure to look about for the cause of the disturbance, and Torridon, perhaps halfway down the bank, would receive a bullet in the back. Then what could he do? He had two horses to manage, now left in the little gorge, and sure to make noise as they went on over the stones and pebbles.

There was only one safe alternative, and that was to shoot the sleeper. It seemed to Torridon that, had Roger Lincoln been in a similar position, he simply would have roused the fellow with a call, allowed him to arm himself, and then have put a bullet through his brain. That was Roger Lincoln, the invincible warrior. But what of himself, the novice of the plains?

He bit his lip with vexation and trouble, and then, stepping a little to one side, he saw with amazement that the prostrate man was not asleep at all.

His eyes were wide open, and he stared before him. Far in the distance, the noise of thunder rolled swiftly upon them. And now the red man stretched a hand before him, toward the north, which was the side to which he faced, and broke into a loud chant.

Torridon felt either that he was in the presence of a madman, or that his own wits had gone wrong.

III

At the first loud words of that song, as though in answer to them, the gray mare, Comanche, and the tall, black stallion rushed up onto the narrow island, snorting with terror. Ashur, as by instinct, made straight for his master. The mare crowded at his side.

At that the voice of the prostrate Indian was raised to a higher key, and, although the words were perfectly unknown to Torridon, he could not help feeling in them terror and exultation combined. For the whole body of the Indian was now pulsing with emotion.

Now the thunder grew, and, glancing back over his shoulder, Torridon at last saw the cause of it. He saw a steep wall of water plunging down the northern branch of the river, while the southern fork remained as dry as ever, only a small trickle of water meandering through the center of the bed of sand and pebbles and boulders.

He could remember that in the many tales of Roger Lincoln there had been descriptions of just such floods as this, caused by heavy rainfall in the hills, when the heavens sometimes opened and let down the water in sheets. Sweeping into the courses, sluiced off the naked brown hills, those waters then began a headlong descent, sometimes smashing open beaver dams and adding the treasures of those waters to the original flood.

Among such phenomena this must have been a giant, for the strong gorge was crowded with the water almost to its brim.

Out of the frothing current whole trees were flung up, like the arms of a hidden giant rejoicing in his strength, and, as the wave plunged on its way, it sliced away the banks on either side, so that a continual swath of trees was toppling inward as though brought down by a pair of incredible scythes.

Whether madman or monster, the prostrate Indian was a human being. What would happen to this tottering little island when the vast wall of water struck it? Already, at the thunderous coming of the flood, the trees trembled; a fissure was opened inside the big tree that leaned out from the bank toward the north.

Torridon caught the sleeper by the naked shoulder and shook him. Under his hand he felt the flesh cold as earth, and covered with an icy damp. And though he shouted and pointed toward the rush of water, the other would not stir. He merely cast out both hands before him and began to shout his chant more loudly than ever.

And then the water struck. There was an instant visible and audible blow. It shook Torridon so that he almost fell, and the gray mare was flung to her knees. The big tree at the side of the island lurched halfway to a fall, with a sound like the tearing of strong canvas in the hands of a giant as the roots were snapped.

The whole forward point of the land was torn away, and huge arms of yellow spray leaped fifty or a hundred feet in the air. The rain of their descent drenched horse and man, and the air was filled with a sort of brownish mist so that Torridon could see only dimly what followed.

He was sure of death, but he yearned to see death coming clearly.

Then, at his very side, the whole edge of the island went down. Vast froth was boiling at his feet as he staggered back against the side of Ashur. Out of the maddening waters a tree trunk, stripped of its branches in the ceaseless mill of the tumbling flood, was shot up, javelin-wise—a ton-weight javelin—flung lightly through the air. It rose, it towered above them, and it fell with a mighty crash—upon the motionless Indian, as Torridon thought in his first horror. But then he saw that the still quivering trunk lay at the head of the red man, its dripping side mere inches away from the skull that it would have crushed like an egg.

And the wall of water was gone. Its thunder departed into the distance with the speed of a galloping horse, and, behind it, it left the gorge with a rushing current. The air cleared from the mist. In those currents Torridon could see boulders spinning near the surface like corks. He was more amazed and bewildered by the force in that aftercurrent than he had been by the face and forefront of the flood.

Yet that storm of water decreased with wonderful rapidity. In a few moments the gorge was hardly ankle-deep with a sliding, bubbling stream, and the wet, raw edges of the ravine dripped into the currents.

Then Torridon could look around him, and he saw that they stood on a little platform barely large enough to accommodate the two humans and the two horses. In the very center stood one thick-trunked tree, and doubtless its ancient roots, reaching far down, had been the one anchor that the moving waters had been unable to wrench away. Otherwise, man and horse must have gone down like straws in that dreadful mill.

The Indian now rose, though with great effort. He staggered, and had to lean a shoulder against the trunk of the tree. Then he threw up both his hands and burst into a chant louder than any he had uttered before. He seemed to be half mad with joy. Sometimes in the midst of his strange singing, laughter swelled in his throat. Tears of extreme joy shone in his eyes.

Torridon would have put the fellow down as a hopeless madman, but something in that ecstatic voice and in the raised head told him that the warrior was speaking to his creator. It was like a war song of triumph, it was also like a great prayer and a thanksgiving.

As for the meaning, Torridon had no clue, but he waited, determined to be wary and cautious.

Never take your eyes from a hostile, night or day, Roger Lincoln had said. *He'll count coup on you while you're asleep, and take a scalp, even if he can't get a hundred yards away before vengeance overtakes him.*

When the song of the Indian ended, it seemed as though life had ended in him, also. He slid down the trunk of the tree until he lay crumpled at its base. His eyes were open and glaring; there was a faint froth on his lips. Torridon assured himself that the fellow was dead. But when he felt above the heart of the red man, he was aware of a faint pulsation, feeble, and very rapid and uneven. The body that had been so clammy to the touch was now burning with feverish heat. He was not dead, but he was very sick.

Torridon looked from their crumbling island across the long leagues of prairie that stretched on either side of the trees fringing the watercourse.

The temptation was plain in him to be away from this place and turn his back on the sick man. He knew nothing about such matters, but even a child could have told that, left unassisted, the other would die before the sun went down.

Then strong conscience took hold on Torridon. He set his teeth and looked about him, determined to fight off that death if he could. If he had been but six months on the plains, he might have had another viewpoint, filled with the prejudices of the trappers and hunters of the frontier, but to him now this was simply a human being with skin that was not white.

First of all he must get the man from the island, and that would not be easy. Then for a safer place to which to take him.

He went down to explore, the stallion and the mare slipping and stumbling after him down the sheer side of the bluff. From the bed of the stream he turned up the southern fork, and he had not gone a hundred yards before he discovered what he wanted—an opening among big trees on its bank, with a promise of present shelter.

He returned to the island, the two horses following close at his heels. The terror through which they had passed was still upon them. No doubt they felt that only the mysterious wisdom of the human had saved them from being caught into the whirl of the waters. Now they crowded at the heels of their protector. He had to wave them back as he climbed up the slope again.

He found the red man totally unconscious now. It was a limp body that he took into his arms and half carried, half dragged to the verge of the descent. There followed Herculean labor, getting his burden down to the level, but once there the task was much easier. He managed to fold the Indian like a half-filled sack over the back of the mare, because she was lower, and because Ashur no doubt would have bucked off such a burden as often as it was entrusted to him.

But Comanche went cheerfully along under this burden, and she climbed the bank of the southern fork and so brought the sick man to a new home.

The Indian had recovered a little from his trance. The violent jarring and hauling that he had received started him raving. And as Torridon lifted him from the back of the mare, the red man uttered a howl like the bay of a hunting wolf. Torridon almost let his burden fall as he heard that dreadful cry, but afterward the other lay still on the grass, muttering rapidly, his eyes closed or rolling wildly when they opened.

First of all he was dragged onto a blanket. Then with all the haste he could, Torridon prepared a bed of branches, made deep and soft as springs, and covered the top with soft sprigs of green. On this he heaved the Indian with difficulty, for the man was of a big frame, although greatly wasted.

Then there was a shelter to be erected. Torridon had seen enough woodcraft to know something about how it should be built. He had with him a strong hatchet. Rather, it was a broad axe-head, set upon a short haft, and with this he soon felled a number of saplings. The bed he had built close to the trunk of a big and spreading tree. He found a great fallen branch, dead for so long that it was greatly lightened in weight, but still tough and strong. Some fallen limbs rot at once; in others the wood is merely cured. It was all he could do to work the branch near the chosen spot and then to raise its lighter end and lodge it in the fork of the sheltering tree.

This branch now became his ridgepole. Against it he laid the saplings, and in a surprisingly short time he had a comparatively secure shelter. Afterward, when he had more leisure, he could complete the structure with some sort of thatching. In the meantime he had a place that would shield the sick man from the night air.

It was dark when all this had been done, yet he worked on, taking off the packs, arranging the contents within the tent house, and then preparing food.

For his own part, he was ravenously hungry, but when he made a broth of the jerked venison and offered it at the lips of the sick man, the latter clenched his teeth and refused all sustenance. Torridon heaved a cruel sigh of relief. It might be that he would be freed from his captivity by the immediate death of the red man.

IV

That early hope was not fulfilled. For three days the Indian raved and raged and muttered day and night. For a week after that his fever was still high. And then it left him.

If left him a helpless wreck, a ghost of a man. His belly clove against his spine. Deep purple hollows lay between the ribs. His face was shrunken mortally. With his sunken eyes and his great arch of a nose and his projecting chin he looked like a cartoon of a predatory monster. But his wits had returned to him. He lay on the bed and rolled his eyes toward Torridon, and there was, for the first time, sense and life in that glance.

Torridon was enormously cheered. He fell to work with all his might to complete the task that he had pushed forward so far and so well. He had arranged small snares. Each day, out of them he took rabbits and small birds, and he cooked little broths and then stronger stews, and the red man ate and gained slowly in strength.

Torridon knew something about the care of fever patients. At least that they must be fed only a little at a time. Certainly he overdid caution and delayed the recovery of the red man's strength, but every step forward was a sure step, and never once did the convalescent beg for more food, even when there was a raging fire of hunger in his eyes.

Weeks passed before he could sit up; a long time before he could stand; many days before he could walk; many more before he could ride.

But that was not an empty time for either of them.

He who is raised with a book in his hand comes to need mental occupation as much as he needs food. As for the hunting, it was easily done. Much game followed the course of the stream, up and down. The work around the camp was small, likewise, and, when the brain of the sick man cleared, Torridon spent the remainder of each day with him. And since talk was impossible until he had mastered the language, he set about the study of it.

Never did student make such progress. He himself had been a schoolteacher for four years, cudgeling information into the dull heads of the Bretts. Now he had himself for a pupil and he drove himself remorselessly. He wrote down every word that he heard and memorized it, going patiently over and over the list. There were many sounds that were hard to duplicate with the alphabet. For those sounds he invented symbols. And as he progressed in his talk, he still kept paper at hand and jotted down the corrections that the convalescent red man made.

And, before long, talk could flow freely between them, particularly since, in their conversation, the red man did most of the speaking. For he had much to say, and furthermore he knew how to say it.

His name was Standing Bull. He was a Cheyenne warrior. In the lodge at home he had two wives and three children. He was young, and he was rising in his tribe, and then trouble came to him. He explained it to Torridon as follows.

Eleven times he had been on the warpath. On these excursions he had been very successful. He had brought back many horses, forty or fifty, according to varying counts, for the narrator seemingly allowed himself some latitude. But, more than horses, he had taken three scalps, and he had counted no fewer than eight coups. Of this he was enormously proud.

"What is a coup?" asked Torridon, very curious.

"A child with a gun may take the life of a strong warrior from a distance," said the Cheyenne, "or a child with a bow may shoot from the darkness and kill a chief. But when a coup is counted it is different. I charge in a battle. I see an enemy. I have a charge in my rifle, but I do not shoot. No, instead of that I keep the bullet in my gun. I rush my enemy. He fires at me. I stoop and the bullet flies over my head. He snatches out a knife. I swerve away from it, and, reaching from my horse, I touch him with my coup stick. It is greater than the killing or the scalping of him."

"But why?" persisted Torridon. "If you kill him, then there is one less enemy for you and your people. That is a great advantage. You may say that it proves you are a greater warrior than the other man."

"That is true." The Cheyenne smiled. "The white men are wise and do clever things. They do many things that the Indian cannot do. The Indian cannot make guns, for instance. Well, still Heammawihio gives the red man some gifts that he does not give to the white man. He gives him understanding of many things.

That is only right and fair. You would not want the white man to have all the understanding, White Thunder?"

That was the name he had given to Torridon, because, apparently, he had come into the life of the Cheyenne with a white face, and on the wings of the thundering rush of water that so nearly carried them all into another life.

"No," agreed Torridon. "Of course the Indians have understanding."

"And the most important thing of all is the counting of coups."

"How can that be?" said Torridon, amazed.

"Look," said the warrior. "What is the greatest thing you wish to have?"

Torridon thought only a moment. "A good woman," he said.

It was the time when the Cheyenne was halfway toward his natural strength. He could raise himself on his elbows in order to look his companion straight in the face.

When he made sure that Torridon was not jesting, he lay down again with a murmur that was half a grunt.

"Women," he said at last, "can be bought for horses, or for beads. Women are very good," he added hastily, for he always showed the greatest tact in saving the feelings of the white man, "because they cook and keep the lodge clean and fresh, they flesh hides and cure them, they make clothes, and, above all, they may bear man children. But, nevertheless, there are other things that you white men want. What are they?"

"We want money, I suppose," said Torridon, who found it rather difficult to look at life in such a naked fashion. When he looked inward, he hardly knew what would evolve from the mist.

"Money, money," said the Cheyenne almost harshly. "Well, you want women for wives, and you want money. What else?"

"To do something important."

"Like what?" said the warrior.

"Like...well, building a great house, say. Or making beautiful pictures."

Standing Bull was hardly able to suppress his scorn. "A great lodge," he said, "is very well. It is good for little children and for women, and for old men, of course. But for young braves there is no need of a better lodge than this."

Torridon thought at first that the other meant the wretched shelter in which he then lay. The leaves of the branches had withered now, and with the passage of every wind there was a sad hushing from the crumbling house of leaves. But then Torridon understood that the gesture of the Cheyenne indicated things beyond—the wide blue dome of the sky—it was the evening of the day—and the dim mountains and pillars of cloud beneath it.

He had no answer to this remark. It was hardly possible that he could explain the beauty of architecture to the red man.

"As for paintings," went on the Indian, "it is true that they are good, too, on a lodge. A wise painter lets the spirits know that they are reverenced. Also, the colors are pleasant to the eye. But though paintings are sacred and pleasant, I never have seen a painted buffalo that looked as much like a real buffalo as this withered branch looks like a whole strong tree planted in the ground."

"There are other kinds of painting," suggested Torridon.

The Cheyenne overrode this suggestion with a sweep of his arm in which the muscles were beginning to grow again. "I ask you what you want and you speak of women, money, lodges, paint. Now let me tell you what the Indian wants. He does not want to have many women. Just enough to do the work in his lodge. He does not care for money or for more than a few painted robes to hang on his lodge. But he cares for something else. What he wants to have is many souls." He paused, triumphantly staring at the white man. "I rush in toward my enemy, I avoid his bullet. I take the cut of his knife in order to touch him with my coup stick. Because, when I do that, some of his soul runs up the stick and passes all over me, and nobody can wash away that new soul that I have stolen. It is mine. I, Standing Bull, have counted eight coups. Who will say, then, that my soul has not been made greater and stronger?"

"What makes you so sure of that?" asked Torridon. "Though I know that you are a brave man, Standing Bull, still I think that the three braves you have killed and scalped are a greater proof of your courage than all your coups."

The Cheyenne smiled and closed his eyes a moment, a sign that he was thinking hard. At last he shook his head. "Do you know that our word for white man has two meanings?" he asked.

"Yes," said Torridon. "I know that you use the same word for spider and for white man."

"This is the reason," said the Cheyenne. "The spider is more cunning than all other things. It can walk on the air. It can hang in the wind. So does the white man. He, too, can do strange things. He even has thunder canoes, I have heard, though that is hard to believe. But you see that there are some things that the white man cannot understand, and that he cannot do. Well, counting of coups is one of them.

"But you, White Thunder, stay with me a long time and listen to me. When I go back to my people, I am going to make a scalp shirt, and then I shall be a chief. The young men will follow me on the warpath. You shall follow me, also. Now you are a wise white man. I shall make you a wise Indian. And when you are that, then who will be so wise and so great in the world as White Thunder?"

He paused and made a little gesture, palm up. It was as though he had offered to Torridon his own soul in the palm of his hand.

V

There was only one thing that seriously overclouded their relations, and that was when Torridon told the Cheyenne that he could not remain with him very long, but, as soon as the warrior's strength had come back, Torridon must make the best of his way across the plains to find Fort Kendry.

When he first asked after Fort Kendry, the Cheyenne had let him understand that he himself knew the way to it perfectly and could direct him so clearly that a child traveling by night could have found the place. But when he understood his companion's fixed determination of going there, Standing Bull grew sullen and even angry.

"Why should you go to the fort?" he asked. "What is there for you except what they have taken from the poor Indians? But when you go there, you will have to pay for the things that are there." He added bitterly: "White men do not give away for nothing. They want money and many robes." He added, by way of coating this bitter comment with sugar: "No one is so clever as a white man. You will not gain when you trade with them, White Thunder."

"I don't want guns or robes," said Torridon patiently. "I only want to find a girl there."

"Ha!" cried the Cheyenne. "A woman!"

"She is promised to me as my wife," said Torridon.

"A woman. A woman," repeated the Indian, and then closed his eyes as though to check a torrent of scorn that was ready to burst forth from his lips. "Tell me, my brother," he said at last, "is this woman young? Or is she an old squaw with many robes and horses?"

"She is young," said Torridon. He smiled a little, and then added: "She has no robes or horses. None at all, I suppose."

"She is strong, then?" said the warrior. "She knows how to flesh skins and how to make soft moccasins and how to bead and do quill work?"

"I don't think she understands any of those things," said the white man. "Certainly she isn't big or strong. She's very small."

Again the Cheyenne was forced to close his eyes. "Her father promised her to you? Then he was lucky to find a brave who would take such a...woman." Obviously he had left out the word "worthless" in his pause. He added: "Is she plain, or pretty?"

"She?" said Torridon. Then his breast heaved and his heart swelled. He was talking to a wild Indian, but he had been silent for a long time. "She is the most beautiful creature that ever was made."

"So?" said the warrior. "Then long before this, some other brave has come and taken her. If you offered five horses for her, he has offered ten. She is gone to his teepee. Think no more about her. A woman cannot make the heart of a great brave sore for many days. Very soon he takes another squaw. If you want wives, you shall have them. When you come home with me to my people, I shall find you the daughters of great chiefs. I shall pay the horses to buy them for you. I shall fill your teepee with everything that you need. Then you will be happy?"

He smiled expectantly, and Torridon was forced to answer slowly: "There is no other who can take her place." He added: "Any other woman would be horrible to me."

"Look at me while I speak the truth with a straight tongue," said the Cheyenne. "One woman has strong hands and fleshes many robes. Another knows how to do bead work swiftly and well. Yes, there is a difference between women. But take two wives in the place of this single one."

Torridon hunted through his mind. He saw that it was useless to delve into the mysteries of love with this man. "You have many horses?" he asked at last.

"Many...many..." said the warrior, smiling with pride.

"Are they all the same?"

"No. There is a bay stallion that is worth all the rest."

"Look at me," echoed Torridon. "I speak with a straight tongue, too. Your stallion, I think, is worth all the rest. Perhaps, however, he is not worth as much as that gray mare?" He pointed to Comanche, grazing nearby. And as though she knew that she was under discussion, she lifted her lovely head and looked toward them with confidence and affection.

The Cheyenne regarded her with a burning glance. "It is true, it is true," he muttered, as one who had had that thought often in his mind before.

Torridon whistled. Black Ashur came bounding and stood before them. "But," said Torridon, "though this mare is very fast, Ashur leaves her standing behind him. Though she is very strong, he will run twice as far as she can run. Though she has a great heart, he will die for me."

"Is it true?" asked the Cheyenne, the same greedy fire in his eyes. "Yes, it is true," he answered himself with conviction, "because he has the eye of a chief. Like a chief in council he holds his head. And he runs on the wind. My brother is a great chief among the white men, or he would not have two such horses."

"Now," went on Torridon, "if there is such a difference between horses, can there not be such a difference between women?"

"Certainly not," replied Standing Bull with warmth. "Does a woman carry a brave to battle? Is his life depending on her? Does she give him the speed to run away from danger? Does she give him the speed to overtake his enemy and strike him down? No, no, White Thunder, you are very wise. All white men are wise. But this is a thing about which you will know when you grow older."

Torridon gave up the debate with a shrug of his shoulders, for he saw that he was facing a wall of rock.

They talked of many other things in the days that followed.

Finally he began to support Standing Bull from the shelter and out under the open sky, and lead him to a blanket where he could sit for hours, drinking up the strength-giving sun and breathing deeply of the pure air.

He was a huge man, standing. He was two or three inches over six feet, with great, spreading shoulders, and arms of an almost unnatural length, set off with huge hands that Torridon could hardly look upon without a shudder of fear. In the old days he had known only two men who impressed him so much. One was Roger Lincoln. But that hero was like Achilles, formidable rather in skill and speed, and graceful surety of all his ways. He was strong, also, but not a giant of power. A giant of power was Jack Brett. He had shoulders as massive as those of the Cheyenne. Perhaps hard labor and the carrying of packs through the woods had given him even a greater force than that of the Indian warrior, but Standing Bull had something of the speed and grace of Roger Lincoln united with the massive might of hand of Jack Brett.

Rarely could an uglier face than the Indian's have been found, with its great, predatory nose, its wide, thin, cruel lips, the eyes, buried, small, terribly bright and restless, and the chin curving well out. He looked like a very god of battle, and as such Torridon looked upon him.

Lying prone in the shelter of the house of leaves, he could care for and pity Standing Bull, but once the giant was erect and walking, in spite of himself Torridon was daily more and more afraid. He remembered, with increasing frequency and force, the warnings that he had received from Roger Lincoln—an Indian never must be trusted to the hilt. *Give him hope, watch him, use him when you can, but recall that always he is as treacherous as a snake.*

Torridon, hearing those warnings in the old days, had come to feel that red men were men in form only. And these warnings had been reinforced by stories of midnight massacres, rum-inspired outpourings of murder and cruelty and frightfulness. And all these tales rolled up in his mind and he believed them all when he looked upon the terrible form and face of the Cheyenne.

The very voice of the warrior was like a roll of drums, a heavy bass that reverberated. And when Standing Bull stood outside the tent and shouted with joy because of the goodness of the sun as it burned upon his thin face, Torridon shook as though thunder had pealed in his ear.

At last a day came when the warrior was seen walking beside Ashur, while the latter regarded him cautiously from a corner of his eye.

"Tell me, brother, which horse shall I ride when we go back to my people?"

"Which will you have, Standing Bull?"

"The gray horse is a strong and a wonderful horse. She runs as fast as leaping lightning, but she is not like the black stallion. Only to sit on his back across the plains to the teepees of my people..."

Torridon smiled. "The black horse is like black thunder. He is full of strength and wickedness, Standing Bull."

"Good," said the warrior. "Saddle him and you will see that I fit the saddle."

It was his way of saying that no horse could throw him. Torridon half believed that he was right, and he was worried. Once the brave felt the magic of Ashur beneath him, would he be persuaded, except by a greater force than Torridon could show, to part from the stallion?

However, now he was committed, and he saddled Ashur with care, and lengthened the stirrups to fit the great legs of the chief. He stood at the head of the horse and watched the Cheyenne leap into his seat.

"Now," said Standing Bull.

Ashur crouched like a cat.

"Be wary," warned Torridon, and stepped back.

Wary was the other.

Nobly, nobly, in another day, Roger Lincoln had sat on the back of that same Ashur, until flung senseless to the ground. The Cheyenne rode in another manner. He was like a panther clutching the back of a wounded bull. And it seemed to Torridon that Ashur had found a master of sheer force at last.

Yet there was an undiscovered spirit in the stallion. He seemed to expand in size, in force, as the seconds flew. He grew a flashing black monster, more in the air than on the ground. And at last, out of a whirl of bucking, out of a dizzy spinning, the Cheyenne emerged headfirst through the cloud of dust, rolled over and over, and then lurched drunkenly to his feet. Blood was running from ears, nose, mouth. But he laughed.

"It is true," he said. "Heammawihio has made such a horse for only one man. Take him, my brother. I am smaller, now. I shall sit on the gray mare."

And he laughed again, in the most perfect good nature.

VI

This was the reason that, when they started back over the plains for the Cheyenne village, the Indian was on the gray mare, Comanche. He was hugely delighted with her, and, taking her for a racing course in the most headlong style, he came plunging back to Torridon and assured him that there was nothing among the horses of the Cheyennes that could keep pace with her. He even invited Torridon to race the stallion against the gray, but Torridon put off the suggestion.

He was very willing to believe that Standing Bull felt great obligations to him as a deliverer in time of need, but he could not help remembering the many tales of Roger Lincoln, and sometimes the warrior looked at Ashur with such glittering eyes that Torridon almost felt a knife planted in the small of his back. So he refused to race against the mare, and, when Standing Bull let her stretch away faster and faster—when they were cantering side-by-side—he allowed the mare to go off into the lead and refused to let Ashur measure strides with her.

Eventually Standing Bull gave up his curiosity. Instead, he returned to the tale of the thing that had sent him out to lie on the island by the side of the river. Several times before he had begun the narration, but always had broken off, letting himself be diverted from the point of his talk like a man who is unwilling to tell of things that are too unpleasant.

What had happened, as Torridon eventually found out, was that Standing Bull, in the midst of his rising glory as a fighter, had returned with a war party and found a party of Sioux blocking their way. In the skirmish that followed, all was going well until Standing Bull, giving way to an ecstasy of battle glory, charged in among the Dakotas and tried to count coup on one of the chief braves among the Sioux.

He almost had succeeded, and he grew tense with grief and trouble when he recalled that he had been so close to endless glory. But the Sioux had swayed from the charge and managed to reach the head of Standing Bull with a stroke with the butt end of his rifle. It floored Standing Bull.

When he came to, he found the Dakotas had been forced to retreat before they had a chance to take his scalp or settle him with a knife thrust. But by the time the singing was gone out of his head, he discovered that he had lost that which was more precious to him than the very hair on his head—his medicine bag. He and all the party had searched the ground where the battle was fought. They had scanned every crevice. But the bag was gone and poor Standing Bull was in a frightful state of mind.

"But what is a medicine bag?" asked Torridon.

"The soul of a brave," said the warrior, and would not explain any further.

However, Torridon in the past had heard enough references to the medicine bag to make him understand that the Indians actually felt the immaterial soul of a warrior was connected with his medicine bag.

With his soul gone from him, Standing Bull found that all his former achievements were looked upon as lost with the medicine bag. He would not be accepted as a member of a war party. His voice would not be heard in the council. And he determined that something desperate must be undertaken in order to change the condition of his life.

The medicine men and the wise sages of the tribe could not advise him. He determined, therefore, to leave the tribe and go forth to make new medicine with the help of the spirits. As a young man goes to consult the future, so Standing Bull went out to lie in danger until a sign was given to him. He had selected the little island where the river forked. It was considered an enchanted spot. Here he lay for four days, never turning from his right side. At last came the thunder of the water; the white man and the two horses rushed up to him, and Standing Bull's soul was filled with joy, for he felt that this was indeed a direct sign from heaven.

To Torridon this story seemed at once amusing, pathetic, and worthy of inspiring fear. He could understand, after he had heard it, that attitude of the Cheyenne toward him, as though he were a personal possession of Standing Bull, and all that he had with him a part of the property of the brave. Heaven had brought him to Standing Bull. Therefore, being from heaven, he must be treated with respect, consideration, gentleness, but at the same time he belonged to Standing Bull. He had been given to Standing Bull in a dream straight from heaven, a dream so powerful that it had not faded as other visions are apt to fade, but had materialized into flesh and blood and iron.

It was easy, too, to understand why Standing Bull had disliked the thought that Torridon wanted to go to Fort Kendry. Furthermore, it was not really right that a man from heaven should want to go to any place other than the abode of the brave to whom he had been sent as a material dream.

It made a situation so ludicrous that Torridon could have burst into laughter. It made a situation so grave that he was ready to quake with fear. He had serious thoughts of making an attack upon his companion, and then riding off to take his chance on the prairie, but the prairie to him was as unknown as the uncharted sea, and, besides, to attack the warrior would have been no less difficult than to attack a wolf. He slept with one eye open; he was ever on the alert, and Torridon began to submit to his fate with a growing apprehension of what it might lead him to.

So they voyaged across the plains. The weather was clear. Sometimes little clouds of purest crystal white, filled with brilliance, blew rapidly across the sky; otherwise it was washed clear. And all day the heat was blinding and burning in its intensity, and the face of the plains quivered with the heat waves that danced endlessly upward. Often from the burning of the sun against his shoulders, Torridon groaned, and then his big companion would look sharply at him.

"Speak louder, louder, brother," he would say. "When the spirits wish to use your tongue, speak with a loud voice, so that I may hear."

Torridon would shake his head and declare that it was only the heat of the sun, but, when he said this, Standing Bull merely smiled a little, secret smile, as though he knew a great deal, and would not press the subject with too many questions. He was willing to be patient with his strange captive.

In the heart of Torridon there was that mingled fear and curious expectancy that filled the old explorers, sailing for the first time through unknown seas, and he turned pale when, on a day, Standing Bull raised his arm and pointed into the eye of the sun. Beneath the sun, like a thickening of the horizon mist, thin clouds were rising—smoke!

"It is there," said Standing Bull. "Presently we shall see our people."

The confusion in the Cheyenne's mind was revealed by that speech. In part he looked on Torridon simply as a white man. In part, the white man was a messenger from heaven, a bringer of luck and medicine to him. And, in part, Torridon was actually a Cheyenne himself, because he had been sent down by the Great Spirit to that tribe.

To a logical and educated mind the three points of view would have been impossible, of course. But Standing Bull could separate the three thoughts. He used them one by one and looked upon his companion in the fashion that was most convenient at the moment.

Presently Standing Bull checked the gray mare. He gestured before him where arose a few swellings of the ground. "Shall I cross the hills and ride in to the village?" he asked.

"You know what is best to do," said Torridon.

The warrior exclaimed impatiently: "Why do you keep back your knowledge, White Thunder? Do you wish to do me harm? Or do you think that Standing Bull is a fool? No, no! I am not a fool. I know that you have understanding of everything. Otherwise, why did Heammawihio send you to me? Now, be kind to me and tell me what I should do?"

Torridon half closed his eyes. But he saw that it was useless to argue and protest. To Standing Bull he was a miraculous creature. He consulted, therefore, his own disinclination to go into the Cheyenne village.

"We should wait here," he said at last.

The brave smiled with satisfaction. "They will come out to find me, will they not?" he said. "They will come out and escort me into the city? They will give me honor, White Thunder?"

"They will." Torridon sighed.

Standing Bull in a vast excitement dismounted, took out his paints, and straightway began to blacken his face. Next he brushed out the mane and the tail of the gray mare. He rubbed away the dust that covered the bead and quillwork on his moccasins and leggings. He combed out his long hair over his shoulders, and he began to put added touches of improvement, such as streaks of paint on his brawny arms. In a few moments he was a brilliant and terrible form, and Torridon looked upon him with awe.

"My heart is filled with impatience, White Thunder!" exclaimed the brave. "Send them out to me soon!"

He hardly had spoken when a boy riding without a saddle galloped a horse over the verge of the hill, swept toward them, and then with a sudden shout wheeled his horse and rushed away. Standing Bull could not speak. He was throttled by emotion and literally bared his teeth like a wolf as he waited.

He was on his horse again, wrapped in his buffalo robe, magnificent and grim, when a cavalcade of half a dozen warriors came over the hill and galloped toward them. The Cheyennes spread out suddenly in a fan, and with a war yell they charged. Torridon glanced at his companion, but he saw a faint smile on the lips of Standing Bull—a smile which that hero was struggling to suppress.

A rush of horsemen, a sweeping cloud of dust, and then they wheeled and came up. Keen glances they flung at Torridon; he felt his scalp prickling on his head.

"Brother!" cried a magnificent youth who seemed the leader of the six riders. "You come with your face blackened. Have you taken a scalp with no harm to yourself? And have you brought this prisoner back with you?"

"Rising Hawk," said the other, "I have been on such a trail as no Cheyenne ever walked or rode before. But this is not the time to speak of it. There is medicine to be made before another word can pass my lips."

VII

There was a murmur of eager contentment among the others. They seemed to accept the fact that this was a mystery about to be carried into their encampment. Four remained as a sort of guard of honor; two raced their horses off over the hill, and by the time that Torridon with the others had climbed to the crest, there was a stream of rapid riders swinging out toward him.

He saw a village of lofty teepees that flashed clean as metal against the sun, and between them and the village was a river, fallen very low. The flats on either side of the stream were covered with corn, but so dust-sprinkled that it was hardly visible to the eye at the first glance. Only by the margin of the stream was it a strong green, as though there it had been irrigated.

Out from the big circle of the village riders were breaking—men, women, boys, little girls. Each horse, as it struck the shallow stream, sent a white dash of spray flying high, and then the rider lurched on up the nearer bank.

Torridon felt that the end of the world was flying upon him. The riders came in a vast tide of noise, with arms brandished. Guns exploded. Wild whoops cut at his ears. And around him poured the tribe.

A huge warrior, naked to the waist, drove straight at him with axe lifted, the sun flashing on it. That flash glanced in the very eyes of Torridon. But the blow was not driven home. The brave went on by with a war yell that stunned the brain of Torridon, and in place of the axe wielder, a spearsman was galloping, bent low over the mane of his horse, and with his lance point leveled at the breast of the white man. This time, surely, the steel would slide home through his breast. No, at the last instant the point was raised, glanced over his shoulder, and another terrible cry dinned in his ears. A procession of terrible forms rushed against him and went by, leaving him untouched. Then a naked boy was dancing beside him, threatening him with a knife whose blade was at least a foot long, and sharpened to an airy edge.

Torridon felt that devils had flooded the world. He would have shrunk from this terrible peril, but his nerves were as numb as though paralyzed.

He heard the exultant voice of Standing Bull beside him: "My brother is fearless. He who has ridden down from the sky on the white thunder, what would make him tremble on the earth?"

He could not answer this friendly and proud remark. If he opened his lips, he felt that a scream would come from them.

The riders had formed in a vast, irregularly eddying circle. Dust clouds boiled up. Through the dust he saw the frantic shapes gleaming, men like polished forms of bronze, terrible in action.

And slowly they moved on—they were the focus and the center of the storm. They crossed the creek. They entered the village. They were pushing through solid masses of horses, men, dogs that writhed away before them and closed again behind. The heat became intense. Dust choked Torridon. A knife thrust between the ribs would have been a happy ending to this prologue of terror and burning sun and confusion.

A woman screamed above the din. She was a young squaw, holding an infant boy high above her head, a naked little statue of red-gold in the flash of the sun. Standing Bull did not so much as turn his head, and yet Torridon knew, by instinct, that they had passed one of the wives of the brave.

Before them the crowd began to split; there were warriors working with a sort of organization to push the rest to either side, and so a way was opened to the front of the biggest teepee that Torridon yet had seen. It was painted yellow below, and black above, spotted with little yellow crosses, and on either side of the doorway buffalo bulls were painted with a good deal of skill, and above the doorway a green crescent moon.

In front of the lodge stood a very old man. The arm with which he held his buffalo robe about him was withered like the arm of a mummy. The flesh was gone from his face, but, instead of making him look wrinkled and old, the skin was stretched a little, like parchment. It gave him rather the look of a starved boy than of an old man, and the eyes were bright and bold as the eyes of a child.

Standing Bull dismounted before this ancient, greeting him with the greatest respect. Torridon himself was motioned from his horse and dismounted. His knees sagged under him. A breath would have staggered him, so completely was he unnerved. He felt reasonably sure of death. He would almost have welcomed such an ending, but it was the means that he had in his mind like a nightmare. He had heard the great Roger Lincoln tell of Indian tortures, of splinters thrust under the nails of the victim, and then lighted, of the tearing and shaving away of flesh, of slow roasting over fires.

Those were the images that drifted rapidly between the eyes of Torridon and the strange forms around him. He hardly knew how he was brought into the teepee. But there he found himself seated, with Standing Bull beside him. The old chief, called High Wolf, who seemed to be the head of the tribe, sat facing the doorway. Presently others entered. Finally ten men had come in, each carefully passing behind the backs of the others, avoiding moving before anyone, until they came to a place where they could sit. They were like ten senators at council. Torridon did not need to be told that the ten chief men of the tribe had gathered here for deliberation of some sort. The youngest among them were Standing Bull and that graceful brave, Rising Hawk, who first had come out to meet them.

Outside, the noise was dying down, but when the lodge flap was dropped, the dust clouds were still rising. It was hot in the lodge, although the lower edges had been furled to admit the passage of a draft. It was hot because of the intense sun beating down from above, and because, also, of the fire that burned in a heart-shaped excavation in the center of the lodge with a steaming kettle on it.

"Everything is here," said High Wolf. "You may eat."

Standing Bull raised his hand, big as a shield, heavy as metal. "First we must be purified," he said. "Everyone here must be purified. There is a great medicine in this lodge, High Wolf."

The old man glanced at Standing Bull. The turning of his eyes was like the stirring of two red lights, but Torridon guessed shrewdly that it was pleasure that moved the great chief.

He himself then took wisps of sweet grass, ignited them, and, waving the smoke to the earth, to the sky, to the four corners of the heavens, he muttered a chant so rapidly that Torridon could not understand the words. Then he carried the smoke to all the guests. They washed their hands in it. This, apparently, was a degree of purification.

Still the ceremonies were not ended. Five small pieces of meat were taken from the pot, and one placed in the palm of High Wolf's hand, and the other four at the four points of the compass. Then, inverting his hand upon the palm of his left, he allowed the meat to remain there and offered it to the four directions.

The eating began after that. Torridon found a large portion of unsalted buffalo flesh before him. He ate it greedily. He hoped that food would give him sufficient strength to put an end to the faint tremor that was running steadily through his body.

It did not take long to consume the food. After that the pipe was produced by High Wolf. He filled it with a preparation of tobacco and dried leaves of the sumac, flavored with buffalo grease. After that he blew smoke to the earth, to the heavens, and to the four points of the compass, murmuring a phrase with each puff. Then he passed it to his left. So it went to the door, but apparently it could not cross the doorway, and was passed rapidly back from man to man so that it could begin again on the farther side.

This smoking was done with absorption, without speech, and each man held the pipe in a way that differed slightly from that of others.

At last it was empty.

High Wolf turned to Standing Bull. "Brother," he said, "Heammawihio is a stern master, but he always is just. We were all sorry when you lost your medicine bag. We wondered what you had done that was wrong. Now we hope that it was taken away from you only in order to inspire you to do some great thing. I think you are about to tell what the great thing may be. We are all ready to hear. We all are your friends. To me you are as a child. Therefore, open your heart and we will receive all your words."

After this courteous invitation all eyes turned upon Standing Bull, and Torridon saw that the braves were in an actual fever of excitement.

That huge warrior, however, remained silent for some time, staring at the ground, and then raised his head on its bull neck and glared up through the smoke hole toward the sun-whitened sky above them. Then he picked from the floor of the teepee just before him a small handful of little pebbles and grains of sand. This he spread smoothly on the flat of his palm, and then puffed it away. There remained two little glittering pebbles, and these he carefully put away in his pouch.

It seemed to Torridon that this was the maddest sort of nonsense, but all the other braves watched it with the most absorbed attention and respect.

"Now," said Standing Bull, "I have asked the spirits of the air and the under the earth spirits to listen to me. If I say anything that is not true, may they strike me with as many knives as there are grains of dust in that which I have just blown off my hand. If I say the thing that is not true, may they strike me with as many arrows as there were grains of dust, also."

He paused and looked about him from face to face, and every one of those dignified warriors inclined his head a little as though acknowledging the tremendous force of this oath.

"For the thing I am about to tell," said Standing Bull, "is hard to understand. I am going to tell you how I sent my soul up to the Sky People, and how my soul came back again with this man and the two horses and all that was with them besides."

VIII

Up to this point Torridon had remained more interested in the possibilities of his future fate than in the talk around him, but at this prodigious lie he could not help glancing down sharply to the ground, prepared to hear the outburst of laughter that would greet the statement of Standing Bull. But there was not a sound.

And when he glanced up again he saw that there was not the slightest indication of mirth in any face. With eyes overbright, the warriors listened, hanging on the words that were next to be spoken. Standing Bull was in no hurry. As one prepared to allow his audience to grow expectant because he had plenty with which to satisfy that expectation, Standing Bull was again looking down to the ground. Or perhaps it might be said that his attitude was that of a man rapt in thought, forgetting those around him while he called up again a vision from the past.

At length he slowly lifted his hand, palm up, and extended his long, powerful arm toward the heavens. Then he said: "When I last saw you, my friends, I was less than a man. My soul was in the hands of the Dakotas. Or else it was rotting on the desert in the rains and drying to dust in the suns. I went out to find another soul.

"I had lain down and asked for a dream and the dream only told me to go out from among my people and follow an invisible guide. I saw no guide, but still I was led for a great distance. I was not told to take a horse, and therefore I left a horse behind me. I did not say farewell to my children or to my wives. I let everything stay behind. Nothing matters to a man so much as his soul." Here he paused. He lowered the arm that had been raised as though invoking divine witness to the truth of his words. He went on, after a moment: "I was led through many days of marching. But though I had little food, I was not hungry and I was not tired. I was supported by the thing that led me. At last I came to the place where the great river comes to a fork, and above the fork it has two arms. One arm goes north and the other arm goes west. Where they meet, there is an island." He paused and looked about him for confirmation.

Rising Hawk said gravely: "I myself have seen that island in the last seven days."

"Do you know what it is now?" asked Standing Bull.

"I know," said Rising Hawk, and said no more, as though he intended to keep his information secret until the end of the tale, thereby being prepared to check its correctness. This made all heads turn for an instant toward Rising Hawk. Excitement apparently was rising fast. This story would be corroborated or completely disproved by an adequate witness.

"Good," said Standing Bull. "I do not say the thing that is not true. Therefore I am glad that Rising Hawk has seen the place. But when I came to it the spirit that conducted me told me to stay there and lie down. I lay down on my right side, with my head to the east and with my face to the north. I lay on my right side for a long time, waiting for something to happen.

"After a while I began to grow hungry, but more than the hunger was the thirst, and that thirst was like a fire in me, and all the while I could hear the running of the water among the stones in the bed of the river. Sometimes I fell asleep and dreamed that I was the bed of the river and that the cool water was running through my mouth. But I always waked up and found that I still lay on the hard ground. And my bones began to press through my flesh. My muscles asked me to turn, only a little bit, because they were dying. Still I would not turn. I did not want to get up and go away. I did not care to live if I had no soul. All at once, in the middle of a sleep, a voice said to me... 'Stand up and follow me.'

"I knew that it was a spirit. I tried to get up, but I was too weak to move. Then the spirit said... 'Your body cannot get up, so leave it behind you.' Then I tried to throw out my thought after the spirit, and all at once I felt as though my body were falling down through thin air. The next moment I was standing on my feet. I looked down, and in the starlight I saw that I was still lying on the ground. Then I knew that my soul had come away from my body. I heard the spirit call again. I walked. And at one step I crossed to the farther bank of the river. I could see the spirit now. It was an old man with feathers in his hair. He had the ghost of a war bow and stone-pointed arrows in his hand, and the ghost of a painted robe was flying over his shoulders in the wind. He smiled and reached out his hand. 'Come with me,' he said. He began to walk up through the air. I followed him, and it was as easy to walk up through the air as it was to walk along the ground. Every step we took was longer than the width of this camp.

"After a while we came to the tops of some mountains and we sat down to rest. We could see all the rivers spread out at our feet. Only, to the north and east, there was a shadow on the earth. I said to my guide... 'What is that?' 'It is the land of the Dakotas,' he answered me. Then we stood up and walked through the air again, always going higher, until we reached the clouds. Our bodies were so light that it was rather hard work to walk through them. It was like going in mud. At last we came to the top of the clouds and I saw the sky country filled with Sky People."

He paused again and looked down with a frown. There was a most breathless silence while the others attended this strange narration. Torridon looked to the chief, expecting that his superior intelligence and experience would at once penetrate the deceit, but, instead, the nostrils of the old man were quivering and his hollow chest heaved with a passionate joy and belief.

"When I try to remember what was up there," said Standing Bull with a sort of baffled dignity, "my mind walks through darkness. However, I met many good Indians up there. I remember I heard a sound like ten thousand warriors all shouting for battle. I asked what it was and they told me that it was the sound of the wind whistling through the robe of Heammawihio as he strides across the sky country. I remember, too, that I stood before a man as tall as a mountain. He looked like a mountain when it turns blue in the evening. I kneeled before him and begged him to give me another soul. He said that he would. His voice was like the sound of a great river after the spring floods have begun.

He offered me a soul in the palm of his hand, but I said... 'If I go back and say that is my new soul, my people will not believe me. Give me a soul that they can see.'

"After a while he said... 'You ask for a great deal, but I want to please you. You have fought bravely. I have watched you in the field and I never saw you turn away from an equal enemy. Now I am going to make a soul for you.' He took up what looked like white clay and began to work it with his fingers, like an old woman molding a pot. After a while he leaned and breathed on it, and there was a sound like a nation singing. After that the lump of clay stood up, breathed, spoke, and was a man."

The narrator turned to Torridon. "It was this man," he said.

There was a stir, an intake of breath like a groan. Torridon saw beads of moisture standing on the forehead of Rising Hawk. Not a shadow of disbelief appeared on any face. These people, more simple than children, did not have to be told that it was a fairy tale they were hearing. They were willing to believe with a wonderful faith.

"'This is your soul!' said Heammawihio to me. 'You had better go down to the earth at once. You had better hurry. The Underwater People are very angry because I am helping you. They want to have you and now they are sending down water devils who will destroy your body. If your body is destroyed, of course this new soul will be no good to you.' Then he showed me where a white-headed flood was racing down the river toward the island where my body lay.

"I said... 'Alas, we never can get to the body in time.'

"'That is true,' said the voice. 'Then you must have horses to ride.'

"I saw his hand reach away like the shadow of a cloud that reaches across a valley in a moment. The shadow came back and put two horses beside us. One horse was like silver. One was as black as night.

"'Which horse will you take?' asked the voice.

"I looked at the white mare. She was like silver. I said that I would take her.

"'You are wrong,' said Heammawihio, 'because the black stallion is much better than she. But they are both medicine horses. However, you chose the silver mare, and therefore you must keep her and always let your soul ride on the black stallion. Now you must go, and you had better hurry. When you come safely back to the Cheyennes tell them that they are my people. The air that I breathe is sweet with the smoke that they blow up to me.'

"When he had said this, my soul and I got on the horses. They were only the ghosts of horses. We jumped them off the edge of a cloud and they went down like birds. But when I looked before me, I could see a great distance away, because the sun was shining now. I saw the island. I saw my body lying on it, and I saw the flood coming down faster than we could go. I said to my soul…'What shall we do?' He said to me…'Call to the white thunder.' Then I called, and a terrible noise took hold of us, and white thunder wrapped us around, and suddenly we were standing on the island. I looked about me and found my body, and I got into it.

"When I opened my eyes, the flood was almost on the island. I looked around me. To the eyes of my spirit, the two horses and the new soul had been as real as this knife." He snatched a long weapon from his belt and buried it in the earth with a powerful gesture. Then he went on: "But when I looked at them with the dim eyes of a man, they were no more solid than the shapes of mist that come out of the ground on a moonlight evening. But every moment they got thicker and more real. I sang a song to them and told them to hurry and help me, because I was too weak to move. All at once they turned into two real horses and a real man. He caught me up. Then the flood struck the island. It tore away almost all of it. It tore away the ground that I had been lying on. It made a noise like thunder, and I could hear the underwater devils groaning and shouting with anger because they could not have my body.

"Then White Thunder, which is the name of this man that the Great Spirit sent down with me, took me away and took care of me while I lay very sick, with all my blood turned into fire. After that, when he had made me strong again with his magic and his strong medicine, we rode back to my people." He paused again, sat up to his stiffest, fullest height, and looked across at Rising Hawk.

"Friend," he said, "this is a meeting of the great men of the Cheyennes. Every one should hear only the truth. If you have seen the island, speak and let them know if I have said the thing that is not."

Torridon waited, breathless.

Rising Hawk swallowed and then struck the arch of his chest until it resounded like a drum. "I have seen that island within seven suns," he declared. "It was half as big as this village. There were many trees on it. But when I looked at it again, I saw that it was torn to pieces. All that was left of it was one tree standing, and even the roots of that one tree were washed bare on the north side. So I give my witness that we have heard the truth from our brother."

IX

After the conclusion of this short speech from Rising Hawk everyone seemed to take it for granted that no further proof was needed. Rising Hawk had seen that the island at the fork of the river actually had been almost destroyed. That was enough, apparently, to verify all of the odd tale that Standing Bull had told.

He, like a hero overcome by the mere thought of what he had been through, allowed himself to sink against the backrest and fall into a profound contemplation, but the others chattered like birds. Torridon, who had in mind ten thousand tales of their taciturnity, was amazed to see them talking all at once, like enthusiastic women.

They never for an instant cast a doubt on the story of their companion, but they declared that undoubtedly he had brought a great blessing upon the entire Cheyenne people, because he had carried down from heaven an actual spirit. Upon Torridon they turned their eyes with the frankest curiosity. If he was something more than man, he was also something less than man, apparently, for they remarked frankly and openly on the slenderness of his hands and the lack of weight in his shoulders, and the delicacy of his features, which proved, they said, that he was not really a white man like those other bronzed ruffians who rode across the plains to traffic or fight with the red man.

What divine properties, then, would they expect him to have? Certainly they had seen that he ate food, cast a shadow, possessed a voice.

But they were all like Standing Bull. They never put facts against facts. They believed what they wanted to believe, and the story of Standing Bull was too good to be thrown away. It was such an exploit as gave distinction to an entire tribe. As for the hero, Torridon puzzled over him a great deal. At last he came to the conclusion that in the first place Standing Bull had made up the story out of ecstasy and a good bit of invention mixed together, but, after telling the tale a few times, it had become letter perfect—and convinced himself.

He had plenty of occasions to tell the story. For the first ten days after the return of Standing Bull there was an endless succession of feasts. Some old man would go through the camp, chanting the names of the guests who were invited to a certain teepee to feast. The feasts were all very much like that which High Wolf had given. There was no change in the food offered, there was a great deal of smoke raised after the eating ended, and then always Standing Bull was called on for his narration.

Each time he talked a little longer. He discovered new details that were worthy of development. For instance, when he declared that his spirit had issued from his body, he said that he had looked at his lifeless self with a great deal of interest. He had leaned and fingered the back of his skull. He had admired the breadth of his shoulders and the strength of his neck, and he had looked for a while at his face, for this was the only time he could see himself except by the treacherous help of standing water or a mirror. For the first time he knew himself.

There was a great deal more of this same sort of thing added by Standing Bull, but his auditors never were tired of listening. They were not all new faces at each feast. Indeed, some of the same men attended a dozen times and always listened with the same earnest, amazed attention. Rising Hawk grew so familiar with the story that he knew when the high points were coming, and he used to rise on his knees, and even whoop with delight when he heard the never-familiar marvels of the story.

As for Torridon, the Indians treated him with a certain respect and contempt commingled. He was regarded as a part of Standing Bull, and was significant simply because he was a gift from Heammawihio. He was a sort of fleshy shadow, in other words.

He was glad enough to be thus lightly regarded by these savage warriors. They were such men as he never had looked upon. There was hardly a warrior under six feet in height, and they were built like Romans, for war and effort. He saw no others quite up to the Herculean standard of Standing Bull, who was like his namesake in massive weight and power, but every man in the tribe was a powerful athlete who lived for one purpose—war. Torridon was glad to slip about among them, almost unnoticed.

Standing Bull treated him very well and made him at home in his teepee. It was a good big lodge, as befitted a man who had two wives and three children. There was a middle-aged squaw who had given her master two daughters; she was a sour-faced creature, but a strong and incessant worker. Her companion, the favored wife of Standing Bull, was called Owl Woman, although Torridon never learned why she should have been given the ugly title. She was the young and handsome mother who Torridon had seen lifting her baby son above her head so that the child might behold the return of his father. Ill-matched as the two wives seemed to be, they got on perfectly; there was never a voice raised in the teepee except when one of the children squawked. Torridon himself was equipped with a bed, a backrest, a post on which he could hang clothes and weapons.

He felt that Standing Bull might have gone on forever attending feasts and talking about his heavenly exploits, but now a cloud was hanging over this section of the great Cheyennes. Two days after the arrival of Torridon, the river that flowed past the encampment ceased running and thereafter no water was to be had except in standing pools, which shrank rapidly under the strength of the summer sun. There were plenty of other places to which they could remove to find water, but that would mean the definite abandonment of the corn crop that had been planted here. Already that corn had suffered from drought. The dusty look that Torridon had noticed had been a true sign of coming death, and, if the drought persisted, there might be cruel want in every lodge in the tribe during the winter to come.

In the meantime the medicine lodge was noisy every day with the incantations of the medicine men, making rain. But though they fasted, strained, and sweated copiously, still not a single black cloud would blow up over the horizon.

Something more than a drought was worrying Torridon. From the first he was allowed to walk about the village as he pleased, but when he asked to be allowed to mount the black stallion, Ashur, he was informed that the horse was very sick and could not be used. This, when with his own eyes he could see the big fellow galloping in the distance, the manifest king of the entire herd belonging to the tribe. When he asked for the gray mare, he was given the same response, although she led home the horse herd at night by a dozen lengths when they were raced in from the pasture grounds, Ashur, like a dutiful lord of his kind, ranging in the rear and hurrying on the laggards while the Indian boys yelled like demons.

He was to be forbidden the use of a horse, then. More than this, wherever he went, he could not make a step without close attendance. Two or three young braves were sure to spy him, and they loitered along in the vicinity, as though their own will conducted them. But after this had happened during several days, he began to understand that the Cheyennes were determined that this gift from Heammawihio should not escape from them if vigilance could prevent it.

To be sure his captivity was not heavy, but his heart was off yonder across the sunburned fields, hurrying toward Nancy Brett and Fort Kendry. He was held here, and who could tell when the kindness of his captors might be exchanged for quite another attitude?

Nervously he waited, and as the drought increased, the village grew more dusty, the faces of the Indians more solemn and sullen, just so much did the face of Nancy Brett grow clearer and dearer to him, and every day he sat with her as they had done once before, at the edge of the river where the crimson and golden forest rolled all its colors into the standing water.

On a day when he was walking past the edge of the village, with two or three braves loitering in his rear, he saw a youth of thirteen or fourteen dragging something on the ground by means of two long leather thongs over his shoulders, but, when he came closer, he saw that the thongs issued out of the shoulders. They actually were fastened to the flesh, and from either shoulder a stream of blood ran slowly down, blackening quickly with dust. Held by the rawhide thongs, a buffalo head was dragged behind the boy, who never ceased walking, although sometimes the fatigue or the misery of his constant pain made him stagger for a step or two.

"Why are you letting that boy torture himself to death?" asked Torridon of one of the braves.

"Do you think that he wants to remain a boy forever?" answered the brave curtly. "Is he to be a woman forever in the tribe? No, but a strong warrior who will go on the warpath and take scalps."

"Can he take no scalps unless he does this?"

"If he is not braver than pain, if he is not patient and strong so that he can smile at trouble, who would want to ask him to go on the warpath?"

That answer had to content Torridon, although he had an almost irresistible impulse to cut those thongs and set the lad free. But who can free a man from self-inflicted torture?

He had hardly turned his back on that pitiful sight when he saw Standing Bull riding toward him, accompanied by no less a person than the great old chief, High Wolf. They came straight to him and High Wolf gave him a solemn greeting.

"Oh, my friend," said High Wolf, "you have been among us many days. You have heard the medicine men working to bring the rain and they raise only a dry dust. You see the corn dying by the river, and the river itself is dead. How long will it be, White Thunder, before you take pity on us and bring us the rain?"

Torridon stared in bewilderment. "I know nothing of rain-making," he said at last, with all the gravity that he could muster.

High Wolf shook his head. "You come from the Sky People," he said, "where all these things are understood. Heammawihio will be angry with you if you let his people starve for lack of water. Come! Tell me when you will do something for us."

Torridon looked at him helplessly, but out of that helplessness he began to evolve a thought.

Standing Bull had taken up the argument in the most direct fashion. "If you will not do it from kindness," he said, "then we must put you in a lodge and keep you there. Let the

Sky People come down and feed you and give you water. Or else, if you want anything from us, you must bring down a little rain."

X

The face of Torridon grew pale indeed at this announcement. From the moment he first came among them, he had no expectation of these people, except that they would find death for him, and now that expectation was about to be fulfilled. Fire might be more terrible for a moment, but thirst would be an agony long drawn out. For three days, perhaps, he would lie in the lodge, and, unless fortune sent down the rain, he was a lost man. There was perhaps one slender hope.

He said to Standing Bull: "Let you and I go a little way off and talk together."

Standing Bull went readily enough. He even dismounted, and they stood together out of earshot of High Wolf, who had wrapped himself in his robe and turned his head impatiently toward the south, for from the south alone they could expect rain at this season, it appeared.

"My friend," said Torridon to the brave, "I know that since you came back among your people and told them the great story about the Sky People and your trip to the clouds you have been looked up to as a wonderful man. But just in order to keep that reputation, are you going to see me starved to death?"

Standing Bull frowned. "Why would it be hard for you to bring us the rain?" he said. "When I lay in the shelter that you had given me, very sick, with fire always burning inside me, death kept coming up to my side like a shadow. But you only had to wave your hand, and death ran away again. You know that I should have died many times if you had not taken care of me. When you went away to hunt, I became sick and weak. When you came back, I always grew strong again. You have a stronger medicine than you need to make rain." He uttered this odd argument with perfect conviction.

"Listen to me," said Torridon desperately. "I found you by mere chance. It would have been easy for me to leave you to be washed away by the water. But I stayed with you. I took care of you. Because of that, you wanted me to come to your people. I came to the Cheyennes. Now you treat me as if I am a bad man. You take away my horses. When I walk, you send your warriors to watch me. And now you threaten to starve me to death unless I make rain. I cannot make rain. I know nothing about such things. In fact, no man can make rain. I speak with a straight tongue. Everything that I say is true."

He paused, breathing hard, and the warrior frowned thoughtfully upon him.

"You were not sent to me from Heammawihio?" he asked soberly.

"I was sent to you by chance," persisted Torridon. "I was wandering across the prairie. I had lost my way. I only happened to find you."

"That," said Standing Bull, "is the way that Heammawihio always works. Everything seems simple. He makes it seem so. But there is no such thing as chance. He watches everything. He sent you to me, though you did not know that you were sent."

"Suppose that he sent me to you," argued Torridon, abandoning hopelessly one part of his argument, "does that show that I can make rain?"

"Friend," said the Cheyenne gently, "I went out to do some good thing for my people and for myself. I prayed to the Sky People. They sent me you. Well, you have done something for me. You have answered that part of my prayer. Because of that I am your friend. My blood is your blood. My lodge is your lodge, and my weapons are your weapons." He said this with a voice not raised, but deepened and trembling with emotion. Then he went on: "You have given back my life to me, White Thunder.

You had cool hands. You killed the fire inside me. So I had one half of my prayer granted to me. Now I ask you to grant me the other half. You have done much for me. But what am I? I am only one man. All my people now are in trouble. I wish you to do good to them. Why do you shake your head? Why are you angry with me? Why do you make me sad, my brother? The great chief is very angry because you do nothing for us. Now, even if I wanted to, I could not take you away. He knows that you have great power."

Torridon grew paler than ever, and sweat burst out on his forehead.

Seeing this, the Cheyenne continued more gently than ever: "You do not need to make a great rain. Only a few drops to show that you are trying to help us. Or only bring the clouds across the face of the sky... then our own wise men can make medicine that will bring down the rain out of the clouds."

There was no answer to make to this last appeal, and Torridon knew it. He had made an effort through persuasion and that effort had failed signally. Now he reverted to a thought that had been forming in his mind since he was first challenged. He turned to Standing Bull as a cloud of dust enveloped them, for the wind, which had been hanging for ten days in the north, now was shifting suddenly to the south.

"Let us go back to High Wolf. I shall talk with him."

Anxiously Standing Bull led him back to the impatient old war leader, whose lips were working as he regarded the white man.

"I have talked to Standing Bull, my friend," said Torridon. "He tells me that I must really try to make the rain come. Very well, I shall do my best."

At these words a smile, half delighted and half grim, came upon the face of the old man. "To make that medicine," he said, "tell us what you need. We have horses and dogs to sacrifice. Also, we have painted robes and many other good things, and everything that the medicine men can bring to you from their lodges you shall have... rattles and masks, and everything that you wish."

"Brother," said Torridon, delighted with this speech, "is it true that I was sent down from the clouds?"

"It is true," said the chief, staring earnestly at Torridon's face as though he wished to make surety a little more sure.

"Well, then," went on Torridon, "if the Sky People are willing to grant my prayer, they need only to hear my voice and to see and recognize me."

"Good," said High Wolf. "I know that great things often are simply done. It is not always the largest war party that brings home the most scalps or the most horses. Can we give you nothing?"

"Nothing," said Torridon. "Only give me what I brought to your city. I had some weapons, and a pack, and two horses."

Standing Bull exclaimed suddenly. Torridon dared not look at the warrior, who now cried: "High Wolf, this man has two horses that are as fast as the wind! Once he has them how could he be caught if he wished to run away?"

"That is true, also," remarked the chief. "And why should you need the two horses, my friend?"

"Tell me," said Torridon, his heart beating fast, but his face sedulously kept calm, "in what way I was sent down from the clouds?"

"With Standing Bull. Is not that true?"

"That is true, of course. But did we come on foot?"

"No, you had two horses."

"Therefore I must have them again."

"Why, brother?"

"Because how will they know me? It is a long distance to the Sky People. They are the ones who must send the rain, are they not?"

"Yes, that is true, of course."

Delighted that his trend of thought was accepted this far, Torridon went on: "If I stand and cry from the midst of the prairie, then it is only a small sound that will come up to their ears."

"Not if the right words are used," said the chief instantly, as one sure of himself.

"I myself," said Torridon, "have sat on the clouds and heard the Cheyennes crying out for pity, and even when the whole tribe was crying out together, and the medicine men were shaking their rattles, and the horses were neighing, the sound came up to my ear as faint and as small as the hum of a bee, half lost in the wind."

The circumstantial nature of this account opened the eyes of the chief. He waited.

"But when I heard that small sound and looked down I could recognize the whole tribe. Now if they heard my small voice, they would look down and say it is the voice of White Thunder. Then they would call one another and say... 'Is not that White Thunder calling to us?' And the others would come and look and say... 'It sounds like his voice, but it cannot be he. We sent him off with two horses, one white and one black, so that we could know him easily. But now he has neither of the two.'"

Broke in Standing Bull: "They would simply think that you had lost them."

"How could I lose them?" answered Torridon, smiling. "I have done nothing but good to the Cheyennes, and the Sky People know it. They would never think that the Cheyennes could have taken my horses away from me."

Standing Bull bit his lip. He was silenced for the moment but he was far from convinced. Then the war chief said quietly: "What White Thunder says has a good sound to my ears. We will let him have the two horses to ride out where the Sky People may see him and Heammawihio may hear his voice."

"You will never see him again," said Standing Bull. "He will go to Fort Kendry like a bird through the air."

"No." The chief smiled. "The truth is that, when we send him out, we will not send him alone."

"What will you do?"

"We will send twenty braves to be around him, and all the rest of the people will be not far off to watch."

Torridon blinked. It was a mortal blow to his plan, which had been exceedingly simple once he had the matchless power of Ashur beneath him. "High Wolf!" he exclaimed. "What are you thinking of? To send me out, and surround me with a crowd so that Heammawihio will not be able to pick me out from the crowd?"

"I have said the thing that seems to me good," responded High Wolf. "No man can do better than his best. Now, White Thunder, go and make yourself ready to call the clouds over the sky. Standing Bull, you will bring in the two horses, the black and the silver. I shall prepare the twenty warriors to go with the rain maker."

XI

The first hope that had sprung so high in the heart of Torridon was half eclipsed by the announcement of the powerful escort in the midst of which he should have to work. But once on the back of Ashur, given half a chance to break free, he would take that chance and depend upon the dizzy speed of the great stallion to make the bullets of the Indians miss if they fired upon him. He felt that he had a faint opportunity left, and the process of the festival might offer him a ghost of a chance.

He went back to the village with the south wind so strongly against him that he had to lean to meet it. Through staggering gusts he advanced down the street of the town. The men were pouring out from their lodges. He felt their eyes upon him already with awe. And presently he made out one of their murmurs: "Already he has put the wind in the south. This is to have a real medicine."

"He does not have a medicine," answered another. "He is medicine himself. He is not a mere man. He is neither white nor red."

Torridon, facing that freshening wind, could not help remembering what he had heard over and over again during the past ten days: that the rain wind was the south wind. He looked with a sudden and frantic hope toward the horizon, but his heart fell again when he saw that all was burnished clear and clean.

He went back to the lodge of Standing Bull and there he made up his pack as it had been when he arrived. Other possessions were shifted about with perfect disregard of ownership, in many cases, but his things had been left alone with an almost superstitious regard. He took his rifle and cleaned and loaded it afresh. He saw to his two double-barreled pistols—the real pride of his life—and so he made himself ready to depart.

All this was done in the midst of a great bustling that spread through the entire camp, and finally Standing Bull called to him from without that the horses were ready.

He stepped through the flap of the tent. The silver beauty and the black were there—Comanche, the mare, looking wild-eyed from her long course of freedom in the open fields, and the stallion ten times more so. But they came like dogs to a master.

A little crowd gathered—the children pressing close, the braves remaining at a more dignified distance—but all eaten with curiosity to see the manner in which the man from the sky would handle these horses from the sky. Apparently they saw enough to stir them. Murmurs of delight and wonder rose from them. Their own animals were not trained to be pets, but to be efficient tools in time of need. Caresses were not lavished on them, and the vast majority were merely wild horses that had been caught, knowing no master except sheer force.

When he took the lead rope from the neck of the silver mare, they spread out their arms to keep her from bolting away, and there were murmurs of wonder when Torridon merely turned his back on her. That murmur grew into pleasant laughter when big Ashur actually strode after his master into the tent. So Torridon carried out all his possessions.

Standing Bull bit his lip as he watched. "Do the Sky People need to see all these things?" he asked.

"They see small and they see big," said Torridon. "Shall I have them say to one another... 'That is not White Thunder, but only a man who has stolen his horses?'"

To this, Standing Bull made no rejoinder, but his brow remained dark with suspicion. And he prominently added his finest rifle to his equipment as he stood beside the best of his own horses.

The saddling was done with much care by Torridon. He saw to it that the cinches were well secured, and that the packs were strapped on stoutly. Owl Woman helped, as in duty bound, in all this work. At last the bridles were on. The mare was secured to the stallion's saddle by a lead rope, and then Torridon spoke. At once Ashur dropped upon one knee, almost like a human being making a curtsy, and Torridon stepped easily into the saddle, while the little boys and girls cried out in delight to one another.

Another word and Ashur rose. In his joy he rose sheer up on his hind legs, dropped lightly forward, and leaped high into the air. But Torridon knew these maneuvers. They looked wild and frantic enough to a bystander. As a matter of fact every leap and check was executed with a cat-like softness and grace. It was a sort of system of play, long established between them. Not a morning passed that did not see such gamboling. The silver mare neighed and shook her head, but followed cheerfully beside them, for she understood, also, that it was play.

But the Indians looked on with alarm and wonder. "*Aha!*" they cried in the hearing of Torridon. "Look! There is a man who can ride a horse. Look at that, my friend!"

"Yes, but that horse has no feet. He has wings, only we cannot see them."

Whatever their admiration, they did not allow Torridon to proceed unescorted. High Wolf, properly enough, had given charge of the guard of honor to big Standing Bull, and that warrior took harsh command of the selected men. He had picked a score of the best mounted, most savage warriors of the tribe, and these closed in around Torridon, behind, before, and to either side, as he issued from the camp.

Behind them came a group of medicine men, hideously masked as bears, wolves, devils, fantastically draped, carrying noisy rattles. Behind these, in turn, High Wolf rode alone, and after him the rest of the tribe, following no order whatever, men, women, and children, confusedly together, rushed from the village and spread themselves out over the flat.

Well out in the open, Standing Bull led the way to a small plateau, circumscribed by a narrow and steep-sided ravine, or draw. The ground that it enclosed was almost like an island. Here Standing Bull directed that the ceremony should take place. Torridon groaned inwardly. With the throat of this high island choked with men, the only escape would be to leap a horse across the mouth of the ravine, and that was a spring of such dimension that even Ashur well might fail in the effort.

"Now, White Thunder," said Standing Bull, "we see that you already have called the wind from the right corner of the sky. We know that you can make that wind carry thousands of clouds over us if you speak to the Sky People. Then speak to them, and tell them to have pity on the Cheyennes."

"Keep back from me," said Torridon. "All keep far back from me. Have your guns ready," he added after a moment. "Let every rifle and pistol be charged."

Standing Bull looked curiously at him. It was not the sort of request that he had expected. But he repeated the order, and the few warriors who had not already loaded their weapons immediately obeyed the suggestion.

They drew back to the verge of the little plateau. Torridon was left in the center, surrounded by potential enemies, and feeling half desperate and half foolish, like one who is a charlatan against his will. However, something had to be done. He looked anxiously toward the south, for he had hoped that perhaps this favorable wind might bring up clouds enough to cause some slight excitement. However, there was not so much as a shadow along the southern horizon. Not a trace of vapor was floating in all the wide, hot face of the sky. Torridon sighed.

In the meantime, all those hungrily expectant eyes were fixed upon him. He must do something, if only to kill time. He made the stallion kneel, and, scooping up a handful of dust, he raised his hand high, and released the dust in a long, thin streamer down the wind.

The voice of a medicine man shouted in the distance: "See it and look down, oh, Sky People!"

Torridon raised the other arm and for a long time stared at the pale, empty vault of the heavens above him.

"Oh, God," said Torridon in a trembling voice, and in English, "if there is a God, help me. I don't know what to do."

A mighty hush had dropped upon the assembly. Their eyes were riveted with tremendous concentration upon him. In the distance he could see women holding up their frightened children on high that they might have a better view. A child screamed. The cry was stifled in its midst.

Then, glancing gloomily to the south, Torridon thought he saw a thickening of the horizon line. His heart bounded into his throat. There was no doubt. The dark line grew yet broader. It began to bulge upward in the center.

"Sky People!" cried Torridon in the Cheyenne tongue, "I command you to send the rain clouds and the rain! Instantly send them!"

At the boldness of this talk a soft groan of fear rose from the warriors and then from the masses of people beyond. Torridon shouted: "Fire! Let every gun be fired straight into the air. Standing Bull, repeat the order!"

There was no need for Standing Bull to repeat it. Instantly it was obeyed. Pistols, rifles, and all crashed their volley into the air. Wisps of smoke blew off in ragged flights. And then Torridon pointed to the south. A lofty thunderhead already was hanging in the sky.

"Swiftly, and more swiftly!" commanded Torridon. "Behold, there is the answer!"

Not until he made that gesture did a single eye glance away from him, and now all turned and beheld in the south the lofty shadow darkening the sky. There was a groan of wonder, and then followed an hysterical cry of joy. The rain was coming! Men and women held up their hands to it. Lips parted. People began to laugh.

Torridon felt a strange lifting of the heart. He waved his hand. There was instant, utter silence, save for the murmur of children, quickly hushed.

"Not clouds only," cried Torridon, "but let there be rain, and let there be thunder and lightning!"

A sort of childish ecstasy had carried him away to these words. But now, across the rising forehead of the cloud, there was a glimmer and then a distinct streak of light.

Even the heart of Torridon was overwhelmed with awe. And from the Cheyennes there arose a cry so filled with fear that it was more like a lament than a rejoicing.

XII

There was not so much enthusiasm in Torridon that he failed to notice that none of the braves had reloaded their weapons. Quietly he loosed the rope that bound the mare to the stallion.

Follow he hoped she would, but she must not act as an impediment when he attempted to bound the black stallion across the draw.

In the meantime, the Cheyennes were beginning to give over their silence. An increasing cry of wonder and awe and joy rose from them as the cloud swept closer. It seemed apparent that it was not merely a squall. Its lofty front was crowned with great towers of the most dazzling white, based on terraces of gray, and these, in turn, were solidly founded upon a huge thickness of heavy black, impenetrable, and yet rolled fiercely upon itself. The whole mass of vapor was in the wildest turmoil, boiling up from the bottom to the top, and sinking from the top to the bottom.

As it drew closer, it piled higher and higher into the central sky until it seemed to be occupying those spaces under the sun that the dimmest stars fill by night. Yet also it was so vast a burden that the air did not seem capable of supporting that storm, and the feet of it brushed the ground. Long arms of black were thrust down, and dun-colored mist clouded the face of the prairie.

The forward bulwark of the storm crossed the sun. At once semi-twilight took the place of what had been day, blazing hot and bright. At the same time, small streamers and flags broke away from the upper section of the cloud masses and darted like flung javelins across the heavens to the north—javelins of transparent and jewel-like white that the upper sun turned into separate walls of brilliance.

Heavier arms were flung after them, darker, heavier. The whole sky to the north began to be flecked with gray and with white splashes, and then the first breath of the wind reached the watchers. It came first with a gentle sighing, and then a puff that streamed out the mane of Ashur. He, like the hero that he was, faced this towering wall of dark with pricked ears and perfect complacence. Only once did he turn his head as if to see what went on in the face of his master.

That face Torridon maintained as well as he could in a grave, almost a threatening air of command. He felt like a futile child in the presence of the deity, but he saw that it was well for him to make these grown-up children imagine that he had indeed commanded the elements.

All the time he kept an authoritative hand raised, and now and again he lifted his voice in a harsh chant, something in the tone of the chants that he had heard among the Cheyennes, though the words that he supplied were the sheerest gibberish. Covertly he was watching the Indians of his guard.

They were overcome, like the rest of the multitude. Sometimes they glanced at him, as at the raiser of the winds, but the vast majority of their attention was given to the progress of the great cloud. They drew their robes close about them. They leaned forward, as though the weight of the storm already were beating upon them.

There was only one exception, and that was big Standing Bull. Calmly reloading his rifle and a pistol that he carried in a saddle holster, he then gave his entire attention not to the wind or the clouds, but to the bringer of the rain—to poor Torridon himself. And the latter felt that he would rather have bought the indifference of that one formidable warrior than the carelessness of all the rest of the guards who were around him. He was at least glad that Standing Bull dared not leave his place at the edge of the draw.

There was no doubt that the cloud was bringing copious rain with it. The mist above the face of the prairie now deepened. It became a thick wall, as impenetrable as any part of the storm, brushing the very surface of the ground, and presently Torridon could smell the acrid yet pleasant odor of rain, newly fallen upon the parched plains. The next moment his face was stung.

A cry of approbation and incredulous delight burst from the watchers as the first, rattling volley of the rain whipped them. It was as though they had taken the beginning of this to be merely a great picture, staged with vast effects of light and shadow, but perhaps as unreal as a painting on a buffalo robe. Now they saw and felt the actuality. At their feet the dust puffed up as the great drops hammered against the earth. Upon their heads and faces the volley struck. And with a universal gesture of praise and joy, they threw their arms up to the blackening sky.

The rain was indeed upon them. The overhanging coping of the cloud now was toppling down the northern sky, shutting the whole sky away, dimming the day to evening light, and now even this light grew yet fainter. Beyond the draw were some bushes. They disappeared from sight as a gray wall swept over them.

Torridon shrank. It was like the coming of a solid wave of water. And when the weight of the rain struck him, he gasped for breath; at once, all around him was in confusion, as the half-wild horses of the guard reared and plunged, but only vaguely could he see them—figures guessed at, things out of a dream.

The very voice of the multitude was more than half lost in the roar of the rain, like the roar of a waterfall—but the chant of exultation came in vague waves toward him, split across by the neighing of the frightened horses, as the huge bulk of the cloud itself was split across by the sudden spring of the lightning. It cracked the blackened sky across from zenith to horizon, and the thunder pealed instantly afterward. The earth shook with the sound, and the ears were made to ring.

But by that flash of the lightning, in spite of the rain curtains that streamed from the sky, Torridon was aware of Standing Bull, who at last had left his post and was making straight for him.

He was roused as out of a trance. It seemed to Torridon, in that excited moment, that heaven had indeed answered a prayer from his lips, and that now he was a craven and a fool if he allowed the opportunity to pass without taking advantage of it, no matter how slight it might be. So he called to Ashur, and the stallion quivered once, and then burst into a gallop. The silver mare, who had been crowding against the black horse as though for protection, veered far to the side, and then rushed after, whinnying. But Torridon held Ashur straight for the verge of the draw.

He had marked the place before. It was not, so far as he had been able to judge, the narrowest gap from bank to bank, but the nearer bank rounded off so as to offer a sure footing, and the farther bank was low, and rounded of edge, also—such a landing place as, if a horse slipped, would not hurl him on his back, but give him a chance to scramble up, cat-like.

The thunder burst on them again, with lightning roving wildly through the noise, and, by that burst of light, he saw Standing Bull at the full gallop after him, guiding his horse with his knees, and his rifle raised with both hands.

"Ashur!" shouted Torridon.

And the good horse acknowledged the cry by hurling himself forward at full speed. They reached the edge of the draw. Excited voices shouted from either side, and it seemed to Torridon that hands were reached out to snare him, but now Ashur was away into the air, leaping without hesitation or fear, and flinging himself boldly over the gap.

What a gulf of sullen dark it was beneath them! And already the torrents of the rain had marked the stony bottom with little pools of water, like glimmering silver. They shot high up, they hung in mid-air without moving forward, as it seemed to Torridon, and then they landed with a jar on the farther bank.

Sick at heart, he felt the quarters of the stallion slip away beneath him. But Ashur recovered himself like a monster cat. He scrambled, found a footing, and lurched away across the prairie, while Torridon turned back with a savage exultation in his heart. Now let them follow if they dared.

They dared not.

On the brink behind him, he saw the great form of Standing Bull, with a rifle couched in the hollow of his shoulder. A pressure of the knee made Ashur bound to one side like a man dodging, and that instant the rifle spat fire. The bullet went wide. Not even the sing of it came close to Torridon's ear. Still he looked back and saw the silver mare, brilliant and beautiful even in this rain-clouded light, hesitate on the verge of the chasm and then pitch forward into it.

XIII

It robbed him of half the pleasure of his escape. There was nothing beneath the sun that Roger Lincoln prized more than this splendid creature, and Torridon little liked the thought of some day facing him and confessing that he had come away and left Comanche behind him.

But now he must ride hard. There was faint danger for the moment, but when the rain lifted, if it proved to be merely a passing squall, then he might well come within range of some of their accurate rifles. And with that weapon he himself was so useless that he could not well keep them at long distance.

So he struck out a straight course to the north. He had made what inquiries he could while he was among the Cheyennes, and he had it vaguely in mind that Fort Kendry must be somewhere to the edge of the northern and eastern horizon.

"Four days and four nights," they had said, "on the warpath. Six days traveling on a hunt."

That was eloquent. He determined that he must keep steadily on by the North Star for four days and nights. Certainly Ashur could do as much in that time as the sturdiest Indian ponies that ever bestrode the prairies. Having made his point, he then would venture one day to the right, and, turning back, he would go straight for two days. If still Fort Kendry was not in sight, he trusted that he would be able to circle and cut for trail until he found some path that would lead him into the frontier post. That is to say, unless what he had gathered from half a dozen sources among the Cheyennes had not been all one parcel of complicated lying.

He laid his course with greater and greater temporary confidence. It was true that the first blast and fury of the wind and the rain had diminished, but, although it lifted, he could not see a sign of a horseman behind him. The rain developed into an ordinary pelting storm, not heavy enough to damage the corn, but certainly enough to give it the soaking it required.

Perhaps sheer gratitude in the breasts of the majority would prevent them from allowing a party in pursuit to start after him. But he sighed and doubted that. And then his heart swelled as he remembered that Standing Bull deliberately had fired after him. Surely in all the annals of mankind there had been no deed of more foul ingratitude. Yet, in a way, he understood. In the confused brain of Standing Bull, he appeared as a gift from heaven. The gift had no right to take wings and remove itself. Furthermore, the more valuable a gift had he proved himself—if he could cure the sick and bring the rain—the more bitterly was his loss to be regretted. No doubt, he tried to assure himself, Standing Bull had fired at Ashur, and not at Ashur's rider.

Now that he had made peace with his conception of the warrior, he felt a certain touch of kindness for the Cheyennes. Those upon whom we have lavished our kindness are always those upon whom we shower our most pleasant recollections. And Torridon felt that he had been drinking deep of real life from the instant when he first encountered the prostrate dreamer on the river island.

He told himself that he had been a boy before, but now he was a man, and a real man. Turning his head, then, from this reverie, he was aware of a streak of gray moving across the plain. He turned back with a shout of wonder and joy, and then through the rain mist she came on bravely, tossing her head and whinnying—Comanche herself!

To Torridon, it was like the coming of a welcome and long-trusted friend. For such she was. And if he never had been able to establish in her the same sort of electric understanding that existed between him and the stallion, at least she would come when she was called, follow at his heels like a dog, and do many pretty and foolish tricks, such as sitting down and begging like a dog, with a lifted foreleg. She did a frantic circle around them, slipping in the mud as she turned, and neighing again in her rejoicing.

Then she came up beside them. Torridon could see mud on the saddle, which proved that she had rolled in the bottom of the draw. But perhaps that tumble had been the means of saving her neck. At any rate, she was unharmed, and, when the rain had sluiced the mud from her, she would be as good as new.

He changed to her at once—Ashur had borne the brunt of the fast running during the escape—and pressed along the course. Into his mind, now, flashed a picture of what he had been in the first dreary days after the loss of Roger Lincoln. He had been crushed with despair, totally overwhelmed with loneliness. Now the two horses were to him like two friends, and almost filling the place of humans. Half the terror was departed from the prairies. And if he could not find his goal, he felt that he could endure hunger with calm, and trust to the luck of the hunt to find game. He was far from expert with the rifle, but still he was much improved. He had an excellent weapon, and he had an ample store of ammunition.

That first day was a hungry and miserable one, but, in place of food and of warmth, he had the delicious sense of freedom. Though he scanned the horizon painfully again and again, he had no sight of any living thing, and he made up his mind that the Cheyennes, knowing how peerlessly he was mounted, had determined not to follow in chase.

He found no tree or even a bush large enough to give shelter, when the dark day suddenly grew blacker with the evening. The best that he could do was to make a pile of the packs and then roll in a damp blanket on the lee side of the pile. A wet couch, but nevertheless his sleep was deep.

Once or twice he roused himself, always to find that the rain was pattering in his face. With vague trouble he wondered if this exposure would bring fever on him, but afterward he slept well again, and, when he wakened, it was because of the low, anxious whinny of Ashur.

He looked up. The great, black horse was standing beside him as though on guard, and Torridon sat up in the gray of the morning. The sky was still solid gray with rain clouds, but those clouds were riding high and the horizon was much enlarged since the low and misty weather of the day before. The stallion was pointing his head to the east, his ears quivering back and forth in obvious anxiety, and Torridon stared long at that spot. It was not until he had stood up that he discovered, in the gray, faint distance, faintly moving forms, barely distinguishable.

It was enough to make his heart leap. Frantically he set about saddling and bridling, his fingers stumbling with nervous haste. But he would not allow himself the dangerous privilege of another glance until he was finally in the saddle on the mare. Ashur should be reserved for the last emergency.

In that saddle, however, when he looked again to the east, he saw that danger was rapidly sweeping toward him. A dozen or more Indians, not half a mile away, were galloping toward him. They did not come in one body, but in groups of two or three, widely separated, and strung out in a line from north to south, as though they were sweeping the plains with a great net to catch what fish they could.

He turned the head of his horse due west and sent the mare into a strong gallop. Ashur followed beside her with his enormous stride. There was no need to keep a lead rope on him. By word of mouth he could be as effectually controlled as by a bridle.

But it was only at a pace little short of her full speed that Comanche could begin to drop the wild riders behind, and that by slow degrees. The Cheyennes—he had no doubt that it was they—moved at a terrific pace, punishing their mounts remorselessly, for each warrior had three or four animals in reserve, and the horse herd was brought up in the rear by active boys, who flogged the tired ones up to the company of their fresher brothers.

Still they could not quite manage the rate of Comanche. The fine mare straightened to her work, and the Indians fell gradually off, so that Torridon felt that he could safely swing toward the north again without any danger of being caught by the wing of the enemy in that direction.

To the north he swerved, therefore, but, as he turned the head of Comanche in the new direction, he heard a sound like the screeching of ten devils. And to the west, not a hundred yards away, out of the very bosom of the plain, as it were, upstarted a full score of Cheyennes, with the formidable figure of Standing Bull prominent in the front rank. They charged down at him, yelling like so many fiends, at the full speed of their horses, the heads of the ponies shaken by their fierce efforts.

Torridon turned dumb with exquisite fear. He could call on the gray mare, but the touch of his knee and the grinding of his heel into her tender flank were enough to make her swerve and bolt back.

A bullet hummed past his head. And, as he flattened himself along the back of the horse, he heard a voice of thunder, distinct above the rushing of the hoofs, the whistling of the wind at his ears.

"Stop, White Thunder! Stop, or we will catch you with bullets! Stop, and you are safe as a brother in our hands!"

He would not stop. He had freedom, and the return to his own kind and sweet Nancy Brett all before him. Death was not so terrible as the loss of such treasures. Desperately he rode. But he could not keep on in this direction.

Straight before him the line of riders from the east was storming, drawing toward him in a group now. He could see the flogging of their arms, as they punished their horses. Their wild whoops seemed to check the pulsation of his heart.

Like a fool he had ridden into this open trap. They simply had driven him into the lion's mouth from one side, while the other side waited to catch him. They were brushing him up, as a housewife brushes dust from the floor into a pan. He groaned with rage as well as terror.

Then he drove Comanche to the due north, or a little east of it. She had gone well before. But her speed now startled even her rider.

He thought that he could detect a note of rage rather than triumph in the shouting behind him. Certainly the noise was growing dimmer. With unflagging speed she kept on, running straight and true.

There were two Indians on the right flank of the Cheyennes who were rushing at him from the east. Those were the two on whom the greatest share of the burden of catching him must lie, now. With a falling heart he recognized in one of them that glorious young warrior, that peerless rider and rifleman, Rising Hawk. Like a bronze statue endowed with life he came, erect in the saddle, the rifle ready beneath his arm. His left hand was raised. He was shouting to Torridon to warn him to a halt, and the fugitive saw that he must play his last card now or lose the game forever.

He had Ashur running lightly beside him, turning his lordly head as though he scorned these men of the prairies. Now he drew the big horse closer with a single word. Shoulder by shoulder ran mare and stallion, and it was a simple thing to slip from one saddle to the next. It was a trick that he had practiced many and many a time before, and now his labor was well spent. He was on Ashur—and at his first call the big black leaped away from Comanche as though she had stumbled in full stride.

Like a human being afraid of being left behind, she whinnied with terror, but Ashur was leaving her with every stride.

They were past Rising Hawk, now. Standing Bull's party was far behind. Then Torridon heard the crashing of many rifles. Yet he did not hear the whistle of a single bullet. He wondered at it. Then, glancing aside, he saw Rising Hawk deliberately fire his weapon high into the air.

At last he understood. They would frighten him into surrender if they could, but they would not deliberately harm him. And, as that amazing knowledge came to him, Ashur swept him into a shallow draw just deep enough to shelter horse and rider. They raced a furious mile along its winding course, and when they left it again to bear straight north, Standing Bull and Rising Hawk and all the rest were hopelessly behind, and every moment they were being distanced more sadly. Even Comanche, with all her speed, and without a rider to burden her, was a full two hundred yards behind.

XIV

After the foolish manner in which he had allowed himself to be so nearly snared by the Cheyennes, Torridon lost his confidence. He felt no better than a boy, and an irresponsible one, at that. But two things struck him with a lasting wonder out of this adventure. The one was the blinding speed of Ashur—for never before had he seen it so tested—the other was that the Cheyennes had chosen to spare his life.

He did not try to deceive himself on that point. He had been in their hands, to all intents and purposes. If they wanted his scalp, it could have been theirs for the asking. The twenty rifles that had risen with Standing Bull to block his flight could have riddled him with bullets. But they wanted his life, not his death. And gravely, gravely did he wonder over this state of affairs.

He had the stallion and the mare to carry him, and he vowed that he would give them nothing but short halts for the next two days. Let the Cheyennes follow if they could. So he set his teeth and narrowed his eyes, and embarked upon two days of weary, continual labor and effort.

The weather broke before midday, but, though the sun came out bright and clear, the going was frightfully heavy under foot. The weight of it, however, was not all a disadvantage. He was able to get fresh meat on that account, for the antelope that at last he struck down with a lucky shot was kept in range only by the softness of the ground over which it raced. He paused to roast bits of the best of the flesh. He carried two large cuts of the antelope with him, and with them he could consider the food problem settled on that trail.

After that he voyaged through empty prairie until the fourth day out, when he struck into rolling ground, and in the distance to the north and the west there were tall mountains, dark with forests.

He came to a river, swift and mighty. When he first came to the bank, he was in time to see a drowned tree floating rapidly past and he knew that the stream was not fordable here. He would have to go higher up before it could be passed. So he turned to the left and went on for another two hours until he saw a canoe paddled in the flatter shallows of the stream by two men in frontier costume of deerskin, dark, almost, as Indians, but identified even in the distance by the sunburned paleness of their hair.

Torridon, from behind a great tree, watched them working, their paddles flashing rhythmically, and the wake dotted with small whirlpools where the wooden blades had dipped and pulled. Rapidly they approached. The craft was long and slender, made roughly, but with infinite grace. In the center was a mound, covered with a buffalo robe. A rifle lay at the hand of either paddler, but they seemed to pay no attention to the banks of the stream until—there was a sudden shout. The steersman backed water strongly, and the paddler in the bow shipped his paddle and caught up a long rifle. Lightly he balanced it, and stared straight at the tree that sheltered Torridon.

So alert and keen did the two appear that Torridon felt as though the tree were small protection, indeed. He shouted in haste: "A friend! White man!" And he cautiously exposed himself a little, waving a hand.

The man in the bow nodded. "Come out and show yourself!" he called.

Torridon slowly stepped into view.

"What might you be aiming at?" said the steersman at this.

"Fort Kendry," said Torridon eagerly. "Do you know where it is?"

The bowsman turned and chuckled and the steersman chuckled as well. They let the canoe drift slowly ahead, the faint wake darkening the water behind them. There was not a sound. Then a fish leaped and splashed heavily, but still the two allowed their craft to float on, paying little heed to Torridon's question, but staring at him curiously.

"Do you know?" cried Torridon. "Is it many days away?" He followed them along the bank, imploring: "For God's sake, come to the bank and tell me where I am. I've been lost. . . ."

They laughed again. Either they were mad or else they were callous brutes. Then, as they began to dip their paddles once more, the bowsman called over his shoulder: "Go round the next bend!" And they swept on down the shining river.

Torridon, sick at heart, looked after them until his eyes were blinded by the sun path over the water. He had so yearned to be among his kind again, and this was a sample of their greeting.

He went back to Ashur and mounted him with a sigh. He hesitated. It might well be that the proper course was down the stream, and yet he was curious about what might lie around the next bend. He sent Ashur forward at a dog-trot, the mare following leisurely, picking at tempting tufts of grass, here and there. And so, finally, he rounded the broad bend of the stream and through the margin of trees he saw before him a dazzling flash, as though a powerful glass had been focused in his eyes. He rushed on through the trees.

It was the reflection from a windowpane, and not a quarter of a mile away he saw the tall rock walls of a little fort, with three small cannon topping the walls—each gun hooded to the muzzle with tarpaulin. Around the knees of those strong bastions were scattered huts, lean-tos, dog tents, Indian lodges.

Fort Kendry!

Torridon clasped his hands together. He was very young. And his sensitive soul had been long and hardly tried. He had been through the long valley of death, as it were, and now he hardly resisted the impulse to weep, but let the hot tears tumble down his face. Sobs rose and choked him. These, out of awe of the forest silence, he kept down.

But no, that silence already was broken. Out of the distance came the brisk and ringing noise of a hammer, rapidly applied, and on the heels of it a dog began to howl—a scream of fear and pain, that died in a succession of rapid yelps.

Torridon sighed again. He almost forgot that this was the happy goal; he almost forgot that beautiful Nancy Brett was somewhere in that collection of tents and houses, or in the solid circumference of the fort itself. Between her and him there existed a thick veil of brutal humanity, and this he must try to brush aside. It seemed to poor Torridon, indeed, that the dog had cried out to say the thing that was in his own soul.

Then stifled laughter came from nearby. He saw two men peering out at him, their faces convulsed with mirth. Brutal, savage faces he thought them, more brutal than the face of any Indian. He gasped at the sight of them, and, as he showed fear, a leering joy gleamed in the eyes of the larger of the pair. He thrust himself out into the trail and laid a hand on the bridle of Torridon's horse.

"What're you blubberin' about?" he asked. "Who are you, and where are you goin'?"

"And where," asked the second fellow, stepping forward in turn, but keeping a bit to the rear, "did you get them horses? Who give 'em to you?"

"Who'd you steal 'em from, you better ask?" said the first of the worthies. "Get down here on the ground and let me have a look at that horse."

Torridon shuddered as he heard the command. Many a time a man passed through many perils, through many dark moments, and the cup was dashed from his lips at the very moment when he had won to it.

"D'you hear?" bellowed the first speaker, and laid a hand of iron upon the knee of Torridon. "Down off that horse, or I'll pick you outten the saddle and throw you in the river, you sneakin' thief. That's what you are. I can see it by the coward look of you. Get out of the saddle! Move!"

The miracle had happened to Torridon before, more than once, and, when the supreme moment came mind and forethought vanished. A sheer physical instinct took command. So it did now. Into his hand winked a long, slender, double-barreled pistol, and he thrust the barrels straight into the throat of the other.

"Sufferin' jack rabbits..." began the big man. He paused, mouth agape. His eyes, round and wide, read the face of Torridon as a child reads indecipherable print in a primer.

There was the other, however, to consider. He was circling cat-like to the rear.

"Keep your friend back," said Torridon, "or I'll give you one barrel and try the other on him. Tell him to get here behind you, where I can keep an eye on him."

To his own amazement, the thing was done. Like two awed children they stood before him.

"Now," said Torridon, wicked pleasure coming to him, "tell me if I am a horse thief?"

The first man, rascal though he might be, had recovered from the first shock. He was able to grin down the pistol barrels. "Son," he said, "you got the bill of sale right there in your hand. I didn't see it at first. Matter of fact, I guess you got two bills of sale."

"Then drop your rifles and back up to the trees," ordered Torridon.

It was done, in turn. They let the long guns fall—then slowly moved back, watching Torridon cautiously all the time.

"Only, will you mind tellin' me," asked one of them, "how you filled your hand? Did you have that gun up your sleeve all the while?"

He said it wistfully, and Torridon could not help smiling. Then, at a touch of his knee, Ashur moved forward. The gray mare cantered beside him. He rounded the next turn among the trees and, glancing back, saw that the pair of ruffians had not moved. He was not overjoyed as he went on, but he had an odd interest in the knowledge that those heavy, trustworthy rifles, even in practiced hands, had proved but clumsy protectors at close range, where speed was of avail.

Then his heart began to lift. No doubt he was riding into a brutal society, but it might be that he would find in himself a sufficient manhood to face the members of it down.

He was entering the town. There were no streets. Between the houses the ways were simply surface soil, beaten to a muddy pie by rain and the cutting of ten thousand hoofs. The horses dislodged one foot at a time, with a loud, popping sound. The pedestrians going here and there wore to a man strong boots, clotted with the mud. And altogether it seemed to Torridon the dreariest little patched and crazy quilt-work village that ever he had seen.

And yet it was Fort Kendry.

A thousand times he had heard that name. It had been ringing through the stories that came in from the frontier. It was one of those last outposts of civilization, hardly civilized itself. Men said that the rapid river that slid past Fort Kendry ate a man a day—and nothing done to the murderers. Still he had some doubt, and, calling to a bearded, little, ratty-looking man, he asked if this were indeed Fort Kendry. The latter, in reply, merely gaped, and then broke into loud laughter and went on his way.

He went farther, until he saw a squaw standing with arms akimbo in the door of a miserable shack. He asked of her in English. She merely stared insolently at him, eying him with contempt, and the two splendid horses with curiosity. He tried her in Cheyenne.

She started convulsively and sprang forward. To the bare ankles she sank in the mud. Yes, this was Fort Kendry. Did he come from the Suhtai? Had he been with them long?

Yes, Roger Lincoln was at the fort. He lived inside the fort itself. Had he known in the Cheyenne tribe a great warrior, Yellow Wolf, who . . . ?

Yes, Samuel Brett was here, and living with his niece in the big, square house just outside the gates of the fort. So she poured out answer and question intermixed. But he did not wait to satisfy her curiosity. He merely waved his hand to her and pressed forward. He was, indeed, too choked by the wild fluttering of his heart to be capable of speech.

XV

He went toward the square house that had been pointed out to him. A big man with a square-cut beard was chopping wood beside the building. His brawny arms were bared to the elbow; the axe flew like a feather in his grasp. There was something deeply familiar to Torridon in the appearance of the stalwart. And he called in a trembling voice to know if this were the house of Samuel Brett.

The other turned, axe poised for a stroke. Slowly he allowed it to sink to the ground as he stared, and then he shouted: "By grab, it's the thief!"

And dropping the axe, he snatched up a rifle. Resistance was not in the mind of Torridon. In blank terror he whirled the horse and fled, and heard the click of the rifle hammer, followed by no explosion, then the furious growling of the other.

Before him the gate of the fort was wide open—a double gate, in fact, with men leaning on their tall rifles nearby. Through the gate he fled, and drew rein inside, a badly frightened youth. Loud and angry voices demanded the reason for thus pushing into their midst, without leave begged. Stern faces closed around him, and a hand was laid on the bridle rein.

"Roger Lincoln..." was all he could stammer. "Is Roger Lincoln here?"

"And what d'you want with Roger Lincoln?" asked one while another exclaimed: "By gravy, its Comanche!"

"Comanche, you fool! She's a half a hand taller'n that gray runt!"

"I tell you, I know her. It's *her*. Didn't I match my pinto ag'in' her last year? Didn't she leave him like he was hobbled?"

A crowd of the idle and curious was gathering, and suddenly, through that crowd, Torridon was aware of a tall man stepping lightly forward, his long hair gleaming over his shoulders, a jacket of the most beautiful, white deerskin setting off his fine torso.

"Roger!" shouted Torridon. "Oh, Roger Lincoln!"

Would he, too, have a rifle and curses with which to greet him? No, no! For Roger Lincoln came with a leap. He took Torridon in those slender, mighty hands of his, lifted him to the ground, and held him at arm's length, by the shoulders.

"My boy," said Roger Lincoln softly, "this is the greatest and the happiest and the finest day of my life. Lad, how did you come back to me from the dead?"

They sat in Lincoln's room in the fort. Fort, indeed, by courtesy, for it was held by a trading company and not by federal troops. Hundreds of miles to the east the formal authority of the government ended. With an armed rabble, the fur company held this outpost; according to the whim of the moment it made its laws. Half hotel and store, and half fortress, it ruled the wild country around it.

They had interchanged stories eagerly. The tale of Roger Lincoln was simplicity itself. Out hunting, and not three miles from his starting place, he had been snatched up by a wandering band of Crows, far from their own hunting grounds. Death and scalping would have been the end of him, had it not chanced that the chief knew Lincoln to be a famous man and decided on accepting a ransom. They proceeded straight to the vicinity of Fort Kendry, and there Roger Lincoln had no difficulty in procuring a score of good horses to pay for his scalp.

That done, he secured the best mount be could find and spent two days in letting the Crows learn that no bargain could be altogether one-sided. He had pursued them, caught two stragglers, sent them to their long account, and returned, eager to get back to the spot where he had left the boy.

But, of course, he found that Torridon was gone. The letter placed on the site of the campfire was gone, also. And after hunting in vain for sign that he could follow, Roger Lincoln had returned to the fort, hoping that his young friend might be able to win through to it, even against heavy odds.

Next came the tale of Torridon, hastily sketched in, to which Roger Lincoln listened with increasing joy. The trip to the Sky People filled him with laughter and excitement. And, finally, he caught the hand of Torridon and exclaimed: "You're such big medicine to that pack of wolves that they'll never give you peace! They'll be trying to steal you again, one of these days."

"Don't say it," murmured Torridon. "It makes me faint and weak to hear you."

The frontiersman rested his chin on the palm of his hand and regarded the boy with a smile and a nod. "The same Paul," he said. "The same Paul Torridon. Almost like a girl until it comes to the pinch . . . and then like a pair of tigers."

"No, no!" exclaimed Torridon. "Ah, Roger, if you knew how happy I am to be with you again, and how many times I've prayed to have a man like you with me."

Here they were interrupted by a knock at the door and no less a person than the commander of the fort appeared, a man of middle age, shrewd and hard-faced, to tell Roger Lincoln that he was accused by Samuel Brett of harboring a horse thief.

"It's the case of Ashur," said Lincoln. "Come down with me and we'll face Brett. He's not a bad kind of a man. But they've written to him that the stallion was stolen, and in a way he was. Now's the time to face it out."

He would not wait to hear the protest of Torridon, who had no wish to meet that grim axe man who so nearly had put an end to his days not long before. But down went Lincoln, Torridon, and the post captain together, and found Brett in a high rage. He repeated his accusation in a loud voice. Torridon was a sneak and a thief and a member of a cut-throat family. And he had repaid the kindness of the Bretts by slipping away with their finest horse.

The post captain heard this speech with a growing darkness of brow. "The law ain't overworked in these parts much," he declared. "But a horse thief I hate worse than a snake... it's one reason that I hate every damned Indian I ever seen. And if this Torridon has stole the black stallion... back he goes to Brett. And, besides, I'll make an example of him that'll..."

"Hold on a half minute." Roger Lincoln smiled. "Let me tell you that I found Torridon locked in the Brett cellar. They intended to cut this lad's throat the next day. We had to fight our way out, and, once out, we had to take the best horse on the place to be sure of getting away from the murderers. The horse that we took is the black one. We'll admit that. But I think the circumstances alter the case a good deal, don't you?"

"The damned lyin'..." began Samuel Brett.

"Wait!" interrupted the commandant sharply. "Lincoln, you give me your word that you've told me the straight of it? He took the horse to escape bein' murdered?"

"I give you my sacred word."

"Then the horse belongs to him by rights," said the other, and, refusing to listen to another word, he turned upon his heel and hurried away, leaving Samuel Brett half apoplectic with fury.

Roger Lincoln had drawn Torridon to one side. "Now, man," he said, "while I keep Sam Brett here and try to hold him, get to Brett's house. You'll find Nancy there, I think. Go fast, my boy." He turned to Samuel Brett. "Brett," he said, "if you think that you have a fair claim to that black horse, will you sit down in my room and talk it over with me? Paul Torridon and I don't want to figure as horse thieves."

"I'll talk it over here!" roared Samuel Brett. "Or I'll fight it over here. As for rights, I can show you..."

Torridon heard no more. He had slipped away through the crowd and hastened through the open gates. Evening was covering Fort Kendry. Lamps were beginning to glimmer behind the windows, and the smell of frying meat made the air pungent as Torridon came again to the big square house and heard a woman's voice calling: "Nancy! Oh, Nan!"

From the distance: "Yes, Aunt Mary!"

Oh, heart of Paul Torridon, how still it stood. He hastened through the gloom toward the trees and saw a form issuing from them with arms filled with greenery. He told himself that he could tell her by the mere pace at which she walked, the lightness of her step, and the sense of joy that went before her like radiance before a lamp. She came quickly on until she was aware of his shadow standing against the twilight gloom, and she stopped with a faint cry.

Then, cheerfully: "Are you the new man that Uncle Samuel sent in from Gannet?"

He did not answer. He could not. He heard her catch a frightened breath, but, instead of running from him, she came slowly forward, a small step and a halt, and a step again. The greenery slipped from her arms to the ground. He heard a small whisper, but to him it was all the vital, human warmth of song, and then she was in his arms.

From the door a long nasal wail was calling: "Nancy! Oh, Nan, where are you?"

And Torridon whispered: "She's here. Oh, Nancy, Nancy, how beautiful you are."

And she: "Silly dear, how can you see me?"

"I can see your goodness and your truth," said Torridon. "And I . . . I . . ."

"Nancy!" wailed the caller. "Are you comin'?"

"Never, never," whispered Torridon.

"I have to take these in," whispered Nancy in reply. "I'll be out again in a flash. Wait here . . . I've got to go in . . . she'd never stop calling me. . . ."

"How long will you be, Nan?"

"I don't know. Not half a minute. Not two seconds."

"Nan, I feel as though I'll never see you again."

"Ah, but you will."

"Kiss me once."

"There, and there."

She swept up her fallen load and ran into the brightness of the doorway.

Torridon heard her saying: "I stumbled on the path and quite lost my breath."

"Why, honey," said her aunt, "you look all done in. Set down and rest yourself a minute, and . . ."

And a hood of darkness that instant fell over the head of Torridon, was jerked tightly over his mouth by mighty hands, and strong arms caught him up, crushing him with their power.

XVI

He felt himself being carried rapidly away, and faint he heard a voice murmur, beside the robe that stifled him: "Will you be quiet and make no cry, White Thunder?"

"Yes," he gasped in the Cheyenne tongue.

Instantly the hood was jerked from his head. They were standing under the edge of the trees, he in the huge arms of Standing Bull. He knew that ugly profile even in that faint light.

"No harm, little brother," murmured Standing Bull. "You are more safe now than you would be in your own teepee. I, Standing Bull, have spoken."

He allowed Torridon to stand, but kept a tight hold on him.

And now the shadow of the girl ran out from the lighted door of the kitchen. Torridon saw her, as the Cheyenne drew him back into the shadow of the trees, saying: "Rising Hawk has gone to bring your horse. We would not take you back on a common pony. And all shall be as you wish in the tribe. You shall be a great medicine man among us, White Thunder. You shall be rich, with horses and scalps and squaws."

The trees closed between Torridon's back-turned face and the silhouette of the girl, but faintly, far off, he heard a cautious voice calling: "Paul! Paul!" And then a little louder, in a voice broken with fear and grief: "Paul Torridon! Where are you?"

A rustling passed among the trees before them. They came into a clearing and there were a dozen horses in waiting, and the gleaming, half-naked forms of several warriors. They closed in a whispering knot around Torridon. He did not hear their voices, for faintness dimmed his ears with a dull roaring through which he still seemed to hear the sad voice of a girl calling for Paul Torridon.

And suddenly he groaned: "Standing Bull, if I have been true to you and helped you in bad times, be my friend now. Take your knife and strike it into my side, but don't carry me back to the Cheyennes."

"Peace, peace, peace," said Standing Bull, like a father to a sick child. "Peace, little brother. Happiness is not one bird, but many. We shall catch them for you, one by one. We shall fill your hands with happiness. Behold. Here is Rising Hawk, and the black thunder horse is with him."

Suddenly Torridon was raised and placed in the saddle.

Standing Bull stood close beside him. "If you make a loud shout," he said, "I give you the thing for which you ask... this knife through the heart. But go with us quietly, and everything shall be well. You shall be to me a son and a brother and a father, and to all the warriors of the tribe. Rising Hawk, watch the rear. I ride in front with White Thunder. Ah, ha. This night Heammawihio has remembered us."

And with his feet lashed beneath the saddle, and a lariat running from the neck of the black stallion to the saddle bow of Standing Bull, Torridon was carried out from the settlement. The lights gleamed more dimly through the trees and went out altogether, and presently there was the faint glimmer of water to their left.

They were well embarked on the homeward way—the out trail for Torridon, from which he could see no return. And he raised his head to the broad and brilliant sky, where every star shone brightly, and he wondered why God had chosen to torment him. The sense of Roger Lincoln's faith and truth rode at his side like a ghost, and the beauty of Nancy Brett, but they had been shown to him only to be taken away.

There were no tears in the eyes of Torridon. He had found a grief too great for that.

Standing Bull put the horses to full gallop. They began to rush forward like the wind. Trees and brush and the shining river poured past them, but the calm stars hung unmoved in their silent places above him.

Peyton

I

When the doctor told Hank Peyton that he was about to die, Hank took another drink and closed the secret inside his thin lips, but when, on the third morning following, he fell back on his bed in a swoon after pulling on his boots, Hank lay for a long time looking at the dirty boards of the ceiling until his brain cleared. Then he called for his tall son and said: "Jeremiah, I'm about to kick out."

Jerry Peyton was as full of affection as any youth in the town of Sloan, but the regime of his father had so far schooled him in restraining his emotions, that now he lighted a match and a cigarette and inhaled the first puff before he answered: "What's wrong?"

"That's my concern and not yours," the father said truthfully. "Further'n that, I didn't call you in here for an opinion. The doctor give me that three days ago, Jeremiah." He always pronounced the name in full; he characteristically despised the nickname that the rest of the world had given to his son. "I got you here to look you over."

He was as good as his word, but the only place he looked was straight between the eyes of Jerry. At length he sighed and turned his glance back to the ceiling, a direction that never changed while he lived. "I'm about to kick out," went on the father, "and bringing you up is about all the good I've done, and, take it all around, I'm satisfied." After a moment of thought he said to the ceiling: "You ain't pretty, but you can ride straight up. Answer me."

"Yes," said Jerry.

"You talk straight."

"Yes."

"You shoot straight."

"Some say I do."

"You got a good education."

"Fair enough. But not too good."

"Ain't you got a diploma from the high school?"

"Yes."

"Then don't talk back. I say you're educated and mostly I run this roost. What?"

"Yes," Jerry replied.

"I leave you a house to live in and enough cows to grow into a real bunch... if you work. Will you work?"

"Is this a promise you want?" asked Jerry, troubled.

"No."

"Well, I'll try to work."

"I leave you one thing more." He fumbled under the bedding and drew out a revolver. "You know what that is?"

"The Mexicans call it The Voice of La Paloma."

"They call it right. You take that gun. Before you die you'll hear men say a lot of things about your pa... and mostly they'll be right... but afterward you go home and pull out this old gun and say to yourself... 'He was a crook... he was a hard one... but he had plenty of grit, and he done for La Paloma that made the rest take water.'"

"I shall," said Jerry.

After a time the father said: "Look at my legs."

"Yes."

"The boots?"

"They're on."

"Good," said Hank Peyton. He added a moment later: "How do I look?"

"Like you'd hit the end of your rope."

"You lie," said Hank. "I can still see the knot in the ceiling." And forthwith he died.

When he was buried, the old inhabitants of Sloan said: "Who would've thought Hank Peyton would die in bed?" And the new inhabitants, who were the majority, added: "One ruffian the less."

Around Sloan the government had built a great dam to the north and irrigation ditches were beginning to spread a shining, regular pattern across the desert. Very few of the cowmen took advantage of all the opportunities that water threw in their way, but a swarm of newcomers edged in among them and cut up the irrigation districts into pitiful little patches of green that no true cattleman could help despising. The shacks of Sloan gave way to a prim, brick-fronted row of stores; the new citizens elected improvement boards; they began to boost. Very soon Sloan was extended in all directions by a checkering of graded streets and blocks that the optimists watched in confident expectation. But old-timers were worried by floors so cleanly painted that spurs could not be stuck into them when one sat down; they scorned, silently, the stern industry and sharpness of the homemakers, and many a cowpuncher was known to ride up the main street, look wistfully about him, and then, without dismounting, turn back toward his distant bunkhouse. For of the many faces of civilization, two were turned to each other eye to eye in Sloan, and the differences were too great for composition. For instance, among the cattlemen, law was an interesting legend that in workaday life was quite supplanted by unwritten customs; among the farmers and shopkeepers of Sloan, law was an ally or an enemy as the case might be, but always a sacred thing. From that point of view, Hank Peyton was one of the most fallen of the profane, and therefore the townsfolk drew a breath of relief when they heard of his death.

It cannot be said that even the cowpunchers grieved very heartily, but they respected at least certain parts of his character, and above all they had an abiding affection for his son, Jerry.

For his sake they were both sorry and glad, and it was generally understood among them that, when his father was out of the way, Jeremiah Peyton would shake up the old Peyton place and put it abreast of the times. They waited in vain for the signs of uplift. Jerry was willing enough to talk over changes and improvements with the wiser and more experienced heads among his neighbors, but when it came to tactics of labor he failed miserably, no matter how excellent his strategy of planning might be.

Sheriff Sturgis, who was the only county official to retain his place in the new regime, said: "The trouble with Jerry is that his dad sent him away to school for just long enough to spoil any likin' for work he might have had, but he didn't stay in school long enough to learn a way of sittin' down and makin' a livin'."

This was the general opinion, for, after the death of Hank Peyton, Jerry drifted along in his usual amiable manner. He made enough busting broncos in the roundup seasons to see him through the remainder of the year in idleness, and he picked up from his little bunch of cows a few bits of spending money. The cowmen excused him for virtues of courage and generosity, but the townsfolk saw only the black side of the picture, and in their eyes Jerry was plain lazy. They waited for the latent fierceness of his law-breaking father to appear as the fortunes of the son declined month after month. His personal appearance remained as prosperous as ever, but the townsfolk noted with venomous pleasure that his little string of horses was gradually sold off until he retained only a few cow-hocked, knock-kneed mustangs, and one buckskin mare with the heart of a lion and the temper of a demon. It may be gathered that, by this time, Jerry had reached a point of argument between cowpuncher and farmer. The one faction held that he retained the buckskin because he loved her; the farmers were certain that he kept her only because of her viciousness and the fights that she gave him.

In truth, they could not understand him. Jerry was a tall, gaunt man with heavy shoulders, a pair of straight gray eyes, and a disarming smile; he was, indeed, a mass of contradictions. When he sat in silence, he had an ugly, cold look; when he was animated, he was positively handsome. The cowmen understood him hardly more than the farmers, but they had faith, which levels mountains.

All this time Jerry may have known that he was frequently the subject of conversation, though none, even of his closest friends, had courage enough to tell him what was said; but, whatever he knew, Jerry was content to drift along from day to day, sitting ten hours at a time on his front verandah, or riding to town and back on the buckskin. From time to time the danger of approaching bankruptcy stood up and looked him in the face, but he was always able to blink the thought away—and go on whistling. Only this thing grew vaguely in him—a discontent with his life as it was, a subtle displeasure that was directed not against men but against fate, a feeling that he was imprisoned. In the other days he had always thought that it was the stern control of his father that gave him that shackled sensation, but now the first of the month, and its bills, was as dreaded as ever was any interview with terrible Henry Peyton, drunk or sober. He was not a thoughtful man. Sometimes his revolt was expressed in a sudden saddling of the buckskin mare and a wild ride that had no destination; more often he would sit and finger The Voice of La Paloma.

It was an odd name for a revolver, for La Paloma means the dove, but there was a story connected with the name. Once upon a time—and after all it was not so long before—a little man with a gentle voice came to Sloan, and because of his voice the Mexicans called him La Paloma. He was an extremely silent man; he hardly ever spoke, and he never argued. So that when trouble came his way he put his back to the wall and pulled his gun. In a crisis the first explosion of his gun was his first word of answer, and eventually the imaginative Mexicans called the weapon The Voice of La Paloma. After a time the reputation of

La Paloma followed him to Sloan from other places. A federal marshal brought it and then raised a posse to find the little man. They found him, but they did not bring him back, and with that a wild time began around Sloan, in which the officers of the law figured as hawks, and La Paloma was a dove who flew higher still and knew how to stoop from a distance and strike, and make off with his gains unharmed. He kept it up for months and months until Hank Peyton crossed him. There was an ugly side to the story, of how Peyton double-crossed the outlaw, after worming his way into La Paloma's confidence, and sold him to the federal marshal. Be that as it may, the bandit learned the truth before the posse arrived and started a single-handed fight with Jerry's father. When the marshal arrived, he found Peyton in the cabin, shot to pieces, but with the gun of La Paloma in his hand and the bandit dead on the floor.

It was small wonder that that story kept running through Jerry's head day by day as his inheritance melted through his prodigal, shiftless fingers. Before long, little would remain except The Voice of La Paloma, and, whenever Jerry thought of that time of destitution, he looked at the revolver and remembered the carefree life of La Paloma; there were no shackles on his existence. His commission to a free life was this little weapon, and for a signature of authority it bore eleven notches, neatly filed.

II

The crisis drew near in Jerry's life; the people of Sloan almost held their breath while they watched developments. The mortgages on the old Peyton place were to be foreclosed and neither man, woman, nor child in the town expected the son of Hank Peyton to look quietly on while the land and the house changed hands. The men who held the mortgages had lawyers for agents; the lawyers had Sheriff Edward Sturgis; Sheriff Sturgis had a posse of good men and true at his call; yet for all that he was observed to wear a look of concern. The sheriff was not a student, but he had a natural belief in inherited characteristics, and he had known Hank Peyton when Hank was in his prime. Nevertheless, the storm broke from an unexpected quarter.

Jan van Zandt held one of the outlying alfalfa farms near the Peyton place, and one day he found Jerry's buckskin mare lying with a broken leg in his largest irrigation ditch; she had come through a rough place in his fence and slipped on a concrete culvert. Jan van Zandt sent a Mexican to tell the tidings to young Peyton. In the meantime he got on his fastest horse, made a round of his neighbors, and returned with a dozen men at his back. They sat down with shotguns and rifles near at hand to wait for Jerry.

He came alone and he came on foot, for there was nothing on his place except the buckskin that he deigned to ride. At first he paid no attention to the men, but sat for a long time holding the head of the patient, suffering horse before he shot her through the temple. Only then did he turn to Jan van Zandt. Jan stood with a double-barreled shotgun in both big hands and from a distance he kept shouting that he knew he was to blame for letting the fence fall into disrepair, and that he would settle whatever costs the law allowed.

"You fool, do you think your money can buy me another Nelly?" Jerry asked. Then he went to Jan van Zandt, took the shotgun out of the big hands, and beat the farmer until he was hardly recognizable. The friends of van Zandt stood by with their guns firmly grasped, but they did not fire because, as they explained later, they might have hurt Jan by mistake.

Afterward Jerry refused to bring suit for the value of his horse, but, as soon as Jan was out of bed, he filed a suit for damages in a case of assault. And he won the suit. The cowpunchers rode in singly and in pairs to Jerry and offered their assistance against the dirty ground hogs, but Jerry turned them away. He sold most of the furniture in his house and the rest of the horses to pay the fine, but, with the money, he sent a note to Jan van Zandt warning him fairly that Nelly was still unpaid for and that in due time he, Jeremiah Peyton, would extract full payment. He only waited until he discovered how such a payment could be made.

It was another occasion for Jan van Zandt to mount his fastest horse—he was quite a fancier of fine breeds—and this time he rode straight into the town of Sloan, thrust Jerry's note in front of the sheriff, and demanded police protection. The sheriff was a fat, shapeless man with a broken nose, little, uneasy eyes, and a forehead that jagged back and was immediately lost under a coarse mop of hair. His neck was put on his round shoulders at an angle of forty-five degrees, and, as he was continually glancing from side to side, he gave an impression of a man ducking danger, or about to duck. It was strange to see big Jan van Zandt lean over the desk and appeal to this man, and of the two the sheriff seemed by far the more frightened. His twinkling, animal eyes looked everywhere except at Jan van Zandt until the story was over.

Then he said: "You got some fine horses out there, haven't you, Jan?"

"The best in the county," Jan replied readily, "and, if you pull me through this, you can take your pick."

"You got me all wrong," the sheriff said. "I don't want any of your horses. But if I was you, I'd not feel safe even if I had six men with guns around me day and night. I'd get on my fastest horse and hit straight off away from Sloan."

The big man turned pale, but it was partly from anger. "Are you the sheriff of this county, or ain't you?" he asked.

"Just now," answered the sheriff, grinning, "I wish to heaven that I wasn't."

From anyone else that speech would have been a damaging remark, but the record of the sheriff was so very long and so very straight that not even the farmers of Sloan had dared to think of displacing him. He was a landmark, like the old Spanish church in Sloan, and his towering reputation kept the gunmen and wrongdoers far from the town. The admission of Sturgis that he feared young Peyton, therefore, made Jan van Zandt set his jaw and stare.

"You want me to move?" he said at length. "You want me to give up my home?"

The sheriff looked at him curiously. Sturgis was not accustomed to these homemakers, as yet, but he dimly realized that Jan van Zandt's hearth was his altar and that he would as soon renounce his God as leave his house.

"I don't want you to give up nothin'," the sheriff said. "I want you to take a vacation and beat it away. Stay away three months... and before the end of that time Jerry will be gone... the only thing that keeps him here now is you."

"Go away," repeated Jan van Zandt huskily, "and leave my wife and my girls out there... alone?"

"Good heavens, man!" burst out Sheriff Sturgis. "D'you think Jerry Peyton is a Mex? D'you think he'd lay a hand on your womenfolk? I tell you, van Zandt, the boy is clean... as my gun."

"He's a bad man," Jan van Zandt solemnly said. "Sheriff, I've seen him as close as I see you now, and I've seen him worked up."

The sheriff noted the black and blue patches on the face of van Zandt, but he said nothing.

"He's bad all through, and, when a man is crooked in one thing, he's crooked in everything."

"Listen to me," the sheriff said. "I've lived..."

"Right's right," interrupted van Zandt stubbornly. "One bad apple'll spoil a whole barrel of good ones. That's true, I guess, and if it's true, then, if there was ever any good in Peyton, the bad has turned him all rotten long ago."

Sturgis looked at the pale, set face of the farmer with a sort of horror. He felt tongue-tied, as when he argued with his wife on certain subjects, and all in a breath he hated the narrow mind of van Zandt that used maxims in place of thought, and, at the same time, respected a man who was determined to stay by his home even if he had to die there. The little, bright eyes of the sheriff looked out the window and followed a rolling, pungent cloud of dust down the street; in the narrow mind of the farmer he had caught a glimpse of certain rock-like qualities on which a nation can build. He sprang to his feet and banged his fist on the desk.

"Get out of here and back to your home," he said. "I've seen enough of your face. Peyton says he expects payment for his mare, does he? Well, he has a payment coming to him, I guess."

"I'll give him what the law grants him," said van Zandt, backing toward the door but still stolid.

"Aw, man, man," groaned Sturgis. "You come out of smooth country and smooth people. What kind of laws are you goin' to fit to a country like this?" He waved through the window toward the ragged mountains that lifted to the east of Sloan Valley.

Jan van Zandt blinked, but he said nothing and he thought nothing; he saw no relation between law and geography.

"Go back to your home," repeated the sheriff. "How do I know Peyton is going to try to harm you? I'm here to punish crimes, not read minds. Get on your way. What do I know about Peyton?"

"You told me yourself that if you was in my place..."

"But I ain't in your place, am I? What a man thinks don't count on a witness stand, does it? Legally I know Peyton is a law-abidin' citizen."

"Sheriff Sturgis," said the farmer sternly, "leastways I've learned something out of this talk with you. You call him law-abidin'? I know he's young, but he has a record as long as my arm. D'you deny that?"

The sheriff swallowed. "Mexes don't count," he said. "S'long, van Zandt."

He stood at the window, scowling, and watched the big farmer mount his horse. It was a chestnut stallion, a full sixteen hands tall, clean-limbed, straight-rumped, with a long neck that promised a mighty stride. He made a fine picture, but what good would he be, thought the sheriff, in a twenty-four-hour march across the mountains? Or how would those long legs, muscled for speed alone, stand up under the jerking, twisting, weaving labor of a roundup. The chestnut was a picture horse, decided the sheriff, made for pleasure and short, easy rides. Jan van Zandt disappeared down the street, borne at a long, rocking gallop, and the sheriff turned his glance to his own little pinto, standing untethered, with the reins thrown over his head. The pinto had raised his lumpish head a trifle and opened one eye when the stallion started away with a snort, then he dropped back into his sullen slumber, his ears flopping awry, his lower lip pendent, one hip sagging. The pinto was six, but he looked sixteen; he appeared about to sink into the dust, but, if a choice was to be made between that pinto and the chestnut stallion for a sixty-mile ride, the sheriff would not have hesitated for a second in making his decision. He was so moved as he thought of these things, that he leaned out the window and cursed the mustang in a terrible voice, and the pinto raised his head and whinnied softly.

III

Three days went slowly, slowly, over the head of the sheriff. During that time he was as profane, as slovenly, as smiling as ever, and yet every minute he waited for the crash. His mind reverted to a period fifteen years before when Hank Peyton had been a black name around Sloan. There were two men of might in those days....

Peyton and La Paloma—and only by an act of grace was Sloan rid of them when Peyton killed the more famous bad man and was himself so terribly shot up that he could never draw a weapon again with a sure hand. After that epic battle he had lived on his savage reputation alone, peacefully, but the picture in the sheriff's eye was the old Hank Peyton. Side-by-side with it he saw the son of the gunfighter, equally large, stronger, cleverer, and possessing one great attribute that his father had never known—a sense of humor. Hank had been all fire, all passion, but his son knew how to smile and wait—in fact, the sheriff knew that he was waiting even now to take the life of Jan van Zandt, and the suspense of that expectation was more terrible to him than the most violent outrage Hank himself had ever committed. Looking into the future, the sheriff found himself already accepting the death of Jan van Zandt as an accomplished fact, and his concern was wholly for his own troubles when he should have to take the trail of young Peyton. But sometimes a sinister, small hope was mixed with his worry—a hope that Peyton was waiting so that he could make his kill with impunity. After all, that was the only satisfactory explanation of the long wait.

It was on the third day that the unexpected blow fell. Six men rode into Sloan. They raced their horses straight to the office of the sheriff, and from the window he smiled when he saw the horses mill about as soon as the masters dismounted. They had saved two minutes by racing, he saw, and now they wasted an equal amount of time tethering their nervous horses, for they rode the type of horseflesh that Jan van Zandt rode—blooded fellows with which they hoped to build up a fine stock for saddle and harness. *New horses, new men*, decided the sheriff calmly, as he recognized Rex Houlahan, Pete Goodwin, Gus Saunders, Pierre la Roche, and Eric Jensen. He decided that the blow had fallen when he saw the hulking form of Jan van Zandt himself in the background, and never was a sight more welcome to the sheriff. The six men came for his door in a bunch, wedged in the frame, and struggled for a moment before they sprawled into the room. It gave the sheriff time to finish working off an ample chew of Virginia tobacco, for which he was duly grateful.

"It's happened," said Pete Goodwin.

"He's up and done it," said Rex Houlahan.

"The thing, it is finish'," said Pierre la Roche.

They said these things all in one breath; the sheriff turned and blinked at Jan van Zandt to make sure that he was not a ghost. But he hated to ask questions, so he said nothing. Van Zandt worked his way to the front, and Sheriff Sturgis saw in his face the pallor of a coward cornered or a peaceful man with his back to the wall and ready to fight. He had never seen another man who looked exactly like that and it troubled him.

"Prince Harry," began the big farmer, and then stood with his mouth working while the sheriff wondered what on earth the chestnut stallion's name could have to do with six armed men. "Prince Harry," continued Van Zandt, exploding, "the skunk has got him . . . and I'm goin' to get his hide. Peyton got him . . . Prince Harry."

"Killed him?" asked the sheriff, seeing light.

"Stole him. There's a law around here about horse thieves, ain't there? Well, we're here to use it."

"Young Peyton has a rope comin' to him," added Houlahan, "and we're here to use it."

"There's a law about horse thieves," admitted the sheriff with grim satisfaction, "but it ain't a written law."

There was a chorus of disapproval. It reminded the sheriff that there is one power more terrible and blind and remorseless than the worst gang of outlaws that ever raided a town, and that is a number of peaceful, law-abiding citizens who rise *en masse* for their rights. The sheriff lost all desire to smile.

"Gents," he said, "if I was to see with my own eyes young Peyton climbin' on the back of another man's horse, I'd disbelieve my own eyes. Horse stealin' ain't up to his size. That's all."

Big van Zandt leaned over the desk, resting his balled fists upon it. "How d'you know?" he said. "Seems to me like you're too fond of this Peyton."

"I got to ask you to take your hands offen my desk," said the sheriff coldly. "You'll be messin' up all my paper pretty soon."

In spite of his rage, van Zandt knew enough to obey.

"Who saw Peyton take the chestnut?" went on the sheriff.

"Who else would take him?" asked six voices. And the sheriff gave up all attempts to reason with them.

"Even if he ain't got the horse now," van Zandt said, "it only shows that he's passed Prince Harry along the line to some of his friends in the hills. It ain't the first horse that's been lost around here . . . and the others have gone the same way. Besides, where does Peyton get all the money he blows around town? We have to work . . . he don't do a tap. I ask you, what does that mean?"

The sheriff looked into each face in turn and saw that he could not answer. He only said: "Boys, you may be right. I hope you ain't, but you may be right." There was a deep-throated growl in response, but they were somewhat pacified by this admission. "I ask you to do this . . . take the road down the valley and try to ride down the gent that took Prince Harry."

"They ain't a horse in the valley that could catch him," said van Zandt with gloomy pride.

"I got some money that would talk on that point," said the sheriff calmly. "But all I say is . . . will you do what I want?"

"We'll go down the valley," said Houlahan, combing his red beard, "but who'll go up the valley? We got six here to go down the valley, but where's six to go the other way?"

"I'll go," said the sheriff, buckling on his belt. Their breath of silence admitted that it was a sufficient answer.

"And if neither of us get him?" they asked.

"Then"—the sheriff sighed—"it's up to me to hit the trail. We'll start botherin' about that when the time comes. Now you better be gettin' on your way."

"But what if Prince Harry was taken across the hills?"

"Nobody but a fool would take that horse through the hills," said the sheriff sharply. "He'd bust his skinny legs in the rocks inside of two miles. Now, get on your way."

He followed them through the door, watched them tumble into the saddle, and then race down the street, shouting. Then the sheriff climbed into the saddle on the pinto. He used neither spurs nor quirt to start his mustang into a racing gait, but the pinto, as soon as the reins were drawn taut, broke from a standing start into a long, lazy lope, unhurried, smooth as the rocking of a ground swell. His head hung low, his leg muscles were relaxed, he seemed to fall along the ground, and he could keep close to that pace from sunrise to sunset. Sheriff Sturgis paid no attention to his surroundings for some distance out of the town. He was thinking of the man who took Prince Harry. If he were a man wise in horseflesh, he would keep far from the hills and go straight along the road. The chances were large that he would give his horse the rein for some distance out of the environs of the town; in fact, he would go at full speed until he had passed the forking of the roads, far up the valley—if he were traveling in that direction. Once there, he would be in sparsely filled range land where there were no houses within a day's ride ahead of him, and also where he would have small chance of getting a fresh mount. Realizing this, if he were at all familiar with the country, the thief would dismount and let his horse get his wind, preparing for the long grind through the foothills. After the pause, there was a great chance that the chestnut, winded by the hard riding and soft from the sort of work that Jan van Zandt gave him, would be stiff and almost broken down. The greatest difficulty before the sheriff was to decide on which of the roads the criminal would follow when he reached the forking. That is, granted that he took this direction up the valley.

His last doubt was presently removed from his mind, for, coming to a stretch of road where the prints of horses' hoofs were few, and these only the tracks that followed squarely between the wheel ruts, the sheriff discovered new signs that made him dismount from his horse to examine them more closely. What he found was the print that a horse makes when it runs at full speed—the feet falling in four distinct beats at about an equal distance from each other, and then a long gap where the last hoof leaves the ground and the body of the animal is thrown forward through the air. The sheriff watched these tracks with painful attention, and then, to settle any remaining doubts, he got into the saddle on the pinto and spurred him into a hundred-yard sprint. At the end of it, he reined in the mustang and dismounted again. There were now two parallel tracks of a running horse, but the differences between them were great. The first comer outstrode the pinto by an astonishing distance, and, in spite of the fact that the wind had drifted a good deal of sand into the marks, the indentations of the other horse were much the deeper. It was the track, indeed, not of a cattle pony but of a heavy horse that had enough blood to get into a racing stride; it was the track of a long-legged animal, and the mind of the sheriff reverted at once to the picture of Prince Harry and his long neck, a sign of speed.

Before he remounted, Sturgis looked carefully to his revolver; he even tried its balance, and, after that unnecessary precaution, he climbed into the saddle again and sent the pinto down the trail once more, at the long, lazy lope that held on through the morning, rocking uphill and down dale until they came to the forking of the road. There was no problem here. As though to help his pursuers, the rider of the long-stepping horse had taken the curve short—his prints lay on the side of the road, far from all others, and the sheriff, without letting the pinto fall even into a trot, swung down the left-hand way toward the hills.

Two miles farther on the sign disappeared on the road, and the sheriff cut in a small circle that brought him to a group of bushes, and in the middle of this a spot of bare sand. There was not a single indentation on this sand, but the sheriff appeared to be greatly interested in it. He looked on all sides, and saw no other sign of shrubbery, then he dismounted, and, searching among the brush, he came upon a dry stalk broken across close to the surface of the ground. The wood was so rotten that it was impossible to tell whether or not it had recently been broken, so the sheriff turned and looked fixedly at the center of the sand plot. It showed no sign; there was not the faintest indication of a mound, and sufficient wind had touched the surface to cover it with the tiny wind marks, in long, wavy lines. But apparently the sheriff had reduced his problem to a point where the clue must lie in the sand of this little opening. He stepped directly to the center, dug his toe into the ground, and turned up a quantity of charred sticks.

IV

He sent the pinto back to the road, and now he broke from the lope into a gallop, still almost effortless, but nearly twice as rapid as his former gait. Once, he glanced back, but the sun was comfortably high—it was not far past noon. A full two hundred yards, or more, he had gone before he found the place where the pursued man had cut back onto the road again, and now the sheriff watched the tracks with a new interest. He found, as he had expected, that the gait was no longer a full gallop, but only a hand canter, and Sturgis knew perfectly well that the long back and the fragile legs of such a horse could not stand the gait that was so natural to a cow pony. The rider must have realized this, for presently the marks of the canter went out, and in its place was the sign of a trot. At this gait the animal went along much better. There was an ample distance from print to print and the uniform size of the gap showed that he still had plenty of strength left. Or perhaps his strength was already far gone and the horse was traveling on nerve alone.

However that might be, the sheriff soon ceased to look at the tracks. Instead, he kept his gaze fastened far down the road, and, wherever it rolled out of sight among the hills, he sat straighter in the saddle and his search became more piercing. There were many places where a wary man could take shelter and watch a great stretch of the road behind him. And if it were anyone of this neighborhood, he would be sure to know the sheriff by his celebrated pinto. In that case a wise man would take no further chances, but pull his rifle and wait for a shot.

So the sheriff, as he went deeper into the hills, spurred the pinto to a faster gait. He looked back, now and again, to the road, and saw in two places a milling of many tracks where the pursued had dismounted to breathe his horse. Now he came swinging over the shoulder of a hill with a stretch of a full three miles running straight ahead of him. It was quite empty—not a sign of any living thing in all its distance—but the sheriff swung the pony around with a jerk and headed back behind the hill.

He had planned to catch sight of the fugitive within the next half hour of riding unless the sign he had read had lied to him. This gap of empty road startled him, for it told him either that he had not read the tracks correctly or that the other had left the road. If he had left the road, there could only be two reasons for it. One was that he had decided on a long rest for himself and his mount, which was quite unreasonable at this period of the day. The other was that he had seen the sheriff following, and had recognized the bright coloring of the pinto. The latter reason was by far the best, and the sheriff acted upon it.

Leaving his pinto ensconced in a clump of trees on the far side of the hill, he skirted around the other edge. The road was a slightly graded cut on the side of a long, sharp slope, forested thickly. The chances were great that the rider of the horse, if indeed he were a fugitive from justice and if his mount were the chestnut of Jan van Zandt, would go either for rest or to spy on the pursuit among the trees above the road, where he could see everything and remain himself unseen. It was on this side of the road, then, that Sturgis prepared to hunt, but he paused before beginning, partly because of the danger that lay ahead of him, but far more because above all things in this world he hated to go on foot. It was while he stood among the brush at the roadside, summoning his resolution and letting his bright little eyes rove everywhere among the trees ahead of him, that the sheriff saw a man step out of the forest and go swinging down the road not fifty yards ahead of him. He was so set for the work ahead of him, however, that he had almost dismissed the stranger from his mind and started toward the trees when something in the gait of the man made him pause. It was a hobbling gait, short steps that were uneven, and the sheriff recognized through sympathy the pace of a man who generally moves on horseback alone. More than this, he saw those strides gradually lengthen, as the walker swung into his work, and it convinced the sharp eyes of the sheriff that this was no random hunter, strolling over the mountains, but a man who had recently climbed from the back of a horse, whose leg muscles were not yet all straightened out. Not until he had noted all these facts did the sheriff catch the gleam of spurs, but he had already made up his mind. When he left his horse, he had taken his rifle with him. Now he deliberately dropped upon one knee behind a shrub and sighted among the branches. With the stock squeezed into his shoulder and his finger curling on the trigger he shouted: "Halt!"

It brought an amazing result. Instead of turning with both hands held high over his head, as is the time-honored custom on such occasions, the stranger leaped to one side, at the same time pitching toward the ground and whirling about on his face, so that he struck with only his left elbow supporting his shoulders, and in that hairbreadth of time he had conjured a .45 Colt out of its holster. He lay with the muzzle of the revolver tipped up and down balancing for a snap shot in any direction.

"Not so bad!" called the sheriff.

The man with the revolver twisted to one side, and the revolver became rigid, for the echo from the hillside had made Sturgis's voice seem to come from the opposite direction.

"Drop it," continued the sheriff. "I've got a line on you, bud. I've got your head in the circle, pal."

The other hesitated for a single instant, and then scrambled to his feet, tossing the revolver into the dust. "Well," he said coolly enough, "what does all this mean?"

"It means that I want the other gun," said the sheriff.

"What gun?"

"Don't play me for a fool," Sturgis retorted. "First, turn your face the other way." He was obeyed. "Now shell out your other cannon."

The other produced a second weapon from somewhere in his clothes, and tossed it away.

"All right," said the sheriff, stepping from behind the bush, "you can face this way, friend, after you've got those hands up high."

The hands went up slowly, and with equal slowness the other turned. Sturgis, with intense interest, saw that the fellow had to fight, apparently, before he could force his hands above the level of his shoulders and up into the region of helplessness.

"If you want my money," said the stranger without undue nervousness, "you'll find my wallet in the left hip pocket."

"Thanks," said Sturgis. "Don't mind if I do. Get up them hands."

The arms of the other had, in fact, lowered a little as the sheriff came closer, but now he straightened them again and looked thoughtfully at Sturgis. He was in all respects a man of superior appearance, with a carefully tended mustache, kept clean of the lips, and a pale, rather handsome face with those square cheeks, somewhat puffy at the jowls, that betoken good living. Above all, he had that straight and penetrating glance that comes to men who have directed many others. He kept his hands high up while the fingers of the sheriff ran swiftly over him. He did not even quiver when Sturgis extracted a third weapon—it was a little, double-barreled pistol that hung under the man's shirt suspended from a noose of horsehair.

Sturgis knew now why the man was so averse to getting his hands above his shoulders, for, even if his thumb was as high as his throat, he had still a chance to hook it under the little horsehair lariat and whip out the pistol for the two final shots.
"My, my," commented the sheriff as he cut the string and pocketed the little weapon. "Kind of a walkin' arsenal, ain't you?"

"In this country, apparently," the other replied, "a man needs to be."

"Oh, we ain't so bad around here," said the sheriff. "For instance, we don't lift horses regular." There was not a flicker of the other's eyes. "Suppose you lead me where the chestnut is," he said. "All right now. You can take your hands down."

"Thanks," said the man of the well-trimmed moustache, and he brushed it with his fingertips, studying the sheriff. "For a hold-up man," he said, "you talk in a singular fashion. What chestnut do you refer to?"

The smile of the sheriff widened to a broad grin. "I'm forty-five years old, partner," he said. "If I was two years younger, I think you'd get by, but today you're out of luck. The seat of your trousers is all shiny, the way cloth gets when it rubs on leather, say. And they's a sort of horse smell about you. I say, lead me to that horse, and don't be aggravatin'."

The other shrugged his shoulders and gave up. "It's not worth seeing," he said.

"Dead?"

"It was a show horse," said the stranger. His jaw thrust out and his face changed. "The first time in my life that I've gone so wrong in judging a horse."

"No stamina, eh?" murmured the sheriff sympathetically. "No guts at all. Well, I ain't surprised that you went wrong on him. When them horses first come into the country, they took my eye, too . . . then I seen what a day's work does to 'em and I changed my mind. But I didn't hear no shot . . . how'd you kill the horse?"

"I couldn't risk a bullet," said the other. "Sound travels too far in this country."

"And instead?"

"A knife turned the trick nicely... through the temple, you know."

The sheriff opened both his mouth and his eyes. "You run a knife into that horseflesh?" he muttered, recovering himself. "Well, it's time we started back... sorry you got to walk."

"Not at all," replied the other, apparently unmoved by the hardening of the sheriff's voice. "I'm not going to walk, and I'm not going back."

V

It made the sheriff look again at his prisoner. "Tut, tut," he said good-naturedly, "you s'prise me, partner. What d'you figure on doin'?"

"Sitting down on that rock and talking to you."

"It'll get us back after dark to the town," said the sheriff, "but outside of that it's a hog-ear to me whether you walk back now or after we've talked."

They made themselves comfortable on the rock, each twisting around so that his face was to the other. "Now, what d'you want to do?" said the sheriff.

"I want your horse."

"Yes?"

"And I want you to take back to Sloan the price of the horse I've just ridden to death, along with the price of your own horse."

"Oh," murmured the sheriff mildly, "maybe you'll give me a check?"

The stranger did not smile. "Here's my wallet," he said.

"You count it for me," suggested Sturgis.

So the thief unfolded the leather, and, extracting a thick sheaf of greenbacks, he counted over silently and slowly into the sheriff's hand five bills of $1,000 each and thirty more of the $100 denomination. "One thousand dollars for the horse," said the stranger, "one hundred for your horse, and six thousand nine hundred dollars to pay for your long walk back to Sloan." He raised his eyes from the count, retaining a few bills in his hand.

The sheriff laid the money back on his knee with a sigh. "Sorry," he said.

"Naturally you're sorry that I should underestimate your dislike for walking," said the stranger calmly. "Accordingly I hasten to correct the mistake," and he added to the little pack four more bills of $1,000 each. "Ten thousand nine hundred is the price of that walk back to Sloan. And now, if you'll pardon me, I'll take your horse and hurry along."

The sheriff sat with his shoulders bowed. He looked like a man over whom old age has suddenly swept, unstringing all his nerves, and he squinted up at the stranger with eyes of pain. "Sit down again," said the sheriff huskily. "I hate to say it, but you've no idea how I hate walkin'."

The other sighed, then he sat down and leaned a little closer. "I want you to take note of these things," he said, and checked them off on the tips of his fingers. "Did you ever hear of a horse thief with close to eleven thousand dollars in his wallet? Does it seem possible to you that a man might be making a journey in such desperate speed that he would change saddles from one horse to another without stopping to haggle with the owner of the second horse about a price? Finally do you think it absurd and beyond reason that a man making such a desperate journey would, when it is completed, send back the price of the horse he had taken?"

"I'll tell you what," said the sheriff. "Them three questions are ones that twelve men could answer better than one."

For the first time the stranger flushed. He sat back, gritting his teeth, and looked the sheriff between the eyes. "I have a checkbook with me," he said at length. "Name the price of that walk back to Sloan. It'll be yours."

"*H-m-m*," murmured the sheriff. "I'd a sort of an idea that it would come down to a matter of writing a check."

"Because," said the other earnestly, "you know that my check for almost any amount would be good." He clenched one hand into a fist while he talked, and the sheriff, looking down, wondered at the smallness of the hand, and the whiteness of the skin. "Besides," went on the stranger, "in your heart you're absolutely convinced that what I've told you is the truth. You know that I'm here on business only. You know from my appearance that I'm not a horse rustler. You know that I'm talking to you as straight as my money talks."

"Straighter, in fact," said the sheriff.

The stranger flushed again. "If you're offended because I've attempted to bribe you," he said, "I'm sorry. But I've most urgent need to get across those hills. I couldn't stop to be scrupulous."

"D'you ever notice," said the sheriff absently, "that when a gent starts elbowin' in a crowd most generally he starts a fight that everybody gets hurt in?"

The stranger caught his breath with impatience but said nothing.

"It's that way about the chestnut horse," went on the sheriff. "He ain't worth more'n a thousand dollars, that horse that you turned into so much meat... with your knife. No, he ain't hardly worth more'n a thousand, but maybe he means more'n money to the gent that raised him from the time he was a foal. You see? Look at it another way. You grab this horse and ride on, expectin' to pay for him later. Well, the gent that owns this horse finds him gone, and right off he says that a gent nearby is the one that done the stealin'. He's sure of that, because he knows this young gent hates him. Well, he starts out and rounds up a pile of ornery boys like himself and come boilin' down to my office bent on revenge. They go one way... I go the other. I have all the luck, it turns out, and suppose that gang of farmers misses the horse, which they will, and comes back thinkin' a lot of hard things about the young gent that they first thought done the stealin'. Well, people take it kind of hard around here when a horse stolen, and, when they got a suspicion, they don't always wait for a jury. They go straight to Judge Lynch and get an opinion. You foller me, maybe?"

"I do," said the other, frowning. "You think there'll be a lynching party on account of this chestnut horse... curses on his weak heart."

His face convulsed as he spoke, and for a moment the sheriff sat with his mouth parted over his next word, staring at the stranger. He seemed to see new things in the horse thief—as if it were the middle of night and a match had been lighted under that face.

"I got to tell you another side of it," said the sheriff. "Suppose the bunch of farmers don't lynch this gent I'm talkin' about, but they only muss him up a lot and call him names. Well, he's the kind of a boy that takes hard names to heart terrible bad."

"If I'm not mistaken," said the stranger, "this young fellow won't use his gun more than once in your district. You're the sheriff, I take it."

"My name is Sturgis," the sheriff replied. There was no change in the horse thief's expression. "Yes, I'm the sheriff and my record is pretty long and pretty clean."

"I'm sure it is," the stranger agreed earnestly.

"But," went on Sturgis, "if all the gents I've ever taken was rolled into one, all their tricks, and all their speed with guns, and all their cool-headedness, and all their cussedness... if they was all rolled into one, I'd rather tackle them all over again than tackle this same young gent."

The stranger scrubbed his chin nervously with his knuckles, and then replied: "I begin to see what you mean... but I'd like to see this remarkable young man."

"Oh, he ain't so different," said the sheriff. "He ain't so different from the rest. He's just a split-second faster with his gun...he's just an inch closer to the bell with his slug...he's just a quiver steadier in his hand...he's just a dash cooler in the head. But"—he sighed—"it's surprisin' what a lot of difference a few little things make when they're all added up. You see, this boy had a considerable pile of an inheritance, and he improves a lot on what he got for a start."

"That description reminds me of someone I knew," the stranger said musingly.

"Was it, maybe, La Paloma that you knew?" murmured the sheriff innocently.

The glance of the other twitched across the face of the sheriff like the lash of whip and then back. "No," he said, "who was La Paloma?"

"But I'll tell you what," said the sheriff suddenly, "in spite of all the harm that maybe you've done by stealin' that horse, I can't help lettin' my heart go out to a gent that knows how rotten it is to walk on foot."

"Ah?" murmured he other. Then he drew out a folded checkbook.

"Suppose," said the sheriff, "that I had some dice here. I might take a chance to see whether you take my horse or whether you come back to Sloan with me."

"We could flip a coin," said the stranger.

"Too risky," murmured the sheriff. "If we even had a pack of cards, we could get along."

"Ah," murmured the stranger, and instantly a black leather card case was in the palm of his hand.

"So..." The sheriff sighed. "Kind of looks like you've took me up. What'll we play to decide?"

"Something short?" suggested the other.

"Sure."

"Anything you say will do with me," said the horse thief. "But wait a moment...why not cut for the first ace?" He broke off with a frown, for he suddenly discovered that the sheriff was smiling quietly, straight into his eyes.

"D'you know," said the sheriff, "that I been waiting for this minute for years and years?"

"What?"

"You was always a queer one," murmured Sturgis, "but still I can't understand why you'd ever come back here, Pat."

VI

The silence that followed had an acid quality. It seemed to eat into the mind of the stranger and weaken him. The black eyes lost some of their brilliance, and presently he moistened his white lips, and whispered a curse.

"Don't do it," said the sheriff, shaking his head. "Don't talk like that, because it always makes me sort of uneasy when a gent cusses me . . . even an old acquaintance like you, Pat." Then he added, after a moment during which he looked almost longingly at the other: "Well, I guess we'd better be goin' back." He broke out in a different tone that might have been called cheerful: "D'you remember that it was in a place about like this that we . . ."

"Wait." Pat gasped and reached his hand out toward the sheriff, but, before it touched his fingers, he relaxed and the arm remained suspended in mid-air. "It can't end like this!" he cried. "It can't end like this!" His whole body was shaking, but all at once he straightened out his glance, and his mustache stopped working and bristling. "You're waiting for me to break down, are you?"

The sheriff raised a deprecating hand. "A man like you break down? A scholar and a gentleman like you? Sure I ain't waitin' to see that. I'd be a fool, wouldn't I?"

"Ed, it all happened twenty years ago. It's dead."

"She's dead," agreed the sheriff, nodding.

The other groaned and clenched his fists.

"It takes about twenty years for a good wine to get ripe and all softened down so's a man can enjoy it," said the sheriff calmly.

The horse thief appeared to be buried in thought. "Suppose I were to tell you a story of a fellow who was down and out . . . who'd lived like a hound while he was young . . . who straightened up and tried to be a man afterward . . ."

"Go on," broke in the sheriff. "You was always a fine talker, Pat," he added encouragingly. "You'd ought to make a good yarn out of it. Let's hear it, Langley."

"You know me too well to think I'd whine," said Pat Langley.

"Sure I do."

"I want you to see in one glance what you do if you take me into Sloan and drag up that other matter against me. Out in the West Indies on the island of Saint Hilaire I have one of the finest plantations in the whole place . . . I have a wife and daughter." He drew a second little leather case from an inside pocket. "You'll see their pictures on one side of the card and the picture of my house on the other." He handed the case to the sheriff. "I want you to know that you'll be stepping into the happiest home in Saint Hilaire and ruining two lives, besides mine. But if you'll drop this affair, Ed, you'll step through the doors you see in that picture and halve everything that's inside. If you don't want to be near me . . . and I don't suppose you will . . . you get half of my bank account. More than that. You can see my financial statement and make your own terms. I'm not offering this as a bribe. In the first place, I did you a great wrong. I want to make amends for that wrong, and the only way I can do it is to work on the financial end. At the same time, I want you to see that, after I wronged you, I realized what a hound I had been. I did go straight."

But the sheriff gave back the unopened leather case. "I couldn't look into a woman's face just now, Pat," he said gently. But Langley paled as though he had gained a first glimpse into the mind of the other. A change came gradually over his face. The sheriff, watching in fascination, noted that change and dropped his hand for the first time upon his rifle stock, but always he had kept the muzzle directed at the horse thief.

Yet Langley only said: "Throw me the makings, will you? See if I've forgotten how to roll 'em."

The sheriff obeyed without a word and watched him deftly make his smoke and light it. When he had inhaled the first breath, Langley seemed to find a new cheer. He raised his head and looked about him as he exhaled the blue-brown vapor slowly. "Not so bad," he said. "Better than a lot of the tailor-mades I smoke." He met the eye of the sheriff. "And now that I'm back in it," he said, "this same country isn't so bad. Cleaner air around here than we have in the islands." He drew a long breath and puffed it out again. "Well, when did you spot me first, Ed? I knew you the moment I saw you, but I depended on the twenty years and this mustache... like a fool. I knew you when I was putting my hands up and I hesitated about making a try with that little necklace of mine. Well, when did you know me first?"

"You're a hard man, ain't you, Pat?" said the sheriff quietly. "When it comes to the pinch, wife and child can go hang."

"You thought I'd weaken, didn't you?" He chuckled.

"It wasn't your face that told on you," said the sheriff, "though it gave me a bit of a shock. Made me start thinking. First of all, when you threw yourself at the ground. That made me guess... that old trick, you know. But all those things were hints pilin' up in the back of my head. Then I got my first real clue when you twisted your eyes at me when I mentioned La Paloma. Funny way you have of glintin' at a gent out of the corner of your eyes, Pat. But what sewed the thing up in my mind was the cards. You always used to have cards with you, and, if it came to a choice in a pinch, you liked to cut for aces."

The horse thief looked calmly at him and tossed his cigarette butt away. "Speaking of cards," he said, "I wonder if she knew that you'd played cards that night?"

The rifle trembled in the hands of the sheriff, but Langley did not wince.

"I was drunk," the sheriff replied.

The other chuckled. "We've all heard that sort of talk."

Sturgis began to breathe through his mouth, as though he had been running.

"To go back to the beginning," said the horse thief, "suppose you and I were to have an even break for our guns. Just you and me with nobody to look on. We take anything for a signal to start for the butts... say the next time that hawk screams. And the fellow who drops is left for the buzzards. If you get me... why, you did it making an arrest of a horse thief... if I get you, I take the pinto along over the hills."

"I'd like the idea." Sturgis sighed. "Heaven above, how I been prayin' for it twenty years."

"Good old sport," Langley said as he rose. "It's done, then?"

"Wait a minute. In the old days you was always a bit better with a gun than me, Pat."

"But you've had more practice lately."

"You lie," said the sheriff, without heat. "You practice with a gun every day of your life. You have to."

The other flushed, looked swiftly about him, and then saw that he was helpless.

"But aside from that," went on the sheriff, "I think the way of the law is a pretty good way, mostly. It gets at the insides of some gents in a way that powder and lead can't. Suppose I was to blow your head off. You wouldn't feel nothin'. I'd feel sort of better afterward, but what would you feel? Nothin'! But s'pose you get sent up for a little while... for stealin' a horse. That wouldn't be bad. Not the prison, but after you got out, Saint Hilaire would have the news. I'd take care that they did. You're proud, ain't you, Pat?"

"I'd kill you," said the other thoughtfully. "I'd kill you as sure as heaven when I was out."

"I don't cross no bridges till I come to 'em," the sheriff replied. "Besides, I know the warden of the state prison. Maybe he'd let me come up and pay you friendly visits once in a while. And then maybe I'd get so fond of havin' you where I could see you that I'd hate to see you leave. So I might want to dig back twenty years and get something else that would hold you the rest of your life. Or if I got tired of seein' you that way, I might even get something that would hang you, Pat." He bit off a large corner of his Virginia leaf and stowed it gingerly in his cheek. "You see how many sides there is to the thing, Pat?" he said gently.

"I see one thing," said the other with equal calm. "Twenty years has drilled through your thick head and put some sense there."

"Well, the day's wearin' on. S'pose we start back. I hate to make you walk."

"Don't mind me," said Pat heartily. "I generally walk every day on the island, and I'm in pretty' fair trim."

The sheriff climbed on his horse, and, as he did so, the other stepped to the side of the road, whistling, and leaned over. "Stand up!" called the sheriff. The other slowly stood up and showed his teeth under the black mustache. He kicked the revolver away. "I almost had it," he confided to the sheriff.

"My, my," murmured Sturgis, smiling. "Wasn't that a close chance, now? I'll tell a man." He motioned down the road ahead of him.

"Certainly," said the horse thief, "I always like to go first." And he stepped out into the road.

"The same old Pat," the sheriff said reminiscently. "You was always prime company."

VII

The things that the sheriff did not know about the farming element around the town of Sloan were supplied to him by a seventh sense. It all fell out as he had warned the horse thief. First the posse, led by red-bearded Rex Houlahan, swept like a storm down the valley. They rode hard and they rode well, and they had the fastest horses within two hundred miles of Sloan, except Prince Harry himself. In fact, the six were chosen men of courage, for, in recruiting his posse, Jan van Zandt had not even applied to the cattlemen, knowing their answer beforehand, and of the farmers, these six were the only ones who cared to come within rifle range of Jeremiah Peyton. Jan van Zandt knew how to pick his men both for the horses they rode and for their personal grit, and one day he might sit in the state legislature for just such qualities as he showed in this crisis.

He wanted Prince Harry back. The horse was the culmination of a long labor of breeding that ran back through two generations of the van Zandt family, and it would take another two generations to get him back, but the affair was more than the matter of one horse. It was the culmination of the ill feeling between the two main classes of population around the little town. To be sure, the majority on both sides remained quiescent. Of the farmers there were only the six, and of the cattlemen there was only Jeremiah Peyton. But if matters came to a showdown, the entire populace was apt to rise in arms and a class war result. The imagination of the sheriff had not stretched as far as this, but the calculation of Jan van Zandt had. And he figured that in the ultimate struggle the odds would be with the farmers in about the same proportion—six to one. However, as far as the sheriff's predictions ran, they were correct. The posse rushed down the valley, flogging their spirited nags every jump of the way. And when they reached the end of the valley, where the foothills sprawled out to a flat and the muddy old Winton River went straggling into the desert beyond, they drew rein and looked about them. There was still no sign of a chestnut horse before them, and, when Rex Houlahan looked down to the road, for he was the most Western of the lot, he did not find a trace of a recent hoof print before them.

There was a rumble in the posse, but few words, and they turned back up the valley. At the town of Winton they stopped for lunch—it was already afternoon—and lay about mumbling threats against the universe in general and thieving cattlemen in particular. In the afternoon they started on up the valley. No sooner had they taken the road than they discovered new grievances all brought upon them by the hound who had stolen the chestnut stallion. Every one of their horses was stiff and sore from the unusual hard work of the morning; their delicate limbs were meant for it no more than the legs of Prince Harry had been meant to stall off the dogged pursuit of the sheriff's pinto. Rex Houlahan's bay mare had been raised from a delicate foal like a child in the family; now she was desperately lame in the off foreleg and Rex went stamping down the road on foot, gnashing his teeth behind his red beard, with the mare following him like a dog. Within a mile she was going chiefly upon three legs, her head nodding far down at each step, and Houlahan's heart was too full for utterance.

For some reason, none of the other five cared to break in before the big Irishman. They let him walk ahead, and they followed in a somber group. For five miles not a word was said, and then, without sound or signal, the whole procession stopped in the road. The bay mare lay down at once in the dust. As for Houlahan, he turned and cast one long look at his horse, and then he noted that they were opposite the house of Jeremiah Peyton. In fact, anyone with half an eye could see the master of the shack sitting on the front verandah, tilted back as usual against the wall. To be sure the chestnut stallion was not in sight, but, as the posse had explained to the sheriff that morning, the absence of the horse proved nothing. He might have been passed on to compatriots in the foothills beyond, thieving cowpunchers who well knew how to send horses along by subterranean courses and bring them out a hundred miles or more away to be sold innocently to the first high bidder. All these things ate into the hearts of the farmers as they sat the saddle, breathing the pungent alkali dust that the feet of their weary horses stirred up. Most of all the idle form of Jeremiah stirred them. Idleness in their Middle Western scheme of things was the all-surpassing sin. Then Rex Houlahan cursed once, softly, and started across the fields. The others followed him.

How it happened that Jeremiah Peyton, the son of Hank Peyton, himself the chief figure of many a tale of border war against the Mexicans, calmly sat on his porch without a weapon near, while he watched six of his enemies come across his land toward him, no one in Sloan could ever imagine. Men were to scratch their heads over this mystery for days and days. The only explanation lay in the profound contempt that he felt for these dirt grubbers and land hogs, as he had been known to call them to their faces. He did not even look up until they were close to the porch, and, when he did look up, he did not rise. He merely whittled on at his stick. First he looked at the tops of their hats, then he whistled to the sky, then he called negligently to an old yellow cur that skulked across the porch away from the strangers. Last of all he appeared to notice the silent, stationary group that sat in their saddles, armed to the teeth, before his porch. Most of all, there was Rex Houlahan on foot, and nearest to him. Although the loss was Jan van Zandt's, Houlahan was the spokesman.

"Peyton," he said.

The boy looked into the face of the big man and smiled, but did not answer. It was a needless insult, and the hands of the posse gathered their weapons closer.

"Peyton, we've come for you," Houlahan said.

For the first time the meaning of the men came to Jeremiah Peyton. In truth, he had despised them all so heartily that up to this point he refused to let his reason tell him what the general silence and the guns meant. Even now as he stood up and stretched the muscles of his magnificent, lithe body from fingertips to toes, he felt that he could dispose of them all, his naked hands against their guns. But the puniest man in the world, if he is possessed of a rage that does not pour itself forth in words, will command the respect of the strongest man. Peyton looked again, grudgingly admitted that the six were picked men of their kind, and that they were dangerous.

"'Evening," he said, running his eyes calmly from face to face. "Climb off your horses and rest yourselves."

"We'll rest when we're through with you," Houlahan replied. Up to that time he himself did not exactly know why he had led the way to confront Peyton, but, as soon as he spoke, the words struck fire in him. The growl of the posse behind him urged him on, and in another moment mob frenzy had them all by the throats.

"Particularly me," interjected Jan van Zandt.

Perhaps if Jeremiah had returned the smooth answer, he might have turned away wrath. Instead of that he saw the spark of fire in all eyes and deliberately chose to pour oil upon the flame.

"Before you're through with me," he said, smiling in his odd manner straight at the brown-faced farmer, "you'll be an old man or buzzard food. Get away from that door."

For Houlahan had slipped over until he was near the front door of the house, thus hemming the master of the place against the wall. As he spoke, he swept his hand behind him, to the hip, and seemed to close his fingers over something.

"The rest of you hound dogs," Jeremiah ordered, "get off my land before I drill you for disturbin' my peace." And, in the midst of the crisis and his bluff, he grinned at his own joke.

They had scattered back like fire before wind. Every man was behind his horse or getting there as fast as he could. Houlahan, with a moan of anxiety, reached one of the small wooden pillars that supported the roof of the verandah and seemed to be hiding there—hiding from the slug of a Colt .45 behind four inches of rotten pine. Even now Jeremiah would have been safe if he had used this moment of confusion to leap to the door and into the house. That would have begun a battle of which the mountain desert would still be talking, but with his big boy heart swelling with scorn he stood there and laughed in their faces and waved them away.

Then Houlahan saw from the side that there was no bulge of a gun on Peyton's hip and he screamed in a voice gone thin and piping with exultation: "He's bluffin' without a gun! Take him alive!"

The posse waited for no second invitation. The alarm of the instant before had strung their nerves to the breaking force, and, now that the fear of bullets was removed, they flung themselves from their horses and plunged at Jerry. He would have stayed there to meet them even at these odds, but he had that Western horror of being overmatched by physical odds, of being reduced to impotence by numbers. He sprang like a tiger for the door, and Houlahan rushed to meet him with a wailing cry, like one who struggles in a lost cause. There was a base of bulldog in Houlahan. A driving blow met him as he came in, and the whipping knuckles of Jerry laid the cheek bone bare, slicing the flesh neatly away, but, although Houlahan fell, he fell forward and clutched blindly with both arms. The arms wound around the legs of Jerry, and, although he dropped Houlahan the rest of the way to the floor with a crushing blow behind the ear, the Irishman had done his work. Before Jerry could shake his feet clear and gain the door, the five were on him. He swung about as the avalanche struck. He broke the nose of Pete Goodwin; he slashed wildly at Pierre la Roche and Gus Saunders; he sent Eric Jensen rolling away with his arms clasped about his midriff, and then Jan van Zandt came up behind Jerry, raised his .45 like a club, grinning, and Jerry went down, inert.

After that, Jan stood guard over the fallen, with the muzzle pointed at the head of the cowman, while the rest of them picked up Houlahan.

Even after Jerry himself had recovered enough to sit up and sneer at the revolver that Jan van Zandt pointed at his head, Houlahan was still the object of main interest. At length they patched up the gashed side of his face, although blood still trickled beneath the bandage that they had made from one of Jerry's sheets. But even after he had gained his feet, Houlahan came staggering, punch-drunk, and wavered before Jerry, the son of Hank.

"Ah, man, ah, man," Rex Houlahan said. "That was a wallop ye handed me." He grinned a lop-sided grin at Jerry, and then seemed to realize for the first time where he was and what had happened. "Tarnation!" he gasped. "I thought I was back in Brooklyn at old Rinkenstein's saloon. Now you, get up on your hind legs." And he stirred the captive with the toe of his boot.

"The spur's the thing for that," put in Jan van Zandt, and, although Jerry was already rising, he assisted by rolling the rowel of his spur across Jerry's leg. Little pinpoints of crimson began to show through the cloth, and the posse laughed.

VIII

A moment later they were silent, stunned, as they realized that Jerry had risen to his feet in perfect silence. Neither the touch with the toe of the boot nor the spur or the burst of laughter had brought a word from him. One by one they began to realize that, unless they killed this man, he would most infallibly kill them.

"Get a rope," Jan van Zandt ordered. It was not the first time in his life nor was it the last that he would seize the highest note of public opinion and give it a voice. A rope was found and a tree likewise, and they brought Jerry beneath a promising branch. Of the six men, five, at least, were anxious to get the thing done with as quickly as possible, but somewhere in the depth of Houlahan a spark of revolt rose.

"Is this a lynchin', maybe?" he asked, as Jan van Zandt placed the noose over the neck of Jerry Peyton. "It ain't," he answered himself. "This is justice. It being justice, he's got a right to be heard. Ain't that the law for horse thieves?"

"They ain't any law for horse thieves," remarked Gus Saunders. "But make him talk, if you want to. It'll be amusin' to hear him lie."

"Sure," Houlahan said. "All right, bud. Come out with the truth. Did you steal Prince Harry?"

The accused smiled in the face of the Irishman.

"Speak up," said Houlahan. "If you can prove that you didn't, which you can't, we'll let you go free." He stepped back, astonished. "Are you goin' to let yourself swing without sayin' a word?" he asked. "Are you goin' to give up a chance to talk for your life?"

The glance of Jerry Peyton went from face to face in the group and they stirred uneasily. They knew that he was examining their features so closely that neither time nor beard could ever mask them from him. If his destruction had been a matter of mob pleasure before, it now became a cold duty. They looked at each other, and they found the same answer in every eye.

"But he's got to speak up," protested Houlahan. He touched his bandaged cheek tenderly, and then went on: "If he don't want to confess, make him. Listen to me, partner, talk out and you'll have the weight of the crime off your soul. You'll die so easy, you won't feel the rope hardly."

The same faint, derisive smile met him.

"Let me try him," Jan van Zandt offered. "The things he don't answer, we'll figure is answered yes. You all take note of that because the sheriff may want to ask us some questions later on. Here, you." The eyes of the prisoner were focused far above the head of the big farmer, and now he caught Jerry by the chin and twisted his head. "Look me in the eye and tell whatever truth there is in your lying heart. You hate me, don't you?"

Not a muscle of Jerry's face altered.

"You see?" said Jan van Zandt. "He admits that he hates me... Jan van Zandt, a peaceful, law-abidin' citizen. That'll be remembered. Next... did a horse of yours get killed by accident on my place?" He turned to the others. "He admits that a horse of his was killed on my place. Keep all this in mind because it's leadin' somewhere. Now listen to me, Peyton. Did you refuse to go to court like an honest man and get your price for the horse that was killed?" His triumph shone in his bronze face as he noted to the posse: "You hear that? Now listen! Did you write to me afterward that you would get your own price for the mare? You did. They's other witnesses to that. Last of all... did you wait till you got the chance and then steal Prince Harry, that's worth ten times anything your mongrel buckskin was ever worth?"

The smile of infinite contempt played again over the lips of Jeremiah. Jan van Zandt, with a sob of grief and hate, drew back his heavy arm and struck the prisoner across the mouth. It threw the body of Jerry back against the rope, but when he staggered erect again, although a white mark enclosed his mouth, there was still the ghost of the smile upon it. It was not the patience of the martyr; it was that sort of stifled rage that overwhelms a man and makes him cold. He found an unexpected intercessor here, for Rex Houlahan caught the arm of the big farmer and jerked him back.

"Don't do that again," he said savagely. "He's got his hands tied behind him, ain't he? He's helpless. He's goin' to be hung like the horse thief that he is, but I ain't goin' to stand by and see him insulted. Not a man with a wallop like the one he packs." He grinned at Jerry with something akin to affection. "Nobody can hit like that unless it's born in him, Jerry. It's a shame you can't live to work in the ring. But there's one thing more, boys. We can't string him up until he's confessed. It ain't right, and I won't stand for it. He's got to say enough to save his soul... if it can be saved. Besides, we'll need more than dumb talk when the sheriff asks his questions."

"Make him talk, then," said Jan van Zandt, "but don't lay hands on me again. It ain't healthy, not by a long ways."

"I've laid hands on worse ones than you, son," said the Irishman as he bent his attention on the prisoner. "Lad, I give you the last chance. Will you talk or do we have to make you talk?"

And when Jerry remained silent, Houlahan gave directions swiftly, and the others obeyed. They fixed running nooses in both ends of another rope, threw it over the branch, and tightened the nooses around the wrists of Jerry. One jerk brought him off the ground, his long body, with the arms above his head, swaying back and forth. He seemed gigantic. There were two men on one rope and three on the other. Houlahan stood in front of the prisoner and talked up to him. He had control, being the inventor of the expedient.

"Jerry," he said, "I see you're fighting hard. You'll stave it off for a while because your arms are strong. But pretty soon the muscles begin to crack... they get that tired... and then they give way and the pull comes under your armpits. Then you feel it down your ribs and across your shoulder blades. Then it takes you in the joints of the shoulders and you begin to think your arms are comin' out of the socket. You're a heavy man, Jerry, and, when your muscles give out and your hands feel dead, you'll have all that weight just hangin' on the tendons around the shoulder. Boy, don't be a fool. Talk up. Say what you done. Tell me the truth. Whisper it, if you don't want the rest of 'em to hear, and I'll never tell a soul. But you got to tell the truth before you die... you got to, or we'll keep you up there by the wrists until you yell for the pain of it."

As he approached the latter end of his talk, he grew more violent, raising his voice, but, when he ceased, there was still no response from Jerry. After that, Houlahan stood under the motionless form and watched with his own face twisted into an agony of sympathy. Presently the shoulders of Jerry slumped down, and all his weight rested with a jerk on the joint itself. His muscles had given away at last, and, although it brought a groan from Houlahan, there was not a sound from Jerry. Houlahan began to whisper advice—telling Jerry how impossible it was to resist—begging him to give up and speak. Then the head of Jerry, which had hitherto remained proudly erect, toppled forward with another jerk and remained hanging low. From behind, he looked like a headless form. Houlahan threw his arm across his face. He went toward the men at the ropes.

"Jan," he begged, "go take my place. I can't stand it."

And big Jan van Zandt went and stood under the body they were torturing. At the first upward glance he blinked and shrank back a step, but he came close again and looked steadily into the face of Jerry. He was so fascinated by what he saw that his own expression escaped from his attention. For some time the men at the ropes watched his change of face, and then, incredulously, they saw a smile come on the lips of Jan van Zandt. Houlahan cried out. With one accord the others slacked away and the limp form crumpled against the earth, the legs and arms falling into crazy positions, as though they were broken. The Irishman straightened the limbs. Jerry had fainted. One by one the rest of the posse looked in his face and shuddered.

"There ain't a thing to do but wind him up this way," said Jan van Zandt, drawing his revolver. "He'll feel no more pain and we'll have done our duty. Stand away, boys, and turn your backs."

There was a whine from Houlahan as the Irishman came between. He was sobbing with rage. "So help me," he said, "but I think you like doin' this dirty work."

"I got a duty as a citizen to perform," Jan van Zandt said.

"You got a duty to be a man."

"D'you mean to say you want this... to live?"

"Let the law handle him. Turn him over to the law."

"They'll get no evidence. He'll be turned loose. D'you want the son of Hank Peyton on your trail, Rex?"

"If they don't keep him in jail," said Houlahan firmly, "he won't be able to use a gun for two weeks with them hands, and we'll have a chance to think of what's next. Heaven knows I don't want Peyton on my trail, but I'd rather you turned me by inches than have that face hauntin' me the rest of my life. Boys, get out the buckboard, and we'll take Peyton in to the sheriff."

They had spent their first fury in the rush on Jerry, and, for the blows he gave them, they had tortured him to senselessness. Pierre la Roche and Gus Saunders hitched two of Peyton's own mules to the buckboard they found behind the house. They placed him in the body of the wagon. La Roche drove, and Houlahan sat in the wagon watching the inert captive. The others followed with the horse slowly, and, before they reached the town of Sloan, Eric Jensen and Pete Goodwin had dropped back and tried to fade away into the darkness. But the rest cursed them back into the procession. No one would be allowed to dodge his share of the responsibility.

"Suppose he dies," Houlahan had shouted from the wagon, "d'you think I'm goin' to be the only one to take his body in?"

So they closed up after that, and, taking that mysterious comfort that comes out of numbers in any crisis, they began to talk to one another about other things.

Finally the wagon reached the main street of Sloan. It was unavoidable. Before they had gone a hundred feet the word spread. Men, women, and children poured into the street. The word was taken up. The posse had caught the horse thief, and the horse thief was Jerry Peyton.

Men rode their horses beside the wagon and looked at the prostrate body within. Then they stared at the faces of the posse and raised a cheer. Five minutes before, the six farmers were beginning to drop toward despondency. Five minutes later, they were traveling in the midst of an ovation. Voices in the crowd of townsfolk took up a shout for a lynching. They wanted it then, and in the main street of the village. But Rex Houlahan stood in the wagon with his red beard blowing across his throat and no one made an attempt to seize the thief. The wagon halted before the jail.

IX

Usually mob scenes did not attract the sheriff. It was a silent tribute to the remarkable noise that the crowd set up this day before the jail, that Ed Sturgis himself came through the heavy door and stood at the top of the wooden steps. His hat was pushed far back on his head, allowing his unruly hair to pour beneath the brim and straggle almost to his eyes. It was always a sign of weariness when Ed Sturgis wore his hat in this way, and when he was weary, he was not a pleasant man. The crowd was afflicted with the usual mob blindness, however. All it saw was the sheriff standing at the head of the steps with his hands on his hips, grinning down at them. The mob gathered itself up in a big wave that washed up the steps and deposited six heroes all about Sturgis.

"They done it!" cried scores of voices. "They put one over on you, Ed. They got the thief. They got Jerry Peyton!"

An unusual phenomenon followed. The wave of noise was met, now, by a contrary wave of silence that began in the immediate neighborhood of the sheriff and, spreading first to those about him, gradually worked its way over the hundreds in the street. Also a path opened before Sturgis down the steps and he went down through the opening with an acre of silent faces in the street tilted up to watch him. He climbed into the body of the wagon and was seen to bend over the body of Peyton. Then he stood up.

"Is Doc Brown here?"

A fat man pushed through the crowd and laid his hands on the edge of the wagon.

"Take this boy, Doc," said the sheriff, "and do what you can for him." The words carried distinctly up and down the length of the crowd.

"All right," said the doctor cheerily. "I'd as soon take care of a horse thief as another. A case is a case."

"Who called Jerry a horse thief?" the sheriff asked. He spoke gently, but once more his voice carried to the outermost edges of the crowd. "What fool called Jerry Peyton a horse thief?"

No one answered. The six brave men on the steps remained tongue-tied.

Then Doc Brown said: "Well, I'll be hanged."

"Take this wagon back to Jerry's place, and half a dozen of you put him to bed," the sheriff ordered. "Doc, you stay with him." He turned and went up the steps and opened the door to the jail. "Come in, boys," he said. "I reckon I got room for you all in here."

The six looked at one another. Then they met the smile of the sheriff, and finally they trooped in single file through the door.

"Let me understand this," Jan van Zandt said, when they all stood in Sturgis's office. "You stick up for a thief... a horse thief, Sheriff?" His voice rose as he remembered something from a book. "You want to arrest us because we handled a crook? I tell you to look out, Sturgis. Maybe we didn't have no warrant for what we done, but we taught a lesson that was needed. And we don't need a warrant, because we're the voice of the people."

"You're the voice of a coyote," the sheriff replied sternly. "I recognize it by the whine. Don't talk back to me, Jan. Don't even look back to me. Don't none of the rest of you do nothin' but smile pleasant at me. All of you sit quiet like little lambs, which you are. Don't none of you stir a hand nor raise a head. Because I'm plumb fed up. I'm fed up so much that I'm puffin' inside and I'm lookin' for action." He methodically made a cigarette and lighted it. "Speakin' of horses," he said nonchalantly, "they's a chestnut horse lying in the woods up in Dogberry Cañon. It's been run through the temple with a knife because the no-good horse give out and the gent that stole him wanted to get rid of all that useless horseflesh. Maybe you'd like to see that horse, Jan?"

The farmer dropped his head into his hands and groaned. At another time such grief, and particularly for a horse, would have moved the sheriff, but now he let his eyes rest fondly upon Jan through a long moment, and then moved them lingeringly across five other faces.

"Well, boys," he said, "I think I've changed my mind. I ain't goin' to jail you. And they's a sad reason why. Jerry Peyton is goin' to get well."

The six quivered under the stroke. Jan van Zandt raised his head and gasped. "And when he gets well," said the sheriff sadly, "he'll be callin' on you to pay you some attentions. He's like the rest of the Peytons. He's like his father. He's thoughtful. I seen his wrists. It'll be four weeks, near, before he can handle a gun. Well, boys, I guess that's all. I wish you all four weeks of good luck."

Jan van Zandt parted his lips to speak. The sheriff leaped straight into the air and, coming down, smashed his fist upon his desk. "Not a word out of you, you sneakin', man-slaughterin' coyote. Git out, you and your pack!"

The six in the same silence rose and put on their hats, and slunk through the door, and silently down the steps to the street. There they parted and the sheriff from a window watched them split apart and travel in different directions. After he had seen this, he turned and made his way through the office to the little wing of the jail where the prisoners were kept. There was only one man there. The sheriff took his way down the little corridor between the bars of tool-proof steel and the wall. He sat down on a folding stool that leaned close to the bars, and, while he rolled another cigarette, he looked with interest upon Pat Langley behind the bars. The latter lay in a vest and stockinged feet on his bunk, and, although he was immediately aware that another person had come, it was some time before he laid down his newspaper.

The sheriff spoke first. "I got some news that'll interest you," he said.

Pat Langley yawned deliberately. "Yes?"

"You mostly remember what I said the farmers would do to Jerry Peyton?"

"Is that his name?"

"Old Hank's son."

The prisoner whistled.

"Well, they done it," said the sheriff.

"Strung him up, eh?" said Pat Langley, losing interest. "Did he pot any of them?"

"They must've got him when he didn't have a gun," said the sheriff. "They all had the signature of his fist, right enough. I could've told from a block away that they'd been talkin' to Jerry by the look of their faces. I disremember when it was I seen him arguin' with four Mexicans in the street one day."

"Does he make the yellow boys his meat?" Pat Langley asked scornfully.

"Mostly he don't pay no attention to 'em," said the sheriff. "But sometimes he gets his feet all tangled up in 'em, and then he just cuts his way out."

"In self-defense?" inquired Langley.

"Sure." The sheriff grinned. "Otherwise, I'd've arrested him long ago, wouldn't I?"

"Of course," said Langley, smiling in turn. They seemed to understand one another perfectly.

"But comin' back to the Mexicans," went on Sturgis, "they was all a husky crew and they took him with a rush while his back was turned and his hands was full of the makin's. It was a pretty sight to foller, if your eyes was fast enough to see all that happened. I disremember, as I was sayin', most of the details, but toward the end I recall Jerry steppin' on the face of one Mex while he belted the other in the jaw. Pretty soon he come up to the door of the jail...he had all the Mexicans tied together. 'I hear you been havin' dull times in your boardin' house,' says he to me. 'So I been drummin' up some trade for you.' And then

I got a good look at the faces of them Mexicans, and their own mothers wouldn't've recognized 'em. Well, that's the way the six farmers looked today," concluded the sheriff.

"But they hung him, eh?" said Pat, rising upon one elbow to listen.

"Nope."

Pat stretched himself out again, yawning.

"They only hung him up by the wrists," said the sheriff, "to make him confess, I guess. His arms are sure a rotten mess to look at just now. They hung him up till he fainted dead away. D'you ever hear of such foolishness?"

"Foolishness?" Pat questioned.

"Sure... to hang him up and then let him get away alive. Damned foolishness. And now," continued the sheriff, "what'll happen when the boy is on his feet and shoots Jan van Zandt full of holes?"

"Why, when that happens," said the man of the black mustache, "you'll have to go out and get Jerry Peyton." He sat up and laughed. "By heavens, I hadn't thought of that."

"You got an ugly laugh, Pat," the sheriff said.

"When I read of your demise," said Pat, "I'll give you a tender thought, Ed. But do you know that this terrible Peyton of yours interests me? I wasn't a bad hand in a pinch in the old days."

"I'll tell a man," said the sheriff gently.

"And now," went on Pat Langley, "I feel a lot better. As a matter of fact, Ed, it was pretty clever of you not to try a hand-to-hand scrap of it... out there in the Dogberry Cañon. How did you tell I was in shape?"

"By your hands," said the sheriff. "The rest of you is pretty fat, but your hands is as skinny and quick as they ever were." He stared fixedly at Pat Langley.

"Well," said Pat, "what do you see? Me in a suit of stripes or yourself eating Peyton's lead?"

The little animal eyes of the sheriff went up and down. "D' you know, Pat, that I got a funny thing to tell you?"

"You're full of funny sayings," said the horse thief coldly.

"There you go," murmured the sheriff. "You always have tried to read my mind, Pat. And you always have read it wrong."

There was something sad about the voice of the sheriff that made the other man frown at him.

"Out with it," he said. "What's the funny little thing?"

"Well, ever since I laid eyes on you out in the road up there, I been tryin' to convince myself that I hate you, Pat, but I don't convince worth a cuss."

X

As for Langley, he rolled off the bunk, and, coming to the steel bars of his cage, he took two of them in his small, strong hands and looked steadily through the intervening space at the sheriff. He contented himself with that long, steady gaze, never saying a word. The sheriff blinked once or twice, but aside from that he met Langley with a sad, calm regard.

"For instance," said the sheriff, "when I brung you in, I went down to write the charge ag'in' you onto the little hotel register that I keep for my guests. Well, somehow I couldn't write down the number that means larceny after your name. Couldn't do it, Pat. I couldn't even write down your name."

"Are you playing a little game?" asked Langley, and he pressed his face against the bars in his desire to look through the little eyes of Ed Sturgis and get at his mind.

"Me?" queried the other in surprise. "What sort of a game do I need to play on you now, Pat?"

It was quite unanswerable. This truth gradually became clear in the mind of Langley. "I can even explain why you feel this way," he said with a sudden change of voice.

"You was always a great hand at explainin'," murmured the sheriff, but, although Pat Langley shot one of his sudden glances at Sturgis, he was able to read nothing in the bland face of his old companion.

"This is why," Pat said. "In the old days I did you a great wrong, Ed. You have kept that in mind all these years, you see. You've been hating me all this time and wishing and waiting for a chance to get back at me. Is that the truth?"

"I guess it's pretty close to gospel, old-timer."

"But down in your heart," continued Pat Langley, "all the time you weren't hating me so much as the thing I had done."

The sheriff blinked again. "I don't quite follow," he murmured.

"I mean this," Pat said hurriedly. "Outside of that one thing I did, I was always square with you. I played straight. I backed you up in every pinch. You remember?"

"That's true."

"So all these twenty years," said Langley, "you've been concentrating to hate that one thing I did. It was a mean piece of work. I don't deny that, Ed, and not once during these years have I attempted to excuse it to myself."

"Go on," said the sheriff, and a little spot of white had come in either cheek. "Let's leave that go."

"Let that pass." Langley nodded. "And when you saw me today, it was a man you couldn't recognize. You found that you didn't hate that stranger you met in the road. It wasn't until you found out what his name is that you began to hate him. Is that straight, Ed?"

It must have been to conceal his emotion that the sheriff looked down and placed his hand above his eyes. He was thinking, and it was some time before he could raise his head and look at his prisoner again. When he did so, it was to say: "Pat, you're right."

The other turned, and, since he dared not raise his voice and, above all, allow the sheriff to see his face, he turned and walked to his bunk and stood with his back to the sheriff and his head fallen.

"What's the matter?" asked the sheriff cheerily, after a time.

"It's because I can't help thinking what a hound I was," Pat Langley said, choking. "And you . . . Ed . . . when all's done, you were the finest friend I've ever had."

"Tut, tut," the sheriff replied. "D'you mean that?"

"Do you doubt me?" cried Langley, whirling on his heel. "Now that I'm here and down and ruined . . . do you doubt me?" He waved to the bars, to the wretched bunk.

"Yes," agreed the sheriff, "sometimes the steel slats work through the blankets and sort of leave a pattern on a gent's back. Them bunks ain't what I'd recommend to anybody that likes to lie soft at night."

To this naïve speech the reply of the horse thief was another of the flickering, bright glances, but there was apparently no mockery in the face of the sheriff.

"What I'm chiefly sorry for," said Langley, "is that I've left you in another mess by this unfortunate episode of the chestnut horse."

"Yep," agreed the sheriff, "that's a pretty bad mix-up, all right. Tell me, honest, Pat, did you figure on sending back the price of that horse when you got to the end of your trip?"

"So help me, I did," Langley said, and there was a ring of truth in his voice.

"My, my," said the sheriff. "You have changed a pile, Pat. Well, I'll tell you about this Peyton. I tell you I fear him, and I do. You remember his dad, don't you?"

"Old Hank? Of course. I had a run-in with him, you remember."

"And came out on top. Yes, I remember. But Hank was a fast man and pretty accurate, and his son is a shade better. But why I fear him is because he has all my luck. No use runnin' foul of a man that has your luck."

"How did he get it?" said Pat Langley with interest. "But to tell you the truth, Ed, you're a fool to fear any man under thirty. It takes a certain age to harden a man's nerve, and the boy could never stand up to you."

"Not unless he had my luck, I wouldn't bat an eye about him."

"*H-m-m*," Langley said. "That makes a difference, of course."

"It was just before I come to Sloan," the sheriff continued. "First place I landed when I headed West was in Nevada, and I hit her when she was wide open and roarin'."

"I've always regretted missing those days in Nevada," Pat Langley said, and sighed.

"Sure, you would have been right at home," agreed the sheriff.

Again Langley looked to discover proof of double-entendre, but he found nothing.

"I was some green," the sheriff went on, "in those days. I was all set up to find trouble. Knew how to shoot, I thought, and at a target I was some handy boy. So I got all togged up with a brace of gats and a frosty eye and went about with a chip on my shoulder. Particular, I had one gun that was a beauty. It was a new model, just out of the shop, and she worked like she had brains of her own. In fact, it's a pretty old model for a Colt today, but in fingers that know their business it don't have to take a back seat to nothin' right up to this minute."

"I think I know that old model," said Pat.

"With that gun," the sheriff continued, "I felt like Hercules, and then some. And so one evenin' I run into a little gent in a saloon. We was playin' cards and I seen him palm a card once... then I seen him do it again. For that matter, they was a couple of the other boys that I was sure had seen it. But they didn't say nothin'. At the time, I wondered why, but I didn't stop to ask any questions about who this gent was. I just give him a call and then start for my gun. Well, Pat, he got me covered before I had my forefinger on the butt of my gun. He seen I was a kid and mostly a fool, though, and he didn't feel much like action, I guess. Anyway, he let me off with a bit of advice, and he took away both my guns for safekeepin', he said, to keep me out of trouble."

"Funny you never told me this story before," Langley said.

"When I knew you," said the sheriff, "I was still too young. The thing was too fresh in my mind, and I hadn't reached the stage when I could tell about the lickin's I'd had in the past. Now, I can grin about 'em."

"*H-m-m*," Langley said thoughtfully.

"But the point of that yarn ain't out yet. The name of the quiet gent that got my guns was La Paloma."

"The devil you say," murmured Langley.

"The devil I do say," said the sheriff calmly. "It was sure La Paloma, though he hadn't picked up that name yet. And that gun he got from me was the one he always packed later on. That's the gun the greasers called The Voice of La Paloma, he used it so handy."

"But what the devil has that to do with your luck leaving you, Ed?"

"Why, just this. The chap that got La Paloma... that was two years after you left... was Hank Peyton, you see? And Hank got The Voice of La Paloma and passed it along to his kid. So Jerry has my gun... and whoever had any luck trailin' a gent that had your own gun? It's more'n that, Pat. The kid puts an awful lot of stock in that gun. I figure he ain't practiced with anything else since he was knee-high. And if he didn't have it, he'd be up in the air. You see how everything turns around it? He's got my luck. My luck is his luck. There you are, and when Jerry Peyton bumps off the first of them farmers... I wish to heaven that he'd get the whole crew of 'em at once, for my part. I got to go out on the trail of a gent that has all my luck pulling at his holster. I'd as soon jump over a cliff. I wouldn't be no surer of dyin' that way."

As he concluded this gloomy story, his eyes dropped to the floor and remained there, studying the shadow. It gave Pat Langley a chance to lift his own glance and observe every detail of the face of the sheriff. He even permitted the faintest hint of a smile that might have been either contempt or scorn to touch his lips. Then he brushed this smile away and came close to the bars.

"Ed," he whispered.

"Well, Pat," the sheriff said absently.

"I have a little proposition that might interest you."

"Fire away, old-timer."

"You say you haven't put my name in the book?"

"I haven't."

"And no one knows that I'm here?"

"Not a soul." He looked quickly into Pat Langley's face. "What are you figurin' on, Pat?"

"On playing your game and mine with the same hand, old boy."

"Go on, Pat. You was always a hand at sayin' surprisin' things."

"Ed, you've already admitted that your old grudge against me is dead. I'm simply a burden on your hands here. Well, let me out of this mess. Give me a horse and a gun. I'll doll myself up in a mask and slide over to the house of this young Peyton, do the robber stunt, you see? Turn things upside down, and finally take his gun and bring it out to you. Then you'll have your luck back and I'll have my freedom and a horse to go on my way. What d'you think?"

"I can't think," the sheriff said. "Gimme air."

XI

It was on the second night following this that the sheriff and Pat Langley rode out of Sloan and took the way down the valley. They cut across the fields, and came by a generous detour behind the house and farm buildings of Jerry Peyton. They had the clear mountain, star-like, to guide them, and even by that dull light they made out the dilapidated outbuildings. There were broken gang plows and worn out two-horse rakes standing about, silent tokens of Jerry's complete failure as a farmer. They dismounted beside a big barn, and, when they passed the open door, they could see the stars through gaps of the roof. The big haymow was empty, and the long row of stalls on either side of the plow contained not a single horse or even a mule. Pat Langley noted this and shrugged his shoulders.

"Makes me feel like the devil," he muttered to the sheriff. "Hate to see a place go to ruin. I remember when the Peyton place was a comfortable little farm. Old Missus Peyton was a wonderful cook, too . . . and *now* look at her kitchen."

That wing of the house presented a roof that sagged far in.

"You got a tenderness for houses that you never used to have," commented the sheriff. "Maybe that comes out of the coin you've made in Saint Hilaire."

The other made no answer; he was taking stock of the place rapidly.

"I don't see your point in not giving me a gun with teeth in it," he said angrily to the sheriff. "Suppose that young devil in there can use either one of his hands . . . he'll punch me full of lead when I shove this empty bunch of iron junk in his face."

"He can't raise an arm, let alone handle a gun," said the sheriff. "He can't even feed himself. The neighbors have to come in and take care of him like a baby."

"Ah, that's it. Then I'll have some of these handy neighbors about when I slip in?"

"Not a one. They'd leave him before now."

The sheriff felt the glance of the horse thief for him through the starlight, discontented with the vague outlines of the face he saw.

"I leave it to you to warn me in case anyone comes," said Pat Langley.

"The old sign," said the sheriff. "You can depend upon that."

"Well, here goes," and, lifting his hat a little, a curtain of absolute dark rushed over the dim face of Langley.

The sheriff whispered: "Are you nervous, Pat?"

"Nonsense," answered the other. "Nervous? I'm enjoying every minute of it."

"And it won't bother you none to go in there and take that kid's gun away from him?"

"Why should it?" Langley retorted. His tone had changed since the mask covered his face; in fact, there was a new atmosphere around the two men.

"I mean, him bein' helpless," murmured the sheriff. "It won't make you feel like a skunk to take his gun away when he ain't got a fightin' chance, will it?"

The other chuckled almost silently. "Listen to me, old boy. I left my scruples back in Saint Hilaire. This is a party for me. S'long!" And he disappeared around the side of the house.

The sheriff, after a moment, made a few steps in pursuit, but then he came back to the horses and stood at their heads, lest something in the night should make one of them whinny. He began to rub the pinto's nose nervously, and whisper into the ear of Langley's horse. Yet there was not a sound from the direction of the house. Once the thought came to the sheriff that Langley might give over the attempt to rob Peyton and go away into the night, but on second thought he knew that the other would not risk an escape on foot. The horses caught the man's wish for silence and stood without stirring as they listened into the night, and the silence gathered heavily about them. Then something that was not a sound made the sheriff turn; he saw his companion once more at his shoulder.

They swung into the saddles without another word and headed across the fields at a trot. As soon as a comfortable distance lay behind them, they let their horses have their heads and went at a wild gallop. Halfway back to Sloan they stopped of one accord.

"Well?" the sheriff asked.

The other ripped away his mask and tore it into a hundred shreds, then he tossed the balled-up remnants into the dust. "Not so simple as you'd think," Langley said. He shrugged his shoulders to get rid of some thought. "He's a bad one, well enough, that young Peyton."

"Made a try for you?"

"Oh, no. He sat in his chair and couldn't lift a hand, just as you said, but he got on my nerves. Can you imagine a fellow who sits perfectly still and follows you with his eyes while you run through his stuff?"

"I can," said the sheriff, and for some reason his voice carried a world of meaning.

"The kid was cool enough," said the other. "I went through his wallet . . . it was in the table drawer. 'Help yourself,' says young Peyton. Cheery smile he has, isn't it?"

"Yep. He's a fine-lookin' gent."

"I took the coin. Only twenty bucks, at that, but it would have looked queer if I hadn't taken it. I told him I was sorry to do it, though . . . but being broke . . . he just nodded at me. 'That's all right,' he said."

"Ah," sighed the sheriff. "You spoke to him?" He did not seem displeased.

"Of course," said Langley. "But he changed his tune when I came to his gun rack. I ran through the stuff and found The Voice of La Paloma. Rum name for a gun, eh? I knew it by the make and by the nicks that were filed into the butt. 'Just a minute,' said the kid. 'You don't really want that gun, I guess?'

"'Why don't I?' I said.

"'You don't understand,' says the kid. 'That gun used to belong to my father. It means a good deal to me. The gun you want is the new Colt that hangs next to the old pump gun.'

"'Don't jolly yourself along,' I said to him. 'I know the make of a gun, and this suits me to a T.'

"For a minute I thought I'd have a bit of trouble even with that handless man . . . he leaned forward in his chair. 'You shouldn't do that,' he said. 'Don't take that gun.' From the way he spoke, I had a ghost of an idea that he had twenty men behind his chair ready to grab me. I had to blink at him, and his face wasn't pretty. 'If you're so set on it,' I said, 'I'll leave the money, but I've got to have this little cannon.'

"'Then,' says friend Jerry, 'you're a fool.'

"'So?' I said to him.

"'Because if you take the coin, and anything else you see here, I'll let it go. But if you take that gun, I'll follow you.'

"You won't believe that it gave me a chill to hear him say it? You know me, Ed?"

"I know you well enough," said the sheriff dryly, "but I believe you got the chill."

"I did, all right. 'How'll you get my trail?' I asked the kid. 'You don't know me. If you live to be a hundred, you'll never know my name, and you'll never see my face. Tell me how you'll follow me, partner.'

"He didn't bat an eye. If he knew anything, you'd think he'd keep still about it, eh? Not Jeremiah. He came right out with it in a way that didn't particularly help my nerves. 'I know your height,' he said, 'I know your weight. I know you have black hair with a touch of gray in it and you're about forty-five years old. You have a heavy mustache . . . the mask bulges out around your mouth . . . and your eyes are black. More than that, I know your voice and I know your hands. Those hands alone would give me a clue. They'll leave a sign I can follow. So take my advice, partner, and put that gun back in the case. Because, if you take it, I give you my word of honor that I'll never rest or draw a free breath till I've run you down and killed you like a hound.'

"That was a mouthful for a helpless kid to say to me, when I had a bead on him, eh? I don't ask you to believe it, but just for a minute I had a feeling that I'd like to tell you to go hang, put the gun in the case, and take a chance on running across country on foot. Of course I didn't do what I felt like doing. And here's The Voice of La Paloma."

He extended the old revolver and the sheriff took it and bent his head over it, then he balanced it in his hand.

"Seems like I still recognize it," he said. He examined it, made sure that it was loaded, and then turned the muzzle full upon his companion. "Now," he said, "sit tight and listen to me while I talk."

The other stared. "Well I'll be…" he murmured.

"Easy, friend," interrupted the sheriff. "Don't move that gun out of your holster. Good."

"What's got into your crazy head," said Pat Langley after a moment, "is more than I can make out. If you're going to double-cross me, go ahead. I'm not fool enough to make a break when you have a bead on me. Want my hands up?"

"No. Do whatever you want with 'em. And use your ears to listen to what I've got to say. I didn't know you then, Pat, but the minute I heard about the way you run a knife into that horse, it turned me ag'in' you. And after that, I didn't like the way you tried to bribe me, Pat. Still, I didn't see how low-down mean you could be till later on."

Langley sat with his head canted, nodding. "It's odd," he said, "that an intelligent man like you, Ed, can live nearly fifty years without increasing his vocabulary. Go ahead."

"No, I ain't clever, Pat. But I was clever enough to see that I was in a mess on account of you stealin' the horse and Peyton gettin' beat up for the same thing. I saw Peyton make his kill after his wrists got well. I saw him go plumb wild. I saw Sheriff Sturgis go out to get him and get drilled full of lead tryin' to do it.

"You see, I ain't clever, Pat, but I seen all that, and I thought I'd see if I couldn't make a combination and get out of trouble. Here you were in jail. If I got bumped off, I could hear you laugh. There was Peyton, getting well for a scrap later on. I wondered if

I couldn't get rid of both of you. Well, I played stupid. You bein' a clever gent, I just gave you a lead, and you worked it all out for me. The lead I give you was that cock-and-bull yarn about The Voice of La Paloma. Pat, I thought you were sure fooling me when I saw you swallow that yarn."

Langley nodded again. "I begin to see light," he said calmly.

"Still," went on the sheriff, "I didn't see my way clear out until you told me yourself that you'd make the dirty bargain. You'd go out and take that gun from a kid that couldn't help himself. Honest, though, Pat, I hated to think there was such a yellow-hearted skunk in the world as you are. But you done it. You made the plan and then you went right ahead and took the gun. And now, partner, you're fixed. Far as I'm concerned, you're free. I got no bolts on you. You can ride as far as you please. And as far as the kid is concerned, I'm rid of him, too. He ain't goin' to do no killin' in my county. No, sir. He'll hop on a horse as soon as he gets well, and he'll never think of nothin' until he finds his dad's gun ag'in and gets it back."

"I see," said Langley coldly. "You'll point out the way to Saint Hilaire to him?"

"I'd ought to, I guess," said the sheriff with a sigh. "But I won't. I like to see a rabbit get a fair start before a hound catches him. Well, Pat, I give you a start off from here to Saint Hilaire. And you better use it. Because water ain't goin' to stop young Peyton when he hits the trail. He'll nose you out, old boy, and he'll finish you, a long ways off from Sloan."

"He's free to follow," Langley said. "If the young fool is keen enough to trail me to the West Indies from the border, I'll almost regret that I have to shoot him. But, in conclusion, I have to admit that you've improved your method since the old days, Ed. You were always a bit of a coward when it came to facing me, but in those times you hadn't enough brains to think of sending a substitute after me. So long, old boy."

"Well," called the sheriff after him, "I kind of expected you'd get in the last word! Ride hard, Pat!"

XII

Dr. Brown, besides attending to his patient, kept six anxious farmers apprised of his condition through daily bulletins that were followed with painful interest by the farmers and their wives and children. Their relatives, also, came to read the bulletins of Dr. Brown. With groans of distress they noted the day on which the doctor sent word that his patient was for the first time able to use a spoon. And later still that he was able to work with a very sharp knife and put enough pressure on the edge to cut his own meat.

That was gloomy news to the six. Without waiting longer, Pierre la Roche sold his farm, packed his belongings, and huddled wife and family aboard a train headed for parts unknown.

Then came the day when it was known that the bandages had been finally removed from the wrists of the sufferer and it was only a matter of time before he would have complete use of his fingers and arm muscles. These terrible tidings swept Pete Goodwin and Eric Jensen and Gus Saunders out of Sloan and carried them away to parts as unknown as those that had received the family of la Roche. There still remained Rex Houlahan and Jan van Zandt. Rex held out until Dr. Brown advised his clients that the big cowpuncher was exercising every day, and his exercise consisted largely in faithful practice with weapons. Then Rex Houlahan disappeared from the ken of man. The sheriff rubbed his hands together, and that night he slept well for the first time in six weeks. But when the morning came he found that Jan van Zandt still remained. It troubled the sheriff, this incredible stupidity. He went out and told the prospective martyr some home truths about himself, but Jan van Zandt merely stared at the sheriff and grew a little whiter about the mouth; he refused to leave. The other farmers formed what might be called a protective association, but for some reason they failed to invite Jan to join. Indeed, no one wanted to be seen in his company, or pose as his friend. Over Sloan and all the valley lay the fear of Jeremiah.

The creditors, at about this time, hurried affairs along. They foreclosed, and the shuddering population of Sloan was informed that out of the sale young Peyton had secured only enough funds to buy for himself a fine new revolver, a reliable horse, and an outfit of clothes and food suitable for a long and hasty trip on horseback. On the next day, he took a room in the hotel. On the next day the doctor let it be known that his patient was completely restored. On the next day the friends and relatives of Jan van Zandt came to call upon him, pressed his hand, muttered a word of farewell, and left him hurriedly.

And the morning after that, Sloan wakened with astonishment to learn that Peyton was gone from their midst, whither no man knew, and that Jan van Zandt still drew the breath of life.

The sheriff collapsed when he heard the news, and then he set about hunting for clues. All he could learn was that young Peyton had made inquiries about a man in the neighborhood of forty-five years of age, a hundred and seventy pounds in weight, five feet and ten inches in height, black hair, and bright, black eyes, and a heavy mustache. And he had appeared interested in Sid Ruben's account of a man who answered that description. Sid had passed him in Dogberry Cañon on the way toward Tannerville, apparently. The sheriff ran inadvertently upon this unimportant bit of news; he was observed to go back to his office singing, a little later, and before the day was over Jerry Peyton was forgotten in the routine of Sloan's busy life.

And the town of Sloan was forgotten by Jeremiah Peyton even more completely. Between his knees he had a mud-colored gelding whose savage eye had pleased him long ago in the corral of Sam Wetherby. In his holster was a gun that had fitted into the palm of his hand like the grip of an old friend. On his feet were shop-made boots, at $40, and on his heels jingled new spurs. Around his neck was a bandanna handkerchief of the finest silk and of a screaming crimson. In his pocket a wallet bulged more or less comfortably. Between his fingers the reins slipped to and fro as he kept the feel of the mustang's head, and in his heart was the glorious knowledge that he was free. The mud-colored gelding carried all that he owned in the world; there was no weight of possessions to take him back to any place. He was like a ship with anchors cut away, blowing for a distant port as he galloped down Dogberry Cañon that morning, and he felt as a sailor, long land-locked, feels when a deck heaves under his heels again, and the wind cuts into his face. The stranger with the small, white, agile hands was his goal; there were other ports that he must touch before the voyage ended, Pierre la Roche, Jan van Zandt, and the others, but he pushed these into the background of his mind. He had an oath that would keep his helm steadily toward the man of the mask and carry by all the others until that port was reached.

He had picked up one more important detail, the color of the horse on which the stranger rode when he left Sloan, and with that added fact he had little trouble in picking up another step of the trail at Tannerville. No one remembered the man with the white hands, it seemed, saving Dick Jerkin, the gambler. He had sat in with this man, it appeared. The stranger had given his name as Owen Peyne and he played a stiff game of poker. Dick dropped a couple of hundred in an hour's play and was about to lose more, according to the luck, when a fortunate call dragged him away from this expert, who seemed to read the cards.

So far the trail was simple, for in the direction of Dogberry Cañon, Tannerville was almost the only stop out of Sloan, but beyond Tannerville the towns multiplied. Jerry cast a circle around Tannerville, and, after three days of hard riding and much talk, he came on the clue again. This time the name of the stranger was Bert Morgan, and Peyton smiled when he heard it. For it proved that the man with the agile hands had remembered the threat that Jeremiah spoke; now he was covering his trail. It was in the town of Benton that Jerry found the trail again, and beyond Benton, of course, lies a wilderness, so Jerry cast a line from Tannerville to Benton, and, projecting the line straight ahead, he struck into the desert and went by compass.

The compass brought him to a jerkwater town a hundred and fifty miles from Benton, and in this town of Lancaster the sign of the stranger completely disappeared. No one had ever heard of either Morgan or Peyne; no one knew of a rather stocky man with gray-streaked hair and a heavy mustache who spent money freely and gambled for high stakes. So Peyton, in despair, vented some pent-up wrath on a restaurant that served him a stale tamale, and, leaving a wreck behind him, he went on across the desert, somewhat soothed.

The stranger had not been in Lancaster. Therefore either Lancaster was peopled wholely by fools who could not remember or else the stranger, also striving to leave a difficult trail, had skipped this link in his journey. So it seemed to Jerry, and, traveling still by compass, he went for three more days across the desert until he reached a town that consisted of a crossroads store and three shacks. There they knew neither Morgan nor Peyne, but they were very much acquainted with a gentleman named Harry Wister, who had left one staggering wreck of a horse, bought another regardless of price, and then shot off into the desert again. All this was six weeks before and Peyton thrilled through every long, hard muscle when he thought of the speed of the stranger. For a hold-up man he was a most unusual criminal; he squandered money like a drunken millionaire, and he rode like a demon.

In Sandy Waters he found news of the third change of horses and a white-handed gentleman named Peters—six weeks ago he had gone through, with a two-hour stop. By this time Jerry had heard the face of the man described so often that he almost knew the well-fed cheeks and the bright eyes, and the white teeth that showed when he smiled. Then, five hundred miles from Tannerville, he reached the western and northern limit of the trail. It went out as completely as if the stranger had ridden into running water.

To say that Peyton was discouraged would be to put it far too mildly, but when a man has worked for thirty days at one affair, he will not give it up too lightly. Peyton took out his spite in a street fight. These affairs with fists were something he rarely indulged in, but bumping up against a bunch of half-drunken, savage Scandinavians gave him his chance. It was from every angle a glorious affair. For half an hour the ears of Jerry were filled with a roar of strong language volleyed at him from five mouths. They were all strong men. Even when they fell, they would catch at him and almost drag him down, and Jerry had fought like a wolf among dogs, leaping and striking and leaping clear. So at length, with one eye closed, Jerry shook himself to make sure that he was still holding together, cast one glance at the five disfigured Danes, and then staggered into the little hotel, content.

He slept for twenty-four hours after that. The deputy sheriff, who came to make inquiries about the fight, looked at Jerry as he lay asleep, went through his belongings, and then left, declaring that a man who could sleep more than twelve hours had a clear conscience. The Danes, though beaten, were not altogether discouraged. They mustered their forces, and, as soon as Jerry was out of sight of the town, they gave him a flying start on his journey back to the south and east. But Jerry was feeling too happy to be vindictive. He shot horses instead of men, and, when the informal posse had melted away, he went blithely on his course.

He had before him ten days of riding in circles from town to town, and then, at last, he came upon no less a hero of the green-topped table than Snowy Garrison. Snowy had come across Jeremiah years before, when Jerry was hardly more than a boy, except to those who knew him, and after a slight falling out they had shaken hands and departed one from another, sworn friends.

On this second meeting Snowy was bulging with prosperity. He had a suite of rooms in the hotel—for this was Chambers City—and a little Negro to call him in the morning and put him to bed at night. Also he had a roll of money that choked his valise. And to Jerry he imparted the tale of a stranger who had come to Chambers City with a bright smile and agile fingers, and of how the stranger had gathered three stable citizens together and taken their money with oiled ease, extracting the savings of years painlessly. Then he, Snowy Garrison, proposing a game, was struck dumb to find a man who knew neither his name nor his widespread repute. His nerves were so shaken by thus discovering the meagerness of mortal fame that he straightway lost $3,000 in three gloomy minutes. The play of the stranger finally recalled him to his better self, and, at 12:00 sharp, the stranger declared that his cash was gone and wished to know if a check would be acceptable. Snowy then peered at the well-fed cheeks of the stranger and declared that a check would be a very acceptable tribute. So they continued to play until dawn. The next day Snowy found himself in possession of a series of little yellow slips of paper, each with *James P. Langley, St. Hilaire, W.I.*, written across the back. And every check was drawn upon a New York bank.

"And when I put 'em in for collection," added Snowy Garrison, "darned if they didn't get cashed in . . . all of 'em."

"Some millionaire out for an airing, maybe," said Jerry. "Well, if I had the kale that some of those gents have, I'd get as close to Nature as I want in Central Park."

"You're talking for us both," declared Snowy with emotion.

"But what did he look like, this fellow?" said Jerry, who had fallen into the habit of asking about the personal appearance of everyone since he took this empty trail.

"Middle aged, middle height, medium weight," said Snowy, "but what I noticed first was his hands. They was so small and white, you see?"

Long, lean fingers closed over the wrist of Snowy and burned the flesh against the bones with their grip.

"Spit it out," said Jerry. "Was his hair black?"

XIII

Information was not all that Jerry obtained through Snowy Garrison; he also sat in at an honest game of blackjack, with Jerry's .45 in view on a nearby chair to discourage any tricks from Snowy. And the honest game replenished Jerry's pocketbook, so that, the following morning, he found himself aboard a train with two tickets to New Orleans, an entire compartment for himself, and a bottle of yellow Old Crow. His first impulse was to open his wallet, and in it he discovered more money than he had ever seen there before. Accordingly, hearing voices outside the compartment—for Jerry had never ridden in a Pullman before—he summoned the speakers by beating upon the metal door with the butt of his gun. The voices outside stopped, and then a Negro popped in his head to see how matters stood.

From him Jerry ascertained a few details to help the blank of his memory. He learned that he had appeared in the train with a companion, both hatless and without luggage. He discovered that his companion, obviously Garrison, had wept feelingly over him, placed $20 in the hand of the porter, and assured him that he must put his dear brother, Mr. Jerry Peyton, off the train, head for St. Hilaire in the West Indies. It was from this porter, also, that Jerry learned many other important facts that influenced his future. He heard that in St. Hilaire people would probably be wearing mostly white at this time of the year, and that spurs, in that island, would be an unnecessary part of his outfit. So when the train reached New Orleans, Jerry outfitted himself in whites and bought his first pair of canvas low-cut shoes, a straw hat so flexible that it could be rolled up and put inside a little cane tube, and a ticket for St. Hilaire. In due time, having passed through a season of white-hot sea and then a sea whipped by a hurricane, Jerry found himself seated on the verandah of the American consul's house at St. Hilaire, growing acquainted with a pungent gin disguised in little glasses of milk and getting the feel of a new air.

The consul's house sat on the brow of a little hill with its face toward the sea, "and it's back on Saint Hilaire, thank heaven," as the consul said shortly after Jerry had presented the bottle of Old Crow to him.

At this Jerry stood up, and, looking down the length of the side verandah, he could see all of the town of St. Hilaire. Five big hills, like five stubby fingers, went up beyond the town, shutting out the view of the rest of the island, and St. Hilaire lay in the palm of the hand. At first glance it appeared to be merely a smear of green—a bright, shining green such as Jerry had never seen before—but presently he discovered under the trees a number of little houses that followed the course of streets. They were not streets laid down with any plan. They must have been constructed by engineers who worked on the system of cattle making a path, and, weaving heedlessly from side to side, following always the low ground. If Jerry had taken a coil of rope, shaken it loose, and flung it sprawling in the dust, the pattern it left would have been a fair representation of the plan of St. Hilaire. Looking more closely, Jerry could see some of the houses quite distinctly, particularly a few on the edge of the town nearest him, and he saw that the slant light of the sun shone quite through them. They were more like lean-tos thrown up for the night than lifelong habitations.

"Still," said Jerry, "I kind of like the color of that green stuff, and, speaking personal, if I were to own this house of yours, I don't think I'd sit out facing the sea."

He apparently struck a vital spark in the consul with this last remark. "Color?" said the consul. He started to stand up in turn, but, changing his mind, he merely sat forward in his chair and waved generously along the shoreline of the bay.

It was a graceful little harbor, an almost perfect horseshoe, with one spot of white in the center where the waves smashed into foam on a bit of coral reef. The points of the horseshoe were low sandy bars, thrusting out into the sea. The sand was very white, and the consul called Jerry's attention to it. "It's the sort of white," he declared, "that can't be painted. It's the sort of white that... that a painter uses for the brow of a woman."

At this the cowpuncher gaped, but the consul turned to him with a broad grin. "Have another drink," he said, pushing the bottle across the table.

The astonishment passed from Jerry's face as the consul kicked an inverted dishpan by way of a gong and bellowed to an agile little Negro for ice.

"Have another drink," said the consul, putting some of the ice into Jerry's glass, and spinning it expertly with a spoon held between two fingers, "and don't mind me."

Jerry accepted the drink and, after he had had it, modified the strength of the remark he had intended making. "Maybe that white is all right," he said, "but still it's too close to the sea to suit me."

The consul leaned back in his chair, and, looking first at Jerry and then at the sea, Jerry was sure that surprising words were about to issue from the consul's lips. He was correct.

"Too close to the sea?" echoed the consul, speaking solemnly. "Why, sir, the sea was placed there by God for the express purpose of bringing out the color of that sand spit. And the white sand spit was placed there by God to bring out the profound blue of the ocean."

He sipped his gin and milk and appeared to contemplate either the picture before him, the gin, or his own remark. He was not more than two years older than Jerry, the latter thought, but his hair was already so gray that it would be silver before long. His face would have been noble had the flesh not puffed a little too much about the eyes; also the eyes, though large, were smeared with mist, and only now and then the vital spark showed through. Jerry was so busy watching that face that he forgot to reply to the last remark of the consul.

"It is, in fact, a composition," the other continued. "It's a planned bit of work. The sea, the white sand, the sky...you observe..."

"Wait," Jerry interrupted. "I agree with what you say about the sand and the sky, well enough, Mister Rimshaw, but why the dickens can't you leave out the sea?"

"You object to the sea?" asked the consul sadly.

Jerry scratched his big head and considered. "The sea," he finally decided, "is like a bucking horse that never hits the ground." Unconsciously he laid a hand upon his stomach. "The sea..." he began again, but could say no more.

"The sea," said the consul, in such haste that he drank only half of his glass, "is the only part of Nature where the mind of man is free to expand limitlessly. The sea..." He paused in the midst of his exordium, so absent-mindedly that Jerry was barely in time to reach across the table and direct the stream of gin that the consul poured into his glass instead of upon the floor.

"Say," said Jerry, "maybe you're a painter yourself, in your off hours? Sort of work at it on the side?"

"Sir," the young man said soulfully, "I am an author."

"The devil you are!" cried Jerry, amazed.

"The devil I'm not," replied the other, with some force. "If I'm not an author, what would you call the writer of six plays, three novels, and countless essays, short stories, and verses?"

"I'm not arguing," Jerry said calmly, "I'm just wondering. If you're an author, what are you doing down here?"

"Studying human nature in the raw," replied the consul readily.

"Have another drink," Jerry said, pouring out one. "I sure like to hear you talk. In the raw, eh?"

"And waiting to find an intelligent editor," continued the author. "You'd be surprised, sir, if you knew how cramped the foreheads of our leading editors are. To me, it is shocking."

"Too bad," Jerry said consolingly.

"You can't understand," the author went on, "until you've learned by experience that costs so many pangs of the heart, and so much hard cash spent on paper and postage," he added. "Since I was nine, sir, I have been pouring my heart out on paper. And after a life of labor, the editorial brain of the English-speaking world condemns me to a hole like Saint Hilaire. I ask you, sir, what would you do in a case like mine?"

"Cut out the booze," replied the cowpuncher instantly, "and get into training."

He was astonished to see the author turn sharply in his chair with a broad grin. "That's sound advice," Mr. Rimshaw commented. "After you were in training, what would you do?"

"Sir," said Jerry suddenly, stiffening, "I sort of gather that you're smiling."

"Do you?" said the consul.

"Are you smiling with me or at me?" Jerry asked coldly.

There is a certain tone of voice that brings men up standing with as much surety as the rattle of a snake or the snarl of an angry dog.

The consul blinked. "With you, of course," he said soberly.

"I sort of had my doubts, that's all," Jerry replied, and, leaning back in his chair, he regarded the author with a hungry eye.

"You were about to give me some advice," the author said.

"Oh, yes. Well, if I were in your boots, I'd grab a horse... I mean a boat... and I'd buy a through ticket to the dug-outs where these editors sit around."

"Ah?" said the author.

"Then," the cowpuncher continued firmly, "I'd go in, with a story under one arm and a gat under the other, and find out what he meant by wastin' my money on postage."

"Do you know what would happen?" questioned the author.

"I got an idea," said Jerry blandly. "What d'you figure?"

"You'd never be able to get in to see the editor."

"Wouldn't I?" said Jerry. "Well, well..." And he grinned openly at the consul.

"And if you did," said the author, "and started any fancy talk, the editor would have you thrown out."

"Which?" asked Jerry, his eyes widening.

"Thrown out."

"With what?" Jerry queried.

"With their hands," said the consul, frowning at such stupidity, "and they'd speed you on your way with the ends of their boots."

"My, my," said Jerry gently. "They must be rough men."

The consul turned squarely about for the first time. The mist gradually stirred from across his vision and two keen eyes looked squarely into the face of Jerry.

"Well," said the author, "what the devil are you doing down here?"

"I'm just touring about, studying human nature in the raw." Jerry grinned. He added: "I'd an idea that you'd come here to live."

"Well," said the consul, "the population of Saint Hilaire is about twenty thousand and two, and you'll find about two people that are worthwhile in the place. One of them is yourself... modesty prevents me from naming the other one."

XIV

"Simple," said Jerry, "direct, and to the point. But then I'd like to get the gent in Chambers City who hoisted a flag over Saint Hilaire and said it was the best island for its weight that ever stepped into the Atlantic."

"Who was the bird?" said the author.

"Name was... what the devil? I forget. Middle-aged chap with gray hair and glasses.

"Respectable?" asked the consul.

"Sure, I won some money from him."

"And he steered you for Saint Hilaire? Well, I'll tell you. If you have the price of a ticket home, grab the next boat."

"*H-m-m*," said Jerry, stirring the ice about in his glass. "So far Saint Hilaire isn't so bad. Don't see much wrong with it except the long drive to the gate."

"What did he say about it?"

"Oh, I don't know. Said it was full of trees and people and money."

"What kind of trees?" asked the consul quickly.

"Poker trees," said Jerry, with innocent eyes.

"Ah!" The author grinned. "I see. Well, there are plenty of poker trees. I have one myself that's not so bad. But taking them, all in all, the poker trees that you can climb don't produce fruit that's worth picking, and the ones that are worthwhile are all fenced in."

"I'm some fence climber," Jerry assured him.

"Social fences," the consul and author continued. "Kind of people who give you a cold smile and tea once a year. Oh, this is a devil of a fine place, this Saint Hilaire. But speaking of poker, I..."

"How high do you run?" asked Jerry coldly.

"*H-m-m*," the consul uttered thoughtfully.

"Business is business," said Jerry.

"Oh," the consul replied, "I see. Well, I guess you don't want to talk to me. But I'll give you the layout of the joint. Personally I'd like to see somebody break down a few boards and get through the fence... maybe some of the rest of us could get through the hole."

"Is it worthwhile getting through the fences?" asked Jerry.

"Dear, innocent Jerry Peyton," the consul remarked. "Is it worth your while? Let me tell you a few facts. There are exactly three hundred and thirteen thousand acres of workable land in Saint Hilaire... and the land that can be worked is so rich that all you have to do is sit and smile at it to make things grow. Matter of fact, the hard work is only to make the right things grow. If you can beat the weeds, you have a fortune by the throat. Well, this land is cut up about as follows. A hundred and thirteen thousand acres are held by five thousand landowners, about twenty acres to a shot, and they're all prosperous little farms, at that. Which gives you an idea what the land will do. Then there's another class of farmers... about fifty altogether, and among them they own the rest of the three hundred thousand acres. You figure that out for yourself. Fifty into two hundred thousand is four thousand acres apiece." As he said this, he covered his eyes with his hand and shook his head sadly. "Four thousand acres breaking their hearts growing stuff for you while you sit back and curse the foreman for not doubling the profits so you can have two steam yachts instead of one."

A sort of horror fell upon the face of the consul. He went on: "But that's not all, dear friend. Tarry a while. Of the fifty, forty of 'em have a hundred thousand of the acreage. The other hundred thousand are divided among ten grand moguls, ten little princelets with ten thousand acres apiece."

"What do they raise on this land?" asked Jerry.

"Anything they think of planting. Coffee, sugar, tobacco... God knows what all... and the only things they don't grow are the things they've forgotten to plant. Those ten little kings own the rest of the island. They work together in a clique. They control the forty because they control not only the market but the social affairs of the island. And through controlling the forty they control everything. Suppose I should offend one of the ten? In twenty-four hours wheels would begin to spin in Washington... twenty-four hours after that a nasty little note would be on its way to me... or maybe a cablegram."

"Speed burners, eh?" Jerry interjected.

"Money's no object, of course. By degrees they're eating up the forty smaller fellows, and they're edging out and taking in the little holdings of the five thousand. Give them a few more years and they'll have the whole island under their thumbs."

"And the fifty are the poker trees?" Jerry asked, leaning back in his chair and caressing his lean fingers, never thickened by harder labor than the swinging of a quirt.

"With fences," the consul added, and he looked at Jerry with attention.

"I wonder," said Jerry, "if you know the names of the fifty?"

"I might be able to get a list," the consul replied without enthusiasm. He drummed his fat fingertips against the top of the table. "In a way," he continued, "anyone who acted as a sign post and pointed me on in my journey would have to be considered in. Peyton, I see that you are a fellow of intelligence. This is a devil of a job, and I don't get many asides."

The cowpuncher waved his hand.

"Frankly," the consul continued, "have you enough money to put up a front that will carry you through the fences?"

The fingers of Jerry wandered beneath his coat and touched the butt of his .45. "Between you and me," he said, "the best thing I have is a friend who'll back me for all that's in him."

"He'll plunge with you?"

"To the limit."

"He's a strong one?"

"I've never been able to faze him," said Jerry.

The consul drew out a fountain pen and an envelope and began to write on the back of it.

"Names?" said Jerry.

"Trees," said the consul.

"Suppose you begin with the top of the gang and work down . . . just offhand . . . I like to pick things by the sound of 'em."

"Sure. Well, there's the de Remi family. Old French crowd and the cream of social doings in the island. Then I suppose you could bunch in order the Franklins, the Ramseys, the Parkhursts, the Van Huytens, and the Da Costas. They're all old stuff in Saint Hilaire. There's a newer set, too, that figures in with the old gang... the Quests, the Gentreys, the Langleys, and the Pattraisons. That's the list of the upper ten. They're the Five Hundred of this joint, plus the guardian angels, and the ruling hand. They're the ones I have to kowtow to"—his face darkened—"and they're the ones who pat me on the back and send along the good word... when they think to do it. I make myself handy for them... sort of errand boy, you know, between them and Washington... and now and then they ask me up to tea and tell me to drop in any time. You know?"

Jerry had never been to a tea, but he had learned, among other things in his brief and rather crowded life, that most valuable of all conversational assets, the ability to use a timely silence. He said not a word, and the consul felt that he was wholly comprehended.

"Suppose you begin at the bottom of the list," said Jerry. "This Pattraison outfit?"

"They and the Quests and the Gentreys and the Langleys," said the author, "are a new fry on the island. Of course they're big guns compared with the small landowners, but, after all, the Pattraisons aren't the last word. You know? Old Henry Pattraison is a card. He was a brewer, they say, before he sank a big wallop of an investment in Saint Hilaire... there's a sort of custom here of forgetting the past of a family and judging it purely by its Saint Hilaire record, but a brewer was a bit strong even for Saint Hilaire's customs. They frowned him down, for a while... but after a while they forgot about his past and remembered that he had one of the best estates in the island and that eventually his heirs would be among the social leaders. Couldn't keep 'em from it. So they took in Mister Pattraison. Also, he's a hearty old soul, clean as a whistle and game to the core."

"That sounds all right to me," said Jerry. "Now the Langleys."

"I put them down in the lower flight because they're newcomers like the Pattraisons," the consul went on. "As a matter of fact, Langley himself was in bad odor for a time. As I said before, people are judged by what they do in Saint Hilaire, not by what they did before. Nobody knew what Langley was before he came here, but he pulled a bad one before he'd been long in the island. He got a small holding in the hills... all the central part of Saint Hilaire is hilly, you know... and then before the people knew it he had grabbed almost all of Guzman's property, and today old *Don* Manuel has just a clump of trees and a smile to live on. It's a long story... the one they tell about the way Langley cut in on *Don* Manuel Guzman. Anyway, he got the land, and the de Remi crowd wouldn't receive him for a long time afterward.

"Then Patricia came out. You know the way a girl does? One year she's a skinny kid, mostly legs and elbows... the next time you see her she's in blossom and knocks your eye out with a full-grown woman's smile. Well, Patricia bloomed like that and she's an extra fine flower. Saint Hilaire took one look at her, and then fell all over itself being nice to the whole family. James Langley wasn't overwhelmed. Not by a long distance. He's a frosty sort of chap, anyway... never speak to him, but I come within an ace of calling him Sir James, you see? Well, he saw that Patricia was the biggest social power in Saint Hilaire. He had the young men of the island in the palm of his hand. No matter what their parents wanted to do, their sons were sure to break away and come to the girl... and she's a beauty, man. So Langley sat back and watched and let the first lot of 'em bark their knuckles against his doors without opening to them. Finally he let them in one by one, and he let them in in such a manner that today he's the social dictator of Saint Hilaire. I suppose old Missus de Remi... Madame, they call her... runs him close when it comes to a pinch, but, all in all, Langley is the king. Missus Langley isn't a forward sort, but her husband has the big ace in Patricia and she can be played every day. Nobody has a successful party unless she's there... nobody thinks the landscape is complete unless her face is in the offing. You see? The de Remi crowd itself is helpless against a girl like that. They may regain part of their prestige after she's married, but, if her father uses his head and marries her off to one of the first-flight families, he'll still be the dictator."

"It looks as if the Langley crowd would be a good one to get by the heel," said Jerry carelessly.

"They would well enough, but look sharp there. Langley is a fox. And there's only one word in that house... James Langley!"

"To the devil with him, then," Jerry said coldly. "Let's go on to the next best bet."

XV

Before night, Jerry had a map of the island; before he went to bed he had studied all the main features, and, above all, he knew every approach to the house of James P. Langley. His plan, like the plans of most intelligent men, was eminently simple. He would go straight over the hills, enter the plantation of James Langley, shoot his man, and come straight back to the harbor. There he would hire one of the big launches that he had seen gliding about the harbor and go for the mainland—or for one of the larger islands to the east where there was room for an able-bodied man to hide. With all this arranged in his mind, he undressed, bathed, and retired for a perfectly sound sleep.

In the morning he was awakened by a light weight striking his chest. He sat up and saw a bright-colored bird sitting on the foot of the bed, looking at him without alarm. It was only a sugar bird, on its eternal quest for insects, but Jerry could not know this, and to him there was something preternatural in the wisdom of the little head tucked to one side and the eyes that glittered at him without fear.

"If you've come to advise me, partner," said Jerry to the bird, "fire away."

The bird flew to the windowsill and looked back at him.

"If it's action you want," said Jerry, getting out of bed, "I'm all set." And when the bird at once darted through the window into the open air outside, a thrill went through Jerry. He felt that the omen was good, and at once he began to sing. He was singing again when he left the little shabby hotel after a breakfast of strange fruits and abominable coffee, and hired a horse for the day. That a man should go with music in his heart to kill another may appear unforgivably callous, but, in Jerry's code, it was established so firmly that an insult to his dead father must be avenged with death, that to shrink from it would have been to him what a denial of God is to most men. He accepted a stern necessity, and, although the horse was saddled with a pad that was a novel form of equitation to the cowpuncher, and, although the revolver irked him beneath the rim of his trousers, yet he sang as he rode because he was nearing the end of his quest.

Jerry was so happy, now, that he noted only the fine road before him, and the glossy brilliance of the tropical foliage on either side of him. Sometimes the sun set a whole field of it flashing so that he was almost blinded, but, aside from such times, or when a strange new scent struck him, Jerry paid as little heed to the country through which he rode as if it had been the old familiar way from the ranch to Sloan.

So he came to a great stone fence that ran out of sight on either side, and straight before him was the end of the road, blocked by an iron gate of towering size. On a pillar beside the gate these words were deeply carved in the stone: Langley Manor. And it struck Jerry with a sense of fatal significance that the end of his trail should be the end of a road as well. A Negro boy came out and opened the gate unquestioningly to the white man; Jerry tossed him a quarter and went through onto a winding gravel way that wove leisurely from side to side, fenced with enormous palm trees. Then he saw before him a house with a mighty façade, and twelve pillars of bright stone going up the height of two stories, in the center, about the portico. There were other columns, on the wing entrance. That was where vehicles drove up, he saw. And for a single instant Jerry wondered if he had not come all this distance on a wild-goose chase—for how could the owner of this great estate possibly be the hold-up artist who had taken his father's gun in malice, some three months before?

Imagination rarely took a violent hold upon Jerry's mind, however. Presently he gave his horse to another Negro boy—there seemed a limitless stock of them moving about—and spoke to a formidable porter at the front door—a white man, who felt the dignity of his position. He made way immediately for Jerry and took his hat. Then he asked for the name.

"Tell Mister Langley," said Jerry, "that I wish to surprise him. When he sees me, he'll understand why I don't want to be announced." He continued, smiling broadly upon the other: "Don't even describe me to him." Then, chuckling openly: "In fact, it would spoil the whole business if you tell him what I look like."

The guardian of the door bowed as one who disdained such boyishness, and, having bowed Jerry through the door into the largest room Jerry had ever seen, he disappeared. The cow-puncher made sure that he was alone in the room—it required a full moment to sweep the big floor space and be certain—and then he stepped to the curtain through which the servant had gone. Behind the edge of it he saw the other going unhurriedly up the stairs. And such stairs! They wound out of the level of the reception hall with the dignity of a swerving river. They invited one's eye up, slowly, and, when the glance had traveled for a distance up the stairway, it was easier to look up to the ceiling of the reception hall and appreciate the loftiness of that apartment. As for the room in which he then stood, Jerry now looked about him only long enough to locate a hidden place from which he could command the doorway unseen. There were three that answered the purpose nicely. He chose a great tapestry that a draft from the open window was already furling back at one side. Here he could stand and see everything that passed through the door, yet he would be perfectly concealed. He would call out the name of Langley as soon as the latter entered, step out as he did so, and, when the master of the house turned, he would give him time to go for his gun first. So much Jerry decided as he stood behind the tapestry. Then he began to listen to the silence of the house.

It was so intense that a foolish fancy came to him that his approach had been noted, the servants and the master warned, and now by scores they were softly creeping up to surround the room in which he stood. Yet, a moment later, he realized that it was only the size of the place and the thickness of the walls that cut off the sounds of kitchen life and housecleaning activities which to Jerry were inseparable from the conception of such a dwelling. He thought, now, of the immense importance of the life that he was about to end. It was the power that had built the wall against which he leaned; it was the hand that hung the tapestry before him; it was the will that ordered this very silence. If that life were taken, the whole fabric would crumble. That big domestic who had gone with such leisurely dignity up the stairs, how he would leap as he heard the shot that killed James Langley. What uproar would rush into this room, and after that a quiet, with only one or two women near the dead body

Such thoughts as these unnerve a man. Jerry stopped himself and reversed the direction of his mind. He recalled again how he had pleaded with the robber not to take The Voice of La Paloma; he saw again Hank Peyton making the weapon a death gift to him. And just as his mind had reached that flinty hardness, there was a soft step. He looked, and saw a middle-aged man with black hair and a pair of shiny black eyes standing in the door of the apartment, looking about with a frown of bewilderment. Beyond a shadow of a doubt this was the man. He raised a hand to his thick mustache, and the hand was of womanish slenderness and pallor.

"Langley!" called Jerry, and slipped out from behind the tapestry.

His own hand was hanging in mid-air, ready for the lightning reach for his gun, but the master of the house turned without haste and faced him.

"Get out your gun," said Jerry, keeping his voice soft. "I'm here for you."

The hand of the other stirred, and Jerry's leaped to the butt of his weapon—and then he saw the hand keep on rising until it was stroking the square, rather fat chin. *He'll deny that he knows me,* Jerry thought to himself.

At that moment the master of the house remarked: "So it took you three months to get here, eh?"

"Look," said Jerry, and he glided a step closer, "I'm giving you a square break. You've got a gun on you. Get it out. You can make your move first... I'll allow you that much."

"Tut, tut," the other replied. "Three months of travel and still hot for more road work. My dear boy, you're a perfect demon when it comes to energy."

"I'll count three," said Jerry. "I know you've got a gun, and I'm going to make you use it. When I say 'three,' if you don't draw, I'm going to shoot you down like a hound. You've got nothing else coming to you."

XVI

He counted slowly, and the white hand merely moved from the chin to the mustache. The bluff did not work. It did not even begin to work.

"No one looking on at this scene," Langley said, "would ever be able to believe that you're the son of old Hank Peyton. I'll tell you what, Jerry... men aren't what they used to be. You haven't the nerve to shoot a man in cold blood."

Jerry had seen many cool men in his day—he was fairly cool-headed himself—but he looked on Langley, now, as he might a superhuman creature.

"We'll go into the little room behind you," said Langley. He came to the door and waved Jerry in ahead of him.

"Thanks," said Jerry. "You go first."

The host smiled and went straight to a chair. "Sit down," he said, waving to another.

"I'm easier standing," said Jerry.

"Yes, it does make it clumsy to get out a gun... sitting down... unless you know the trick," he observed tauntingly.

Jerry flushed, and, accepting the challenge, he drew the chair squarely before Langley, and with its back to the wall. He sat down on the very edge of it.

"Very well done," said the other approvingly. "I won't offer you a smoke, however," he added, "because I always feel that smoking with a man is like eating at his table. It's rather hard to treat him as an enemy afterward."

Jerry watched, and his eye was as sharp and steady as flint. "Get into your talk," he said. "Get on with it. But if you've touched a button or anything like that, if you've sent a high sign for some of your guests to come flocking around me, remember that I'll get you before they can get me, my friend."

The host tipped back his head and laughed and laughed and laughed. Jerry watched, fascinated, as the fat throat puffed and shook.

"Dear me," James P. Langley said as his merriment subsided, "I almost like you for that, my boy. You've been reading quite a bit of trash, I see. Buttons to press and trap doors, too, eh? Come, come, you're too old for that."

"All right," Jerry said, leaning suddenly back and smiling in turn at the other. "I'm not in a rush. If this is the game, I'll play it this way."

"Oh, I don't put you down for a fool," Langley replied at once. "You've done two things very well. First, my trail was a hard one to follow. I suppose it was the gambler in Chambers City that tipped you off?"

Jerry shrugged his shoulders.

"You don't need to be reticent on his behalf," said the other, and the well-trimmed mustache bristled a disagreeable trifle. "I know that's the only place you could have learned what you wanted to know. You got him to talk, eh?"

"Also, I won quite a stake from him," Jerry said, and smiled.

"That's item number two for you, then," said Langley. "The third thing is that you're right about the gun. I have a revolver with me. I always have, in fact."

"And you sit like a cur and hear me browbeat you, eh?" said Jerry.

The host grew pale to the eyes. "It's hard to stand abuse," he said. "But I'll have to."

The fighting devil in Jerry welled up into his eyes and ran back to his heart, twice; a cold sweat was standing out all over his body, and he was shaking before that was over, but he had kept from drawing his gun.

"It's hard, isn't it?" the other remarked. "But I've known very few men in my life who could kill in cold blood. You think you can and your nerves are all set for it, but, when it comes to meeting the other fellow's eyes, you weaken, eh?"

Jerry sat very still and thought. Every ounce of mental strength in his brain went into the effort. "Langley," he said, when he had finished the struggle, "I think you're not straight... I think you're a crook."

The other lighted a cigar and puffed at it, then held it poised as though he were listening to an entertaining story.

"I think you're a crook," Jerry repeated, "and a lot of little things along the road to Saint Hilaire have just about convinced me of it. But there's one chance in ten that I'm wrong. I'm not reserving anything. You did a yellow thing back at Sloan. You got me when I was helpless and you took something from me. If you can explain that away, I'll get up and say good bye and never look at your ratty eyes again. That's square, I think. Now explain."

The older man squinted through a mist of smoke. He looked up to the ceiling and then down at the floor. "That's a square opening for me," he said. "But I can't take advantage of it. All I can say is this... the only big mistake I ever made in my life was in rating a very clever man as a fool. You see, I treated the man as a fool, and he took me off guard. God, it seems impossible that I could have done it, now that I look back. He twisted me around his finger. The result is the clever man put me in such a position that I can't explain how I happened to take your father's gun. It's impossible. I could tell you a story, but then you'd ask questions, and your questions would blow up the tale." He puffed again at the cigar thoughtfully.

Jerry raised his left hand and brushed it across his shining forehead without obscuring his sight. "One thing more," he said. "If you give me back the gun, I think I can call the game off now. I'll not try to think it out."

But still the host shook his head. "I've just been thinking of that," he said, "but the clever man saw through even that chance. I can't give the gun back to you."

"Then," said Jerry, "as sure as the sun's going to rise, I'm going to drill you, Langley."

"Tut, tut," said the other. "You've already had your chance and you've failed. I know your mind, lad. I've stepped into it. You can't pull a gun until the other fellow has made the first move. Now, if I were to go for my revolver, I'd get it out, and I'd get it out before you had yours halfway to the mark. I'd kill you, my son... but, when you were dead, what earthly good would it do me? None whatever, and, instead, it would do me a tremendous harm. You see, large things are built on small, and, if I were to kill you, this entire house would topple about my ears."

That whiplash flicker of his eyes went up and down the body of Jerry Peyton and then burned into his face.

"Nothing would please me more," went on Langley, "than a moment alone with you out in the mountain desert... say somewhere near Sloan... where a community is not so shocked by manslaughter. Unfortunately we are some three thousand miles and more from Sloan." He paused and sighed. "And we are on the island of Saint Hilaire, where man-killing is looked upon not as a vocation, but as a sin. You've no idea what a great difference that makes. For instance, if you were to be irritated past the point of endurance... if you were to do the impossible and draw your gun and shoot me... a dozen telephone messages would be sent out instantly from this house, and then the messages would be repeated at the farther end, so that in five minutes the entire coastline of this island would be watched and guarded. Every boat would be inspected to make sure that you were not on it, and little launches with machine guns mounted on 'em would slide up and down the coast to see that you didn't drift to sea."

He had talked so long that the cigar had almost gone out, and he now prevented this evil by puffing rapidly; his head appeared, presently, through a dense cloud of smoke, the eyes glittering at Jerry.

"You see," went on Langley, "this might be called a co-operative system of society. Do you follow that?"

"I'm followin' you so close, partner," said the big man, and he stretched himself in his chair, "that I'm wearing calluses on your heels. Go on."

The host looked at him with singular respect and cold observance commingled; he was thinking of the long, powerful body of a great cat, stretching with sleepy eyes, but incredibly alert at the same time.

"In this co-operative system," continued Langley, "we all work together to make it uncomfortable for the criminal. We don't consign all our legal interests to the hands of one sheriff, as they do at Sloan. Instead, we all step in and catch the disagreeable member of society and exterminate him with no more compunction than one would step on a snake."

"Me being the snake," said Jerry ungrammatically, and grinned.

He was met by a flash of white teeth. "I'm glad you understood so well," Langley went on. "For you are here in the midst of a net. It might be said that you rest on the palm of the hand of society, and, if you bite the skin which holds you, the fingers will close and crush you out of recognizable shape. But, on the other hand, suppose that I were to shoot you down. In that case the danger would not be nearly so great. I would be kept under surveillance, to be sure... but I could readily escape from actual physical danger. On the other hand, a vital blow would be struck at the foundation of my work and ambition. I have said that if I kill you, this house will tumble about my ears. And I mean this almost literally. I am not a mild man in a crisis, and the people of Saint Hilaire would not endure another outbreak on my part. I should find my social position destroyed, the prospects of my family irretrievably ruined, or, at the least, the work of many years blown away in one puff of wind."

He lowered his voice toward the close of this speech until it became no louder than the murmur of a bee buzzing inside a room in a bright, still day. There was also the hidden anger in this murmur; it carried the hint of a sting.

"You're a bright man," Jerry said dryly. "You're too bright, almost. But you can't hold up. You can't stand the gaff. Suppose I pick a time when you have a lot of Saint Hilaire's social knockouts around you... suppose I step up and call you hard... insult you in front of the gang. That'll make you go for your gun, eh?"

There was that same mirthless flash of white teeth, the same bristling of the precisely trimmed mustache.

"In many ways," said the rich man, "you are a child, Peyton. If you did that, I'd simply denounce you to the police as a madman and have you locked up."

"You'd be disgraced, though," said Jerry. "They'd see you're yellow."

"Not at all," said the other with meaning. "Whatever people may privately think of me in Saint Hilaire, my courage, at least, has been placed beyond question. Come, my boy, look about you and see how complete the net is. I speak without passion and without fear of you... your position is impossible... therefore, look about you, admit the fact, and withdraw at once."

With one long, inward glance Jerry obeyed and saw that, as Langley had said, there was no escape. But being brought up against an impenetrable wall, his anger rose. It was a wall of words, after all; it was an obstacle created by the talk of this cool fellow with the glistening eyes. And in his helplessness Jerry let his glance rove. He then saw, close to him, a writing desk of ebony. It was one of those rare bits that are carved elaborately, and yet the minute carving is made subordinate to the line of the piece; the slender legs were yet strong enough and they rose from an adequate base; one would not be afraid to rest the weight of his elbow upon that desk. It was polished until, although it stood in the shadow, it glimmered, as though shining in the content of its own beauty. On the smooth surface lay a paper knife; it was silver, with a handle roughened by emeralds set into the metal, and on the surface of the dark ebony there was a reflection, a white streak for the silver and a green light for the emeralds—so that the knife seemed to be floating. Upon these two things of beauty Jerry stared, for to him they reconstructed the whole fortune of the rich man and signified more than the rest of the house. The desk, carved like a jewel, the paper knife, a jewel indeed, left carelessly upon the surface of the desk—Jerry calculated absently that the entire value of the main street of Sloan would not duplicate that paper cutter. He looked up to Langley and sighed.

"It looks to me," he said, "as though you're right."

"Good," the millionaire said. It was a great mistake, that satisfied nod, for no man, and particularly no young man, likes to have his conclusions taken for granted. But Langley was victorious, he felt, and now he rushed on foolishly: "Of course, I'll see that all arrangements are made for your trip back, and it will be a pleasure to refund the money you have spent on this unfortunate excursion, in fact..."

"The devil!" said Jerry with infinite disgust.

It made Langley open his eyes.

"I said it looked to me as though you were right," said the big man, "but I'll be hanged if I'll go on the looks of it. I can't plug a man who won't pull a gun. You're right there. I can't make you fight by insultin' you in public. Well, there's still some other way I can hit you. I don't know how it is, but I'll find that way... and I'll make you come to me foamin', Mister Langley, I'll make you come to me like a cow bawlin' for her calf. I'll make you come ravin' and beggin' for a chance to get a shot at me. I'll make you want to do murder, my friend." He leaned a narrow, hard fist on the surface of the writing desk. "As a matter of fact, Mister Langley, I don't think that's anything new to you." So saying, he straightened, and backed with long, light steps through the door.

Langley watched him, interested, and then noted the swiftness and ease of the sidewise leap that carried the Westerner out of sight behind the wall. There was an ominous grace about his actions that made Langley think, not for the first time, of some big, half-tamed panther, playing in his cage. But the bars against which Jerry Peyton spent himself were the bars of civilization. While he thought of these things, Langley picked up the paper knife from the ebony desk and looked at it curiously. The hard fist of Jerry had rested upon it, and it was sadly bent. The jeweler would have to look at it.

XVII

The Negro boy before the house of the master had the reins jerked from his hands, and he had barely time to catch a silver coin that was flung to him while Peyton vaulted into the saddle. The little Negro was used to seeing expert riders mount, but something in the manner in which this stranger flung himself through the air and landed lightly in the saddle on a horse that stood a good sixteen hands and a half made the boy gape. He remained gaping while Jerry jerked the horse from a standing start into a full gallop with a merciless twist of spurred heels. Then horse and rider shot off down the road and the shadows of the palms were brushing across them.

It was not the road by which he had come to the house, and Jerry did not care. He went blindly at top speed until the rush of wind against his face had cooled his blood sufficiently for him to begin thinking. In the old days, when he felt after this fashion, he used to jump into the saddle on the buckskin. She took part of the mad humor out of him with her bucking, as a rule, and he spent the rest of it hunting for trouble with the first man he met. Around Sloan men were astonishingly accommodating when it came to providing trouble, but in this infernal island... He brought the poor horse to a stand with a wrench on the reins that almost broke the poor brute's jaw, for through the tree trunks just ahead of him he made out the flash and blue shimmer of the sea. It was everywhere about him, then. It was crowding into his back yard, in fact. He sent his trembling horse out onto the brow of the hill and looked down where the surf came boiling on the beach and then slid back to the deep places. It leaped in tricky currents, and he saw what had been a smooth place before suddenly involved in a deep whirl that sucked the foam under and then threw it up again. To Jerry water meant, on the whole, nothing more than the sleepy old Winton River, and he looked on the ocean with disgust. He remembered, too, the way the ship had ridden the waves, bucking until one's stomach commenced almost to float. So he hated this blue ocean and its green margin; above all he hated it because it drove back into his mind the memory that he was helpless—that he could never escape if he shot down Langley. As if to complete his picture of isolation, as if purposely sent to drive him to a frenzy, a long, low-lying launch sneaked into view around the end of the promontory and glided across the bay. How could he escape from such a seagoing greyhound as that?

He found his horse shaking again, and then he discovered that the animal was terrified because he had ridden so close to the edge of the hill, where the soil crumbled away and dropped in what was almost a cliff to the sea. At the sight of his horse's fear all the mad, sullen child boiled up in Jerry, all the hate that he felt for Langley and the sea and the fate that had sent him to this accursed island. He spurred the gelding until he stood straight up, with a groan, and then struck on all fours in full gallop. He strove to swerve inland, but the iron arm of Jerry wrenched his head over and made him race along the very verge of the cliffs. Sometimes the ground gave way under his pounding hoofs. Sometimes his hindquarters sagged as a miniature landslide commenced and threatened to suck the horse over the brow of the hill, until the gelding was tortured into a hysteria of fear as strong and as blind as Jerry's hysteria of rage. He ran, now, where Jerry guided him. He went fearlessly along that crumbling cliff edge. He even strove to swerve and leap into the abyss when the yell of the cowpuncher rose and blew tinglingly behind him, but the man kept him true to his course, not a foot allowed on the danger side of it and not a foot allowed toward safety. He kept on until Jerry felt the forelegs pounding, felt the hindquarters sag, and knew that the gelding was almost spent. All at once his own passion left him. He swung the gelding over to a firm little plateau and brought him to a down-headed halt. For a moment the panting of the horse lifted him slightly up and down in the saddle. He himself was panting, now that his rage had been converted into weariness, and, when he slipped off the horse and remorsefully patted the flanks of the gelding, he would have given a great deal, indeed, if his prank had remained unplayed.

It was at this moment of depression that he looked over the croup of the horse suddenly, and saw an old man standing on the hilltop above him with folded arms and watching him solemnly. Indeed, his pose was one of almost affected dignity and reserve. He held his hat in his hand, so that it came under one elbow, and the wind was lifting the misty white hair, which he wore rather long for an ordinary man. He stood with one foot advanced in that position of self-control and balance that the world for some reason has connected with that nervous, active genius, Napoleon. For the rest, there was no semblance at all between this man and the conqueror. He was of an attenuated leanness and very tall. Even from this distance Jerry could see that his head was small and his nose large. There was about him a sort of cruel dignity and scorn—it made Jerry think of a bald eagle surveying his kingdom of the air from a crag. He was almost surprised when he saw the old man shake his head in disapproval and became aware that this majestic figure was watching him. Because the other stood with head uncovered, Jerry instantly swept off his own hat and bowed.

Among the maxims of Hank Peyton, uttered when he was drunk but observed whether drunk or sober and impressed even upon Jerry's infancy with brutal force, was the following: "They's three things you got to side-step and handle with a long rein . . . an old horse, an old man, and a woman." There was a little white scar that showed over Jerry's eye when he flushed; it marked an occasion when he was a very small boy and had spoken back to his mother. Hank Peyton had promptly knocked him down with the butt end of a loaded blacksnake. That lesson of courtesy was never forgotten by Jerry, and, if he was ever tempted to forget, the scar reminded him. So he stood with his broad-brimmed hat in his hand and waited for the older man to address him.

As for the other, he stood for a moment surveying Jerry, and finally came down from the hilltop with a long, sure step surprising in so old a man, and as dignified as his standing appearance.

"Good morning," he said. "I am Manuel Guzman."

"Sir," said Jerry, "I'm glad to know you. My name is Jeremiah Peyton, and I hope I haven't been riding over your land."

A cloud came on the brow of the old man, and Jerry remembered what he had heard from the author.

"When you passed that point," said *Don* Manuel, "you entered my estate."

"I'm sorry," said Jerry.

The old man was silent, and a sense of guilt came to Jerry. He felt as if he had been spied upon and a weakness observed.

"I am sorry for your horse," the other replied calmly. "You are a wild rider, Mister Peyton."

Rebuffs were bitter food for Jerry. He had to waste a frown on the ground before him before he could look up and meet the eye of *Señor* Guzman calmly. And then he was surprised to see a smile gradually spread over the lean face.

"For my part," said the Spaniard, "I keep away from my horses when I am angry. Or perhaps it was the horse itself that angered you?"

"The horse is a fool horse," said Jerry gloomily. "Look at him. Winded already and his spirit about busted."

"By a ride on the edge of a cliff," said the old man, smiling more broadly. He looked narrowly at Jerry. "I thought you were going into the sea when you rounded that point."

Jerry looked back. The point was marked by a great boulder of red stone, and between the boulder and the sea drop there was only a meager footpath. Jerry shuddered. "Did I ride around that rock?" he asked.

The old man was silent again and appeared to be thinking of other things. "You must come up to my house with me," he said, "and sit down for a time. Your nerves are upset." Jerry hesitated. "And I have some whiskey you shall taste, if you will."

"Lead the way," Jerry said instantly. "I'm so dry"—he paused to find a sufficient word—"that my throat crackles every time I draw a breath."

The Spaniard chuckled and led the way over the hilltop front that he had just descended. It gave an unexpected view of a low, broad valley, covered with a thick green crop on this side, and, where it went up toward a range of hills beyond, Jerry could see the regular avenues of an orchard. "Once," the Spaniard said, pointing, "that land to the hills was in my estate. However, I have still land enough. Follow me, sir."

And he took Jerry down the slope and up again until they reached a plateau densely covered by a growth of gigantic palms and trees almost as tall. In the center of this little forest there was an opening, where they found the house. It was built solidly of sawn rock, a single story sprawling around a patio with the usual fountain in the center. There was an arcade about the patio, and the stone floor, newly washed, was unbelievably cool to the eye. It was a green rock, worn deeply in places. Here they sat down in the shade, facing each other across a little table. The chairs were never meant for comfort; at least, though the rigid backs may have fitted the form of the *don*, the larger body of Jerry overflowed them. He forgot the chair, however, when a barefooted Negro in white cotton jacket and trousers came pattering out with a tray, and the whiskey and ice and seltzer were arranged between them.

"Are you staying long in Saint Hilaire?" *Don* Manuel asked.

"You put me down for a newcomer, eh?" Jerry replied.

"No old inhabitant rides as hard as that," said the Spaniard, "at ten o'clock in the morning. In the morning and the evening . . . oh, they are reckless enough . . . but at ten o'clock the day begins to fall into a sleepy time and every one yawns and drowses."

"Then," Jerry added, "you make an exception, *señor?*"

"With me it is different," said the old man. "I carry whip and spur within me, and in a way, sir, you might say that I also gallop along the edge of a cliff." He sighed. "To your happiness, *señor*."

Jerry bowed, and they drank together.

There is a period after liquor has passed the lips of two men when they sit and look at one another and can read minds. This brief moment stole over the old man and the young, and they sat regarding each other solemnly.

The white-clad Negro had brought a basket of fruit and knives, but Jerry refused it.

"I don't know how long I shall stay," said Jerry, reverting to the last question. "As soon as my business is over, I leave."

The Spaniard smiled again in his wise way.

"And yet, *señor*," he said, "when I saw you careering along the hills, between the sea and the sky, one might say, I made up my mind that you were a prisoner in Saint Hilaire."

"A prisoner?" repeated Jerry slowly.

"To your interests here," replied the Spaniard coolly. "A prisoner rebelling, however, against his captivity. I can remember a day," he went on, "when I rode very much as you rode along the hills, and I cared very little whether my horse fell into the sea or remained on the dry land." He pushed the whiskey bottle toward Jerry as he spoke, but the latter sat, turning the bottle slowly.

"I can almost tell you why you rode that day," said Jerry.

"*¿Señor?*" queried the old man.

"You had spoken to Langley, eh?" said Jerry. He saw the other quiver under the shock. "Because," went on Jerry hastily, "I've just finished talking to the same fellow."

Don Manuel had raised the glass toward his lips, but now he lowered it again, untasted.

An inspiration came to Jerry. He filled his own glass and poised it. "I think," he said, "that there is a real reason for us to drink together. Once more, to your good health, *señor*."

Don Manuel looked long and earnestly at the American. "I drink," he said, "to the kind fortune that has sent me a man."

XVIII

The casual visit of the morning was extended until noon, and when the noon meal passed there was a lazy warmth in the air that forbade travel. When the evening approached, the *don* showed Jerry through the house, and, stopping in a room where the windows overlooked the sea, he said: "This is your place, sir, until you leave Saint Hilaire." It was impossible to refuse hospitality offered in this manner. Jerry made up his mind that he would make his refusal later on, but then came the dinner, and, after they dined, the night dropped about them and Jerry began to talk. The words flowed almost without his knowledge, and before he knew it he had laid his heart bare to *Señor* Guzman. He had told of the first meeting; he had told of the pursuit; he had told of the scene in Langley's study, and, finally, of his unquenchable determination.

They were sitting in the patio, and after the story was done the Spaniard remained silent for a pause of embarrassing length, looking up at the stars. Finally he went into the house and returned with a candle. He placed it at the other end of the long court, so that the flame was merely a slender eye of light, tilted sidewise with its halo by the steady pressure of the northeast trades, which blow day and night unceasingly over St. Hilaire. *Don* Manuel came and stood behind the chair of Jerry; the young man turned and looked up, but, with his hands on the muscular shoulders of the American, preventing him from rising, *Don* Manuel said: "There is a tale going the rounds," he said, "that at ten paces *Señor* Langley can snuff a burning candle. Yonder candle, now, is about twice that distance, I think."

"Ah?" said Jerry. And as he spoke he whirled in the chair. He did not rise, but the gun leaped out of his clothes and exploded—the flame of the candle leaped and went out. "Confound!" Jerry said at the end of a moment of silence. "Too low or I would have trimmed it."

But the Spaniard went down and picked up the candle and came back carrying it in both hands. He stood, then, peering down at Jerry as though the candle still burned, and by its light he studied the stranger.

"I am out of practice," said Jerry, flushing, "but with my gun in shape and a bit of work to..."

Don Manuel raised a compelling hand and went into the house. When he came out again he said, without prologue: "It is because you have no way to touch the man's nerve, is it not?"

"How can I touch him?" Jerry replied sadly. "Can I get at his property? Can I threaten him in any way? If he had a son, I might manhandle him, but I can't hit a man forty-five years old."

An aria from an opera which had been popular twenty years before Jerry was born came whistling from the lips of *Don* Manuel. He sat with his chin in his hand. At length the music stopped short. "Go to bed and sleep, my son," he said finally. "For you must get up with me at dawn, and then I shall show you the key to *Señor* Langley's heart."

"We're going to his house?" asked Jerry sharply.

"You must trust me," said the old man with a marvelously evil smile. The bitterness of half a life was summed up and expressed by that smile. "Be prepared, for in the morning you shall see the key to his heart."

From the first meeting it had seemed to Jerry that he sensed a base of rock in the nature of the Spaniard, and now he knew that misfortune had not taught him or bowed him. He was as rigid as he had been in the pride of youth, and in the place of the warm blood of the young man his veins were filled with acid hate. Yet evil is usually more imposing than good. Jerry saw, when he lay in bed looking into the dark, that the only reason he had spoken to the Spaniard and told the whole story was because he recognized subconsciously the unholy fire in *Don* Manuel. He trusted to that fire now. And in this trust he fell into a profound slumber.

Once, it was a dream-like thought, he seemed to part his eyelids slightly and look up at the form of the Spaniard in a robe of white, shielding a candle so that little of its light touched the face of the sleeper, but a bright radiance fell on *Don* Manuel. Jerry shuddered—in his sleep. When he next wakened the hand of *Señor* Guzman was on his shoulder.

"Get up," said the host. "Here is a bathing suit that will fit you. You must be thoroughly awakened, so plunge into the tub of cold water that waits for you. When that is done, put on the bathing suit and come into the patio."

It was impossible to deny those eyes, so bright under their wrinkled lids. And before Jerry was fully awake, he had gone through the routine that the host prescribed and stood beside him in the patio.

Don Manuel looked over his guest with an almost painful attention—as a trainer, say, looks over the trim muscles of an athlete—then he nodded as one who knew men. "Come," he said simply, and led the way from the house and over a terrace of grass to a hilltop that overlooked the sea. The sun had not risen. To the east, over a gray mist along the horizon, the tints of the dawn were rolling up the sky, and one cloud, high above the rest, was burning with red fire. It sent a stain of crimson across the sea toward the two on the cliff.

"Well?" said Jerry.

"Are you cold?" said the Spaniard. He himself was wrapped in a heavy cloak.

"No," said Jerry Peyton. Indeed, the air was as mild as a spring noontide.

"Look down to the beach."

It was a drop of a hundred feet, at least. A long, white stretch of sand lay before him, and along its margin the waves rolled, broke into sudden lines of white, and then slipped swiftly up the shore.

"What's next? I see the beach."

"Patience."

It was odd to see the old man assume command. He paid not the slightest heed to Jerry, but began to walk up and down. The northeast wind sent his cloak flapping every time he turned at the end of his pacing. For the rest, he seemed to be looking up into the eye of this wind more than any place else, and a ghostly feeling came to Jerry that the Spaniard was about to receive a message out of the empty air. He, also, began to scan that horizon, and he started when *Don* Manuel stopped in his pacing and pointed suddenly down at the beach.

"The key to *Señor* Langley," he said.

And Jerry, looking down, saw a girl galloping a horse along the beach. She wore a light cloak, which blew behind her, and a scarlet cap covered her head. The blue cloak, the red cap, the cream-colored horse—she was sweeping along the beach like a gay cloud out of the sunrise. A claw-like hand caught the shoulder of Jerry and dragged him down behind a rock.

"She mustn't see you with me," said the Spaniard. "Not now."

"Is this part of the job you plan on, partner?" said Jerry coldly. "Spyin' on a girl?"

The cream-colored horse stopped, and the girl, dismounting, threw away the cloak, slipped the shoes from her feet, and ran down the beach toward the sea. Jerry sat up, and, when the Spaniard turned to him, he found that the boy's face was scarlet, and a white line showed above his eye.

"Did you get me up before sunrise," said Jerry fiercely, "to spy on a girl?"

The Spaniard blinked and then smiled.

And in spite of the lessons of his father, in spite of the scar on his face, in spite of that fine Western scorn of anything connected with duplicity where women are concerned, Jerry looked again.

It had been merely a causeless shock, he decided, as he watched her run along the beach and saw the skirts of her bathing suit fluttering about her. As he looked, the water was struck to white about her feet, and then she dived under the surface.

As the wave rolled swirling to the shore, the Spaniard smiled again at Jerry. "That is the key to *Señor* Langley," he said. "That is his daughter, Patricia."

For a time Jerry stared at him stupidly. "Listen to me, partner," he said coldly, when he had finished his survey of that ancient, evil face. "I come from a place where bad men are pretty fairly thick, but bad men around women don't flourish in those parts. They wither away sudden. They get cut off at the root. You see?"

Don Manuel made a slow gesture, with both the palms of his hands turned up.

"*Señor* Peyton," he said, "you are not wise. I point out to you a way in which you can make *Señor* Langley come to you as you wish, raving, with his gun in his hand, and you insult me for pointing out the way." He leaned over and laid a bony hand on Jerry's arm.

"Do not say it," Jerry murmured, the flush gradually leaving his face.

"That is much better, my son," said the Spaniard. "Now hear me calmly. You will go down to the beach. You will swim. When you come on shore, you will be close to *Señorita* Langley. She will speak to you... you will speak to her. You will tell her your name. She will tell you her name. Is there any harm in that?"

"It looks straight to me," said Jerry cautiously. "What's it lead to?"

"To much," said *Don* Manuel. "It leads to everything we wish. She will go home and remember you. You will be easy for her to remember."

"Me?" said Jerry, wide-eyed.

"Peyton is a simple name," said the Spaniard hurriedly.

"That's straight enough," murmured Jerry.

"And when she goes home, she will tell her father that she has met you. Now, the *Señor* Langley is a stern man in his home. His word is law. Ever since she has become a young woman, the girl is used to hearing her father say... 'Receive this man'... and she receives him, or... 'Do not smile on this man'... and she makes her face a blank before him. There is always a reason. Such a man is too poor, too rich, or one is of the good blood and another is not. There is always a reason, and the girl obeys, for her heart has not been touched. Do you understand?"

"I partly follow you," said Jerry, frowning with the effort.

"A woman is like a blossom," the old man continued, watching the eyes of the American. "For a time she is hulled in green. And after that the green opens and she is stiff petals... a bud. But then, all on a day, a bee touches the bud or the wings of a moth dust across it or a leaf falls on it, and then it opens in that one day and lets the sun come into its heart. It is all in a day... and all in a day a girl steps into womanhood. Is that clear, *señor?*"

"I see something in it," admitted Jerry cautiously.

"But the *Señor* Langley does not see it," said *Don* Manuel. "He is the cold Northern race... his heart is ice... he cannot see the heart of a woman. But I am a Guzman, and I know. Old men and poets know women, my son, and I am a very old man."

"Go on," Jerry commanded sternly as the *don* paused.

"We return, then, to the moment when Langley orders her to see this stranger she has met on the beach no more. He gives her a reason... she is not to make friends with every nobody she meets. Pardon me, *señor*."

"That's all right," said Jerry heartily. "I can see the old boy's face as he says it. Go on."

"She understands that this must be so. Yet she is thoughtful. For when she mentions your name, she sees her father start. It is a little thing... a lifting of the eyebrows. You see? But the girl sees it. She says... 'My father knows this man before.' So she asks her father to inquire about you and find out your past. Perhaps he does it... perhaps he tells her a lie. He dare not tell her the truth, and, if he tells her a lie, who will know it is not the truth?"

"Wait a minute," said Jerry. "You don't know this Langley. She'll never guess it's a lie."

"I am an old man, and I know women," persisted *Don* Manuel stubbornly. "She will know it is a lie, and, also, she has the blood of her father in her and she understands. So she sits in her room and thinks. For one, two mornings she goes to another beach... but there is no good beach in Saint Hilaire but my beach. She cuts her feet on the coral... she wades up to the ankles in slime and mud... and she thinks of the hard, clean, smooth sand of the beach of *Don* Manuel. It will be so." He paused. "Also, she may remember you... you are different from the others, my son." So on the third morning she says to herself... 'What harm in going there? Father need not know. The man is not a viper.' So she comes on the third morning to the beach of *Don* Manuel."

"I follow all this," said Jerry. "Nobody likes to swim on a muddy bottom."

"You understand swimming, my son?"

Jerry thought of the place where the Winton drops into a wild series of cascades. Once he had gone down those rapids, swimming. "Yes, I swim a bit," he replied.

The Spaniard nodded. "That is still better. So she comes back, remembering how you swim."

"But what the devil does that lead to?"

"Everything. The apple of discord is thrown into the family of *Don* James. And the girl has kept a thing from her father."

"I don't like it," said Jerry sullenly. "I... don't like that idea."

"Wait! The apple of discord is thrown into the family. And now the girl sees you every morning... for every morning she swims to keep the blossom in her cheeks that all Saint Hilaire wonders over. Ah, I know. Also, she is come to the time. It is not far distant." He nodded, and his little, evil eyes glittered into the distance. "She knows the bees that buzz in Saint Hilaire. She keeps her petals closed. They are nothing to her. But she hears a new sound. It is a lean wasp, fierce, swift, silent, strange. She opens her heart to it."

"Partner," said Jerry with concern, "this early mornin' air must be going to your head. What the dickens are you talking about?"

"You shall see. The day comes when the girl goes to her father again and speaks of you. Then he has been disobeyed, and the madness comes over him. Have you seen him in his madness?"

"No."

"Ah, ah," murmured the Spaniard, "you have much to learn of *Don* James. Well, you will see it. But now go down to the beach. Go down, my son."

"And in the end?"

"In the end he will know that he has been disobeyed. He will seize his fastest horse and rush to my house. There, I trust, you will not be hard to find."

"Partner," said Jerry, "I begin to get your drift. He'll come ravin'... he'll come for the showdown?"

"He will come and shine like a flame... like the flame of a candle in my patio, *señor*."

But Jerry Peyton was already on his feet and going down the sandy slope of the hill toward the beach.

Don Manuel kneeled and pressed his face close to the rocks as he saw the lithe, muscular figure break from a walk to a jogging trot, and from a trot, as a sudden feeling of exultation came over him, into a full racing gait. A rock rose in his path. He hurdled it with a great leap and went on, his bare feet spurring the sand into little jets behind him. The old man clutched both hands to his heart.

"God give me grace," he whispered. "Let her see him now."

His prayer was answered. She rose from the sea, shaking the water off of her face, at the same time that Jerry struck the shore.

Two strides brought him up to the knees in the water; he shot through the air, disappeared under the heaving front of a wave.

Don Manuel rose and walked stolidly toward his house.

"It is enough," he said. "She has now seen a man."

XIX

As for Jerry Peyton, the slope of the hill face had given such impetus to him that he forgot the girl, he forgot the scheme, he lost himself in the joy of speed, and, when he slipped under the wave, he came up with a long, powerful overhand stroke that shot him through the water. He had never swum in salt-water before, and his swimming muscles, hardened to the work of fresh rivers and lakes, now whipped him along through the heavier, more buoyant ocean. Also, it sent a tingle across his skin. He gave himself to his work. When a wave heaved up trembling before him, he dived and came up in the calm water beyond. Past four lines of waves he swam, and then turned and made leisurely back for the land.

If it was pleasure to swim in the face of the sea, it was marvelous to have the big waves pick one up, unaware, and be thrown bodily toward the land. He came with a crawl stroke, now, rioting in the speed, and with foam about his shoulders. A mass of water lifted around him and tossed him up—when he came down, his knee struck sand. He staggered up the beach, panting, and there he saw the girl, with one hand on her hip and dabbling one foot in the water. He came from a land where the girls have no fear of men, and yet he was unprepared for the directness of her eyes and the fearlessness of her smile. He was striding through the surf, tingling, when her glance stopped him. His broad chest was working like a bellows, filling with that pure morning air, and then her glance stopped him.

"That last wave nearly tumbled you on your head, didn't it?" said the girl.

"Did it? I don't know. I was having too good a time to see. Never swam in the ocean before."

"You let them take you and float you," said the girl, "and you can ride them in . . . like a horse, almost."

He had stopped panting enough to look more closely at her now. He saw that her eyes were black, but they had not the glitter of her father's eyes. He was deeply grateful for that. He had an odd desire to step back so that he could throw her into a perspective and see her clearly—as if she were a mountain. He was surprised by the small, cold touch of awe—something that the Spaniard had said was true, something about flowers between the bud and the blossom.

"Show me how, will you?" said Jerry.

"Of course. Come on."

They went into the water, side-by-side.

"Who are you?" asked the girl.

"I'm Jeremiah Peyton."

"I'm Patricia Langley. Come on, here's a bully wave."

He was amazed by the ease with which she cut the water. Her round, active arms plied the water just ahead of him, and he held back to watch. She stopped in a rocking trough, treading the water. "How far out shall we go?"

"As far as you like," said Jerry.

"Oh, I don't care. I never get tired in the water."

"As far as you like," he repeated, treading water, also.

"But there's the Long Reach," she said.

A wave obliterated them, but, when he came up again, he followed her gesture and saw a white streak out to sea. "What's the Long Reach?"

"I don't know exactly. Some kind of a cross-current, or something like that. It forms from the mouth of the cove, several times a day, and then goes swirling out to sea. If you get caught in it, it's all day with you. Takes you miles and miles out. Billy de Remi was caught in it . . . poor Billy."

The top of a wave spilled over her as she spoke. She came up laughing, and then struck out. "You say when you want to turn back!" she called back over her shoulder, and then the red cap was submerged as she struck out with a driving crawl stroke.

He could see that she was challenging his speed, and she slid through the water with remarkable rapidity, but half a dozen strokes convinced Jerry that he could overhaul her when he chose. He drifted back, and then cut in around her and drew up on the side of the white line of water. Once or twice, as she turned her head for breath, her eye caught his and she flashed a smile at him, but on the whole she was strictly serious business.

She headed straight out to sea, and now Jerry could hear, louder than the noise of the surf behind them, the rushing of the white waters ahead of him. The girl also heard them, but she went straight on, lifting her head clear, now and then, to gauge the distance. An odd thought came to Jerry that she was testing him in this manner, and with a few hard strokes he pulled up even with her.

She came up, treading water, at that. She was white, but her eyes danced and she was smiling. "Shall we go on?"

"Just as you say," said Jerry, and smiled back.

She cast one gloomy look at him and immediately struck out again. Now the sound of the waters ahead filled Jerry's ears, but he kept even with her, and a little ahead, until an arm of boiling water reached out at them. They were swept far from their course and close together. Over the sound of the rushing he heard her cry, then she turned like an eel and hit out for the shore. It was a full minute of hard labor before she made headway. The current came foaming about her neck and made a wake behind her shoulders; once she turned her head and cried again to Jerry, but he, swimming with comparative ease close by, made no effort to aid her.

They were clear of the danger as suddenly as it had come upon them, and she brought her head up, treading water again.

"Why . . . ?" she began angrily.

"Well?" said Jerry, and grinned at her white face.

"It nearly got us!" panted the girl.

"I knew we were all right," he said. "You told me you knew these waters."

All at once she was laughing. "You're a queer one!" she called, and headed back for the line of the surf. He remembered, as he followed, that *Don* Manuel had said she would find him different. In fact, he was so full of many thoughts that he by no means grasped her lessons in surf riding. He saw a big wave take her and shoot her toward the shore, she riding lightly in the crest, and then the same wave caught Jerry, doubled him up, and rolled him over and over like a ball. He came up with sand in his ears, his nose, his mouth, and, in his blindness, staggered toward the waves again, but Patricia came, laughing, and led him up the beach. That misadventure seemed to restore her good humor. She was still laughing when he had washed himself clean again and turned on her.

"In my part of the country," Jerry said, "they don't treat a tenderfoot this way. Five minutes after I meet you, you take me within a yard of drowning, and then you roll me in the sand."

She was pulling on her shoes and lacing them. The instant before she had seemed more boy than girl; now she was wholly woman. And when she smiled up at him, absent-mindedly, he searched his mind for something to say. But his brain was a perfect blank. He looked around him—the sea, the hills, the wind, the sky, the sunrise rushed upon him, and he rejected them all. He wanted to say something, in fact, which would make her forget all those very things. A great gray bird flew in from the sea, and she raised her head slowly up and up, watching its flight—until he was conscious only of her parted lips, her eyes, and the line of her throat.

"I wonder what it is?" said Patricia, standing up and catching her cloak about her. The cream-colored horse came up to her; he was evidently her pet. "It's not a gull," she said.

"Damn the bird," said Jerry with warmth. "I beg your pardon," he added hastily as she glanced at him. "I wasn't thinking of what I said."

"I think you were," Patricia replied not altogether coldly. She surveyed him anew and liked him. "What in the world made you say that?"

"I don't know," said Jerry miserably. "I guess you're pretty peeved about it, eh?" He began to explain with a frown: "You see, I was about to say something when that bird flew over, and..."

"And then I interrupted you?" She observed him still again, for men did not usually tell her when she interrupted them. She had never seen a man who looked quite like that in a bathing suit. His face and neck were tanned and his hands were even darker to the wrist. But the rest of his body was as white as snow, and, whenever he moved, she could see long, unobtrusive, efficient-looking muscles at play. "What was it you were going to say?" she added.

"That's the point," and Jerry sighed. "You've made me forget it."

"You are queer," the girl commented with a light laugh.

"I had an idea you'd think that," said Jerry gloomily.

"Why?"

"Because I feel mostly like a fool." She had a wonderful resource of laughter, effortless and sweet to hear. "Do that again," said Jerry.

"Do what?"

And he answered: "Laugh again... it's great to hear you."

She looked beyond him and saw that the sun was about to rise, her signal to depart for a beauty sleep before breakfast time, but she saw that he was enjoying her immensely, and, for some reason, it meant a good deal to see this fellow look at her with intense eyes. It seemed important, indeed, just to keep that big, powerful body at play.

"I'm sorry that I made you forget that thing," said the girl.

"So'm I," Jerry replied unaffectedly.

"No idea what it was about?"

"It was about you."

"Oh," murmured Patricia. She had been talked to so much by men that she was long past the stage when she glanced away or had to summon a flush when they talked personalities. Instead, she was able to look directly at them, and that always gave her a vast advantage. It always made the men feel that they were inane and that Patricia was formidably clever. But when she looked at Jerry, he seemed too much absorbed in his own reflections to note her. A surmise struck her that he had not consciously intended a compliment—that he was talking as naturally and as simply to her as he would talk to another man—that under the surface of those keen gray eyes and behind that rather ugly face there was simply the heart of a boy. The moment she surmised these things something like a pang went through Patricia. She leaned against the side of the cream-colored horse and she watched Jerry with a wonderful, still look.

"It was about you," he was saying, "and it was important. I'll tell you," he continued, gathering head, "you're harder to talk to than most girls . . . do you know that?"

"No," said Patricia. She even forgot to smile, she was so intent studying him, and she was beginning to wonder why she usually was fencing with words when she talked, to men—even the boys of the island, who she had known ever since they were mere infants.

"Well, you are hard enough," said Jerry. "I never had any trouble chatting with other girls. Nope, not a bit. Any old thing would do to start with."

"Oh," said Patricia.

"But just now," went on Jerry, "I had an idea that you were about to get on your horse and go."

"I am," said Patricia, starting and gathering up the reins. But she did not turn toward the horse.

"I was afraid of that," said Jerry, "so I hunted around for something to talk about. I saw the ocean and the sky and the hills and the sunrise and all those things. You see?"

"Weren't they good enough to talk about?"

"If you're laughing at me inside," Jerry said, "just do it right out loud. I don't mind. In fact, I like it."

She did laugh at that, but not very long. "Go on," said Patricia. For she felt as if she were hearing a story. There was an element of suspense about everything he said.

"What I wanted wasn't any sea or sky stuff," said Jerry. "I wanted to say something about you."

"Oh!"

"Because," explained Jerry, "you seemed more important."

"Oh!" repeated the girl.

"Say," said Jerry, "d'you mind tellin' me what you mean by saying oh, so much?"

"I don't know," murmured Patricia, then added hastily: "I mean, it seems to me that you started the conversation very nicely without that lost remark."

"D'you think so?" said Jerry, and smiled with pleasure. "I'm no end glad of that. I'll tell you something," he said confidentially.

"What?"

"Oh, it isn't important. But I saw you go in swimming from the top of that hill, and, when I came down, I was hoping that I'd be able to talk to you."

"When you came down the hill," said the girl thoughtfully, "were you trying to catch my eye?"

"As a matter of fact," confessed Jerry, "when I came down the hill, my legs got to going so fast that I didn't think about anything but running. D'you ever try it? If it's steep, your legs get a funny feelin' around the knees."

"I'll try it, someday," Patricia said, and smiled. "I'm glad you did talk to me. How old are you?" she asked, apropos of nothing.

"I'm twenty-four," he said, as if it were the most natural question in the world. "How old are you?"

"You look more like eighteen or thirty-five, somehow," said Patricia, thinking aloud. And then: "What did I say?"

"That I looked sort of young," said Jerry. "I don't mind, because I'm growing older every day."

"You have a way of saying things," said the girl, "that makes me want to think them over. I'm still sorry about that lost remark."

"I can't remember what it was about," he answered, studying. "But I can tell you what I meant."

"All right." She kept continually breaking out with eagerness and then checking herself. Perhaps she felt from time to time that she was compromising her dignity.

"It was something to this effect...that it makes me happy to be here talkin' to you." He was looking down at the ground in his brown study as he said this, and she was glad that she did not have to answer. Also, it gave her a chance to look at his face without passing the barrier of his glance. "So happy," said Jerry, looking up quickly, "that I feel sort of grateful."

She put her foot in the stirrup and swung up.

"What's wrong?" asked Jerry, looking behind him.

"The sun," panted Patricia. "It's a way up high."

"Isn't that natural for it to be there?"

"I have to go home. Mister Peyton, why...?"

"Yes? Stand still, fool horse." He caught the bridle close to the bit and took every tremor out of the horse with a twist of his fist. "Go on," said Jerry.

"Why don't you come to call?"

"At your house?" said Jerry.

"Of course."

"I'll tell you," Jerry said, and grinned. "If your dad ever saw me come through the door of your house, he'd start r'aring."

"Do you know Dad?"

"Sure I do."

"Then you knew me all the time!"

"I never saw you before," Jerry replied with equal truth and evasion.

She admitted this with a nod, but now she was frowning as she looked at him; she was concentrating mightily on him. He had been interesting before, but, if her father hated him, he must be important.

"What's Dad got against you?"

"Ask him," said Jerry coldly.

"Something awful?"

"Ask him," repeated Jerry, and set his jaw. She found herself, in an instant, looking into an entirely different face, and it took her breath. Then that metallic light passed away from his eyes. It was a marvelous change.

"Maybe... where... but where did you know him before?"

"Maybe he'll do the explaining," said Jerry calmly.

"Won't you even defend yourself?" cried Patricia.

"Defend myself?" Jerry said, and he smiled. "Why should I? Does your father do your thinkin' for you?"

"Of course not."

"Then you can make up your own mind about me out of what he says. I'll tell you this, though... he thinks I'm a cross between a fool and a rattlesnake."

"But..." said the girl. She stopped, with her lips parted, and it was easy to see that she was troubled.

"I won't keep you," Jerry said suddenly, and dropped his hand from the bridle. "Good bye."

She avoided his outstretched hand. "Why good bye?" she said.

"Your dad won't let you see me again."

"I'm not a baby," said Patricia hotly.

Jerry smiled.

"What do you mean by smiling?" asked the girl.

He shrugged his shoulders, and suddenly she had slipped her hand into his. "*Adieu!*" she called with a delightful accent, and went galloping down the beach.

He stood watching her for a long time, but when, as she reached the point of the beach, she looked back, he had turned and was striding up the hill.

"I wonder what he meant by that smile?" she repeated, and checked her horse to a hand gallop. It was easier to think at that pace.

XX

He did not see *Don* Manuel until they came to the breakfast table together. The cloth was white and crisp, and against it there were some red-hearted melons so sweet and rich that one ate them with lemon. Jerry occupied himself strictly with business, and half of his melon was gone before *Señor* Guzman spoke.

"You had a long chat?"

"Yes," said Jerry.

There was not another interchange of words until breakfast was ended. The Spaniard employed every second of the silence to the full.

"Well," he said afterward, "she is delightful, no?"

"She?" echoed Jerry vaguely.

"No?" insisted the Spaniard.

"I don't know," Jerry replied.

"*H-m-m*," said *Don* Manuel. He added: "It is unfortunate that you don't like her."

"Who said I didn't like her?" Jerry exclaimed. "She's... lovely." He said after a moment: "And the daughter of Langley."

"Well," declared *Don* Manuel after a moment, "you are a happy fellow."

"Do I look happy?" asked Jerry.

"Ah, yes," said *Don* Manuel steadily.

"Well," said Jerry, "I'm sad as the dickens."

"*Tush!* That is too bad. What makes it?"

"I dunno." He looked wistfully at *Don* Manuel. "It's something like seasickness," said Jerry.

"The melon . . . yes." He nodded.

"No," said Jerry, feeling for the place. "It's not my stomach. It's higher. It's an ache." He stood up. "It . . . it makes me feel as if I can't breathe in here."

"We'll step out in the patio."

"*¡Señor!*" called Jerry.

They were in the door; the tall old man looked down at Jerry, and his eyes burned deep in his head.

"Why did you send me down to see that girl?"

"To amuse you, my young friend."

"*Don* Manuel," said the American, "you're a clever devil."

"You are profane," *Don* Manuel remarked dryly, "and yet in a way you honor me."

"She asked me to call," Jerry went on. "I told her that her father would never let me in his house."

"What?" cried *Don* Manuel, and his bony hand dug into the arm of Jerry.

"I told her that he hated me, but she seemed to have an idea that her father might be wrong."

"Kismet," whispered *Señor* Guzman. He snapped his fingers loudly.

"What's that?"

"You were inspired," said the Spaniard.

"She will never come again," Jerry replied, and laid his hand against his throat.

"On the third morning," said *Don* Manuel. "And now, come. We will walk together."

They went again to that highest hilltop that overlooked all the valley and all the coast. Sometimes, from beneath the screen of green and out of the shadows, white spots showed in the sun, the laborers at work on the plantation. "My father, my grandfather, my great-grandfather," said *Señor* Guzman, "owned all this land as far as you can see... and I am the fourth in the line."

Jerry looked at him, and saw at what a price he retained his calm. "I'm sorry," said Jerry.

"For what?" asked *Don* Manuel.

"Because you lost it all."

"It shall be mine again," said *Señor* Guzman.

The American said nothing.

"It is that which keeps me alive," the Spaniard continued. "And the Lord sustains me to regain my heritage. I shall tell you. I am no longer a man... I am a ghost, with a purpose in place of life."

A chilly conviction came to Jerry that he had to do with a madman. That explained the fire in the eyes of the old man, if nothing else.

"It was long ago that I lay on my deathbed," said the Spaniard, "and, while I lay dying, the *Señor* Langley came to me. He had loaned me money... he came to have the debt discharged, and he said that since I was ill he would not burden me with matters of this world... the priest waited even then to give me absolution. *Señor* Langley was thoughtful... he had only some papers that I must sign and then forget about all debts. I had strength to hold a pen and therefore I signed."

"Ah," said Jerry, and his voice rattled in his throat.

"But the good priest," continued the Spaniard, "had heard what Langley said to me. When he came in, he warned me. I looked at my copies of the papers I had signed and saw that of all my estates I now owned only a tiny corner. A weight fell upon me. I lost my senses.

"When I awakened, they were making ready to prepare my body for burial, but I had slept and I had new strength. As I lay there, I knew that I had been spared to get my vengeance. And when after I had waited these many years, in quiet, I saw you, my son, and I knew that He had put a weapon in my hand." He paused, then added: "The heat of the morning begins. Let us go into the house."

Over the valley a mist of the day's heat was beginning to rise. It thickened, and, when Jerry looked back as they went through the trees, all the rich acres behind him and below were as mysteriously clouded as a reflection in a troubled water.

The next morning he went to the hilltop and sat on the rocks, waiting and watching. Nothing came up the beach, and although he remained there until the heat burned his face, there was nothing to be seen but the glare of the sand and the shining water, and some gulls balancing in the northeast wind.

On the morning after that he went again to the hilltop, but there was nothing to be seen, although he waited this time until his eyes ached from peering up and down the sand. He went back to the house, whistling.

"My son," said the Spaniard, "I am happy when I see that you have learned a cheerful patience."

"Are you?" Jerry replied, and smiled with child-like sweetness upon the old man. "Whiskey, *Don* Manuel."

The host clapped his hands twice, and in haste two little Negroes came running. "Whiskey for *Señor* Peyton," said the Spaniard, "and in haste."

All the time that Jerry sat, looking into space, *Don* Manuel walked up and down the patio. He wore his long cloak, as usual, although the day was stifling hot. And when Jerry looked at the cadaverous face, pale as a lichen, he felt that there was truly no good warm blood in the body of the *don*. "A horse," Jerry said, for the hired horse on which he had ridden had been returned long since to the stables by one of *Don* Manuel's men.

Now the Spaniard clapped his hands again. "The bay gelding," the host ordered.

Whereat the man started and needed a second signal and a frown before he withdrew. There was a long pause after that, with

Jerry drinking steadily and alone, until four men came leading a bay horse. They led him as if he were a devil, and in truth Jerry saw a devil in the eye of the gelding. He rose and grinned once at his host. *Don* Manuel bowed, and Jerry vaulted into the saddle.

There followed a terrible five minutes in which the bay became a bolt of red fire, twisting into such odd shapes as only fire can assume, shaking himself from knot to knot. Most of the time he was in the air, and, when he struck the earth, it was only to jar it and spring aloft again. At the end of the five minutes he dropped his tail, put up his head, and cantered softly down the hill. A chorus of silence followed him from the Negroes and from *Don* Manuel, but Jerry rode straight on. The whiskey was sending a genial warmth through his brain and heart, and there was a singular tingling in his fingertips. Jerry recognized that sensation, from old habit, as the signal of an approaching storm.

He rode straight across the island to the town of St. Hilaire and across St. Hilaire to the house of the author. It was nearly noon, but the author was not yet up. Jerry moved two servants from the door and entered.

"Hello!" greeted the author, after being lifted through the air and replaced on his bed. "What the devil?"

"Jeremiah Peyton," said the other.

The consul rubbed his eye open.

"You must have a pretty bad town here," said Jerry.

"Why?" the consul inquired.

"They give you work that keeps you up all night," said Jerry with sympathy. He bound a wet towel around the author's head.

The consul found himself able to see, and therefore leaned out the window and gasped for breath. Presently he stood up again. "Isn't that *Don* Manuel's Lightning that I see down there in the street?"

"No, that's my horse."

"Good heavens," said the consul, clasping his head, which seemed to reel with a thought, "did you ride him here?"

"I asked you about the town," Jerry replied. "How bad is it... to keep you up all night?"

"It isn't so bad," the consul answered, and smiled. "I'm glad to see you riding *Don* Manuel's horse. How are things going?"

"Fair."

"Climbed any fences? Busted through any?"

"No. I'm diggin' under one, though. About this town..."

"It's a quiet place." Again the consul sighed. "But I ran into a bunch of Irishmen last night. I wanted to go home but they wanted to stay out. I didn't feel like hurting their feelings. You know?"

"Sure," Jerry agreed. "How many are there? I like Irishmen."

"Three," said the consul. "They're at the hotel. They have some Irish whiskey, too."

"Only three?" said Jerry sadly. "What do they look like?"

"Their names are Sweeney, Murphy, and Smythe," the consul replied. "They're all over six feet and built right. Why do you ask?"

"You'll hear later," Jerry retorted, and went on his way.

Later he stood at a door of the hotel.

"Are you Sweeney, Murphy, or Smythe?" said Jerry.

"Maybe I'm all three," said the black-headed man at the door.

"Maybe you ain't," Jerry remarked, who lost his sense of grammar when he was happy.

"What the devil is it to you?" asked the black-headed man.

"I've just come from the consul," said Jerry, "and he says you're three fellows... with good whiskey."

The black-headed man did not hear the last part of the sentence. He reached swiftly through the door and dragged Jerry into the room by the nape of the neck. When he was fairly inside: "Now, son, talk sharp. Who told you you were a man?"

"My mamma told me," said Jerry, and smote him upon the root of the nose.

Two large men in pajamas rose on either side of the room out of their beds and watched the fight. Afterward they laid out the black-headed man on the carpet and fell upon Jerry from both sides. The tingle had left the tips of his fingers and was in his shoulders. He hit hard and fast to get it out of him. Finally he sat on a table, looking at his knuckles, which were raw.

"Who told you to come here?" queried the black-headed man, sitting up suddenly on the carpet.

"The author," said Jerry.

"Oh," the black-headed man ejaculated. "I had an idea that he moved in the best circles." He added: "Why don't you have a drink?"

"I was waiting for you to pour it," said Jerry.

"Lift my friends off me," the black-headed man requested, for Jerry had made a heap of the three.

Jerry made a way for the black-headed man.

"Are you feeling better?" asked the Irishman.

"Lots."

"It's this climate," commented the Irishman. "It makes a man nervous in the fists. Here's to you."

XXI

That day was a joyous oblivion, at the end of which Lightning carried Jerry softly and safely out to the house of *Don* Manuel. The *don* came out and superintended while three of his boys carried Jerry into the house and put him to bed. Afterward he sat up all night beside the bed, listening to Jerry snore. At the first coming of gray light he wakened his guest. "It's the third morning," said *Don* Manuel. "Get up."

And Jerry rose like a lark, singing. "She's going to come," he said to *Don* Manuel.

"I know," the Spaniard replied. "I was twenty, once."

Jerry had hardly reached the top of the hill when he saw her come riding around the point of the beach and he ran down to meet her. He stood, panting and holding her hand, while he said: "It's taken three days to get you back, but it's worth the wait."

Then he saw that she was not in a bathing suit, but was dressed formally for riding, with shining leather boots and trousers and a derby hat. There was only one touch of color, and that was a crimson blossom at her waist.

"You were seen in Saint Hilaire yesterday," said the girl coldly.

"It's a fine little town, isn't it?"

"I suppose what's left of it is," she observed.

"I was killing time until you came again," explained Jerry.

"*H-m-m*," said Patricia, but his smile was irresistible.

"Why aren't you going to swim this morning?" asked Jerry.

"Because I have a sore foot," answered Patricia gloomily. She stared accusingly at him. "I cut it on a piece of coral at the other beach yesterday."

"Yep. None of the other beaches are any good."

She remembered something and said, flushing: "Were you so sure I'd come back?"

"I knew you couldn't stand the mud and the coral rocks," said Jerry. "Won't you get off your horse?"

"I have to go right on," said Patricia.

"We could walk the horse the way you're going. It would rest him... besides, he looks sort of winded."

She glanced sharply at him, but he was looking only at the horse. "All right," said Patricia, and got down from the saddle. First she scanned all the hilltops swiftly.

"Are they following you?" asked Jerry.

"Why?"

"To find out if you see me."

"Do you think I've come out this morning just to see you?"

"Sure," said Jerry. "Take my arm."

The sand was deep, and she took his arm, but it was only to steady herself until she could find the right thing to say. "I think you'd better leave Saint Hilaire," she said.

"I'm going to," Jerry replied.

"Aren't you happy here?" asked Patricia suddenly, unreasonably.

"Are you?" asked Jerry.

"Why do you say that?"

"You have big shadows under your eyes. You haven't been sleeping."

"Insomnia is an old trouble of mine," answered the girl, watching him. She sighed when he did not look back.

"I'm glad your foot doesn't bother you in the sand," said Jerry.

"There's a bandage on it," Patricia said instantly.

"Let's stop walking."

"Why?" But she paused with him.

"I'll tell you. The crunching of the sand starts breaking in on what I think."

"They must be light thoughts," the girl commented idly.

"They're still thoughts," said Jerry, lowering his voice.

"Go on," Patricia urged.

"It's not a story I'm telling," Jerry replied, frowning. He began to look straight into her eyes.

"I have to go home," said Patricia suddenly.

"You don't."

"How do you know?"

"The sun isn't up."

Patricia swallowed. "You can't dictate, you know," she said.

"I'm studying up, though," answered Jerry.

"What d'you mean?"

"Why are you afraid?" asked Jerry in return.

"I'm not afraid."

"You look pretty white."

All at once she was leaning back against the shoulders of the cream-colored horse, and he turned his head and looked at her with his big, bright eyes. "I'm unhappy," said Patricia, with her gloved hand at her breast.

It was a glove of some rough, soft leather. At the wrist it wrinkled into many folds, and it was loose over the hand. It fascinated

Jerry. He pored over it with a sort of sad delight. For one thing, it was a deep yellow, and the color seemed to him pleasant next to the crimson blossom.

"Is it connected up with me?" asked Jerry.

"I don't know," said Patricia.

"Are you kind of hollow inside?" inquired Jerry.

"Yes. How do you know?"

"Is it something like seasickness?"

"Yes, but worse... it... it stays with me."

"I know," said Jerry.

"What'll I do?"

"I tried whiskey. I don't know what you'll do." He said more thoughtfully than ever: "I feel the same way. I'll tell you something. I thought that when I saw you again, I'd be a lot better right away. But I'm worse."

"I thought it was this beach," said Patricia. "I'm so used to seeing the sunrise here."

"But it isn't?"

"It isn't," said Patricia.

They stood close, looking miserably at each other.

"I'm never to see you again," said Patricia.

"That's your dad's work."

"He'll send me away from Saint Hilaire if he ever finds out that I saw you again."

"Doesn't like me, does he?"

She said slowly: "I think he's afraid of you. He was never afraid of any other man I ever heard of."

"Well, if you leave, I'll leave, too."

"Would you follow me?"

"Of course."

"It wouldn't do any good. If you followed me, Dad would do you harm."

"Does he tell you why he hates me?"

"He says I couldn't understand."

There was another silence. A gull screamed far away, and the wind blew the sound lazily down to them.

"Will you come out here once in a while?" said Jerry.

"If I can. Suppose Dad has seen me here."

"But you'll come?"

"Yes."

"Shake on that." He took her gloved hand. At the touch, something leaped from his heart to his brain and cast a mist across his eyes. Vaguely he saw that her eyes were wide and that her lips were parted.

"It's a bargain now," said Jerry.

"Of course."

"You have to come, you see."

"I'll come. The sun is coming up, Jerry."

"Good bye." He helped her into the saddle. "Wait a minute," said Jerry.

"Why?"

"Keep on looking out to sea. I'll tell you later."

She smiled faintly, and looked out to sea.

"All right," said Jerry. "You can go now."

"What was it? Why did you make me do that?"

"I saw the sunrise hit your face. It made you look pretty fine."

"Oh, Jerry!"

"What's the matter?"

"Good bye."

He stood back, dazed, and saw her whip the cream-colored horse. He switched his tail in protest, and then sprang away down the beach.

Jerry watched her out of sight, and then went up the hillside more moodily than ever.

"Well?" asked the Spaniard, on the hilltop.

"Were you here all the time?"

"Of course, my son."

"Listen to me, pardner. In your religion you go to a priest once in a while and get a lot of things off your chest, don't you?"

"Of course, there is the confession."

"*H-m-m*," said Jerry. "And you don't particularly encourage other gents to hang around at that time?"

"There must be no third man there, of course."

"Well, keep away from this beach 'round about sunrise, *Don* Manuel, will you?"

"Ah," said *Señor* Guzman.

XXII

A messenger came to the house of *Don* Manuel that day before noon and brought a little envelope addressed in a feminine small hand to Mr. Jeremiah Peyton. Jerry opened it and read as follows:

My Dear Mr. Peyton:

You will be delighted to learn that I have at last come to agree with your viewpoint, and, if you will, I shall meet you on the beach, below the point which bounds the beach of Don Manuel, this evening after moonrise. There is a full moon, and the light should be pleasant, since we have no reading to do.

James P. Langley

All the letters were formed with a very fine line, and drawn out with the most exquisite precision. One felt a certain mechanical perfection, looking at this letter. It was rather like a printed form. Jerry held it close to his eyes, and still he could not see a waver or a scratch.

"A steady hand," said Jerry, and went to his room.

He remained there all day. He felt that he must bring his gun to the point of absolute perfection, and therefore he took it completely apart, oiled and cleaned it, and oiled it again with so delicate a film that it left the tip of the finger clean when one touched the mechanism. The trigger had grown stiff, and he lightened the pull. Then he went through his regular routine of exercise—it had been three days since he had performed, and he found himself stale and rusty. It was not until the nerves along his arm would jump like a twist of lightning that he was content.

All the time *Don* Manuel was walking up and down upon the hilltop, outside the window, a gaunt and ominous form.

Later on, Jerry went out and joined him. They did not speak a word for an hour, but each read the mind of the other. Jerry had a very small dinner, for, as Hank Peyton used to say: "A full stomach makes a slow hand." And when there was a pale semicircle of light over the eastern sea, Jerry said good bye to his host and went down from the hill to the beach.

He was in time, on rounding the point of the beach, to see a stream of silver come from the east across the ocean, which was very still. That light, at the same instant, picked a figure out of the gloom in front of Jerry, made the beach all white, and set the shadow of the figure walking over the white sand; a solitary gull wavered low down against the sky.

"You are in perfect accord with me," said the dispassionate voice of Langley.

"Thanks," said Jerry.

The other paused at a distance of some ten paces. "Am I too close?"

"Makes no difference to me," said Jerry cheerfully. "Close or far off."

"Before we begin," Langley said courteously, "I wish to compliment you on your scheme. It worked beautifully, as you see." Jerry saw the gleam of the white teeth beneath the shadow of the mustache. "The girl is under twenty and she has less sense than I thought."

"Are you done talking about her?" asked Jerry coldly.

"Certainly."

"Begin."

"Suppose," said Langley, "that in order to get a perfectly even start..."

"By all means," Jerry replied.

"We stand with our arms folded, then. We wait, say, for the next scream of the gull, and then both go for our guns. Is that satisfactory?"

"Excellent."

They stood rigid, their arms crossed, their shadows lying long and stiff on the white beach. Once a bird called from the inland, but neither of them stirred. Then came the cry of the gull. The bird had changed its course, and, shooting straight over toward the land, it uttered a clear cry, hoarse as a sea wind. And the shadows on the beach leaped into action.

The arm of Langley shot straight out, for his gun had been worn under his coat, and in folding his arms he had simply settled his fingers about the butt. He flung his arm out, and the revolver exploded, but in the surety of the first shot, or because his arm swung too wide with its impetus, the bullet missed—it merely shaved through the coat of Jerry beneath the armpit as his right arm darted down and came up again, with a flash of metal. Before the finger of Langley could press his trigger the second time, the gun spoke in the hand of Jerry. There was a loud clang as it struck metal, then a brief arch of light as the revolver was torn from the hand of the older man and flung away. He leaped after it with a moan of anxiety, but, when he scooped it up, he saw Jerry standing with his own weapon hanging at his side.

"I'm sorry I didn't get you the first time," Jerry said calmly. "I can't shoot again."

Langley came to him, walking like a cat, so soft and so light.

"I ought to blow your head off while you stand there like a fool," he said. "But I'll give you another chance. The next call of the gull is the signal."

"The gull's gone," said Jerry. "Besides, this is the end of it."

"Are you yellow?" Langley asked with a curse.

"It's out of our hands," Jerry replied solemnly. "Don't you see, Langley? You miss me. You play a dirty trick, getting your gun in your hand before the signal comes... even then you miss me, and I gather it's about the first time in your life that you've done such poor work. I sent my slug right down the alley and... it hits your gun. It knocks it out of your hand without even breaking the skin. Can you understand that?"

"I understand that you're backing down," the other replied.

Jerry could see the heavy mustache bristling. "You aren't cut out to be my meat," he said calmly. "You aren't my size, pardner."

Langley stood without answer. His anger was making him pant.

"You're fat in the arm and fat in the head," went on Jerry, "and you can't stand up to me. Look me in the eye, Langley, and admit it."

"We stay here," said the other, "till one of us is drilled."

"Go home, Langley. I can't pull a gun on you again."

The older man began to work at his throat. He seemed to be stifling. "I don't know why I don't shoot you without argument," he said.

"You're a good deal of a dog," Jerry remarked calmly, "but you can't quite do that. Worse luck for you, Langley."

"By heaven," said Langley, "you refuse to fight, then?"

"I was set for the draw," said Jerry. "I'd have smiled if I drilled you the first shot, partner... if I pulled my gun again, I'd be shooting her father. Is that straight in your head? I'd be murdering her father because I know you haven't a chance."

"Is it possible?" cried Langley. "My heavens, am I listening to this and doing nothing."

"I can't fight you," said Jerry, "so you've got a right over me. I'll give you my word not to see Patricia again."

"Your word?" said Langley eagerly. "Jerry, there's a touch of sound, clean sense in you."

"Keep away," said Jerry. "Stand off from me. I'll not see her until I've gotten rid of your objections. Good night."

"Nothing but a bullet will get rid of them!" called Langley.

Don Manuel saw him come in, and, when Jerry went by, the Spaniard shrugged his shoulders and sat down again, as one prepared for a long wait. But Jerry went to his room and wrote to Sheriff Edward Sturgis, at Sloan.

Dear Ed:

I'm here at the other end of the world, pretty near, and I suppose you're glad to have me here. I don't know how long I'll stick here. I'm at the end of a trail, you see, but a new one may begin most any day.

I'm writing this to ask a favor of you. You know most of the old boys who used to make Sloan the center for their celebrating.

In those times did you ever hear of a fellow named J.P. Langley, middle-sized, with black hair and eyes? He talks like the East, but he walks like a Westerner, and he handles a gun like an old-timer. I've an idea that, if you look back into your mind, you might unearth a pretty sizable record for him, and, if you do, I could use it.

The point is, he's grown proud lately, and somebody ought to remind him of his past. And I can tell by his eye that he has one.

He's fixed well down here. He has millions, they say, and his dugout looks like it. Also, he has a daughter.

Well, good bye, Ed. Here's wishing you better luck than you ever wished me.

And say, Ed, don't you owe me a favor because I lifted myself and a lot of trouble out of your county?

Yours,

Jeremiah Peyton

XXIII

The thing that bothered Jerry more than anything else during the next ten days, or so, was really the conduct of *Don* Manuel. He knew without a word being spoken about it, that Jerry had met Langley; he also knew that neither of them had been killed in that meeting, and yet *Señor* Guzman remained perfectly equable. He protested with something close to tears when Jerry declared his intention of leaving the house and going to the hotel in St. Hilaire, so Jerry stayed on. He was left almost entirely to his own devices. In the silent household of *Don* Manuel he came and went when he pleased, and the servants obeyed him with as much eagerness as they obeyed their master. And Jerry noted this singular fact: that no servant in the Guzman household accepted gifts. He used to think of this, and then remember the quarters he had tossed to the men at Langley's place. Indeed, if he had been a nervous wreck seeking absolute retirement, *Don* Manuel would have been giving him a perfect vacation and rest cure, but Jerry represented some hundred and eighty or ninety pounds of iron hard muscle without a nerve in it, and the inactivity ate into him day by day.

For seven mornings he had risen and gone to the hilltop from which he could look down, before sunrise, on the beach. And for four mornings she came regularly before sunrise and stayed there until the day was well begun. But Jerry never went down to her. By the very fact that she was allowed to come out in the morning he knew, with a melancholy pleasure, that her father was trusting in his own promise not to see the girl. But on the fifth, sixth, and seventh mornings she did not come at all, and finally Jerry gave up his trips.

It was ten days after the letter that Sheriff Edward Sturgis arrived. He came in as much of a hurry as if he had ridden barely five miles and must turn back as soon as his horse was breathed. He, at least, had made no change in costume to suit the change in climate. He had his ancient felt hat, his shapeless trousers, his remarkable sack of a coat, always unbuttoned, just as he had worn them in Sloan. And when Jerry saw the sheriff standing in the entrance to the patio, he was swept directly back to the little town. He had connected Edward Sturgis with the law so long that he immediately forgot all about the letter. Indeed, it seemed quite impossible that the sheriff should have come in answer to any written appeal. So he said as he took the stubby hand of Sturgis: "What's the matter, Ed? Do they want me back in Sloan?"

"Nothin' particular," said the sheriff, and his bright little eyes surveyed every inch of Jerry in a split-second glance. "I ain't heard any special mournin' because you're away, Jerry."

The latter smiled faintly. "Come in and sit yourself down, Ed. I'm some glad to see you." He led the way to one of the tables in the patio. At his direction, cold drinks and strong drinks were brought, while the sheriff sat back and fanned himself with his hat and looked admiringly about on the coolness and upon Jerry.

"Kind of to home here, ain't you?" he commented.

"Old Spaniard runs this dump," said Jerry, who had forgotten to wonder at his own relations with the *don*. "He's a pal of mine. Sort of took me in when I blew down into these parts. But come out with it, Ed. What do you want me for?"

"I don't want you," said the sheriff gently. He finished a drink, and continued to look about him. "This is a rum place, Jerry."

"But if you don't want me, who does?" asked Jerry.

"Durned if I know," replied the sheriff frankly. "I don't know of anybody that hankers after you, particular. Why?"

"You haven't come here to take me back?" Jerry inquired, sitting back in his chair with a sigh of relief.

"Certainly not." The sheriff grinned. "Nothin' pleases me more than to have you do your plantin' of dead men outside my hang-out. Well, I'm glad you're fixed comfortable." He continued to fan himself, always looking about him. He was one of those men who discover interesting details no matter where they may be. And his shoulders were so humped with riding a horse and sitting at a desk that when he looked around he had to move his head in hitches, so to speak.

"Not bad," said Jerry, still looking narrowly at the sheriff. "I hope you're not trying to put something over on me, Ed."

"What makes you ask that?"

"I dunno," said Jerry. He leaned back in his chair again, with one hand behind his head—but his right hand was always free, always unemployed with the fingertips continually tapping lightly on something. No matter in how perfect a state of quiescence he might be, that right hand remained alive, as though it were controlled by a separate intelligence. All of this the sheriff noted.

"You're always set for something, ain't you, Jerry?"

"That's where you're all wrong," said Jerry. "I'm never set . . . I'm just sort of expecting."

"Oh, all right," Sturgis said, and grinned. "Put it that way, then."

"I'm glad you understand," Jerry said. "This is pretty peaceful country, but I believe in goin' prepared for war."

"Get that out of your head, Jerry. I'm not down here gunnin' for you. I'm pretty smooth, maybe, but I don't drink with a man I want to get."

"I know that, Ed. But tell me straight, hasn't your being down here got . . . ?"

"Got something to do with you? Well, maybe it has. Maybe it hasn't."

"Take your time," said Jerry. "I hate to rush a man. Have another drink. You weren't interested in what I wrote about Langley, were you?"

"I seen what you said about him."

"Know him?"

"I dunno. What's he look like? Oh, I remember you told me what he was like. Well, I'd like to look him over."

"I can't take you over to see him, Ed. Him and me, we had a little falling out. In a word, he's a skunk, Ed."

"You don't say," murmured the sheriff conversationally. He settled himself to hear a story.

"He must have millions," said Jerry. "But he made a flying trip up to Chambers City on some queer sort of business, and on the way he took it into his head that he wanted The Voice of La Paloma. Somebody must have told him about it while he was going through. Or else he was an old-timer in those parts and knew all about it already. Anyway, he stuck me up for it when I was helpless with my wrists all bunged up. I took his trail... and here I am. But the way he rode that country up home made me think he was an old-timer there... so I wrote to you to see if you knew his record."

"Have you met up with him?"

"Twice."

"And you're both still healthy... up and around?"

Jerry flushed.

"You must be kind of out of practice, Jerry."

"The first time he wouldn't pull his gun, Ed. The second time... well, I hit his gun with my slug the first shot and then..."

"Well...?"

"I dunno. We just sort of parted, Ed."

"Is he good?"

"Fastest I ever saw. But he tried a crooked stunt. It spoiled his aim. That's why I'm here chinning with you."

"For a boy," said Sturgis, "you're a cool kid. I sort of like you, Jerry. What about this girl?"

The question came so suddenly that Jerry winced. "What girl?" he said.

"The one you talked about in your letter."

"What did I say in the letter?" inquired Jerry, dazed.

"That you were out of your head about Langley's daughter."

"Did I say that? I thought...well, I can't answer you, Ed."

"The girl spoiled your play with Langley, is that it?" asked the sheriff.

"How d'you mean?"

"What's she like?" asked the sheriff suddenly.

"You mean what does she look like?"

"Yep."

Jerry raised his head and studied the adobe wall. His restless right hand was still, and this the sheriff noted. "Suppose," said Jerry, "that you've been to a party and your head is hot, and your mouth full of ashes...well, you step out into the morning and a cool wind hits your face...."

"Is she like that?" the sheriff inquired.

But Jerry was still absent-mindedly studying the wall. "Suppose you've been riding the desert," he went on slowly, "and you drop out of the mountains into a valley full of fruit trees and a spring...and you ride along with the blossoms dropping around you...and the birds fighting in the tops of the trees and..."

"Is she like that?" asked the sheriff with increasing emphasis.

"Suppose," said Jerry, "that you've been playing poker, and the luck's against you, and you step out into the night and look up and see how still the sky is with all the stars close down...."

"Oh, Lord!" the sheriff exclaimed without heat.

"What's the matter?" said Jerry, looking dazed again.

"Do you see much of her?"

"Her father's against her seeing me, you know."

"So...?"

"She came down for a while where we used to meet. But I couldn't fight it out with the old boy...he's her father. Put a mist over his eyes and they're about the same as her eyes, see?"

"*H-m-m*," said the sheriff.

"I couldn't fight it out with him, so I didn't have any right to go sneaking around seeing his daughter. So I promised him that I wouldn't talk to her any more."

The sheriff started violently. Jerry looked at him in surprise, but the sheriff was only crossing his legs, which was a considerable feat, owing to the size of his stomach and the shortness of the legs.

"Well, Ed, the odds were sort of against me. I think he's a crook. But I have no proof. I want to be able to go around and talk straight to him. I want to be able to say... 'I haven't a cent and I've been a rough one, but I've been clean. You've got a fortune, but you're crooked. What you say about your daughter doesn't make the slightest difference to me."

"I follow you," said the sheriff. He added with his characteristic suddenness: "Does the girl miss you, Jerry?"

"I don't know, Ed."

"She came down to your meeting place even after you'd stopped going there?"

"That doesn't mean anything. She likes to see the sunrise there."

"*H-m-m*," said the sheriff. "Well, I don't suppose you could introduce me to this Langley?"

"Not without a troop of cavalry, Ed."

"I'm going out to look him over."

"I'll show you his house."

"You needn't mind. I located that before I came to see you."

"Come back here for the night, Ed. *Don* Manuel will be glad to see you. Particularly if you know anything about Langley's past. He's interested, too."

"Come back here?" echoed the sheriff vaguely. "Oh, yes. Sure. Good bye, Jerry."

XXIV

Langley was a strong believer in efficiency, and he knew that efficiency means a concentration of the executive authority in anything from a nation to a household. And therefore, shortly after their honeymoon ended, when his wife began a sentence with—"I think..."—he promptly answered: "My dear, you're much too nice to waste your pleasantness thinking. Hereafter I'll do your thinking for you." Mrs. Langley was one of those calm-eyed women who know how to look the truth in the face and smile. She saw her husband for the first time, really, but she smiled when she heard him say this. After that she was never known to rebel against fate, and the word of Langley was fate in his household. Only of late, as Patricia grew into womanhood, there had been vague stirrings of revolt behind the calm eyes of his wife, and on this day the storm broke suddenly and without warning on the head of the rich man. She had placed herself between him and the door and lifted her head and told him that whether he willed it or not, her daughter was to be happy.

"And will you tell me," Langley replied, "what I'm grinding my heart out for if it isn't her happiness?"

"She's been in her room...and hardly out of it...for forty-eight hours," said Mrs. Langley.

"She's sick?" Langley asked, changing color.

"The doctor told you that."

"Fever," said Langley. "Nothing unusual at this season."

"The doctor is a fool." It was a strong word for her. It made even J.P. Langley stop—mentally—and look at her again. He had known long ago that she had little tenderness for him, but he had been content with knowing that he controlled her. Also, she was decorative and knew how to make his guests happy; so that it came to him with a distinct shock, as he looked at her this evening, and discovered that she was very close to hating him. "The doctor is a fool," repeated his wife, as though she feared he had not heard.

"He is the best in Saint Hilaire."

"She has a fever," said Mrs. Langley, "but it's a fever of longing, James." She made a little gesture with her palm up, but Langley was thinking so hard and fast that he did not notice. It was a gross error, for when her hand fell back to her side, it gathered into what was almost a fist. "She's in love," she added coldly.

"Give her quinine just the same," said Langley. "Give her quinine and rest. That'll do the work."

"Do you really intend to make her marry who you wish?" asked Mrs. Langley calmly.

"Of course I do. Good heavens, Mary, are you surprised by that?"

"And yet," she pursued, more to herself than to him, "she's more your child than she is mine." She added: "I think you're breaking her heart, James."

"Not in this century." Langley chuckled. "They may be strained, but they don't break. It's out of date."

"Ah," said his wife, and smiled to herself.

It was growing to be a habit of hers, this inward smile, and it always maddened Langley. He stood rubbing his mustache, and smiling in jerks. "There's one trouble with you, my dear," he said. "Ever since the first baby died."

"James!" she cried faintly.

"I've got to say it," he persisted. "Ever since that, you've an idea that every man is a baby. By heavens, I think you're fond of this infernal snake in the grass without ever having seen him."

"I like what Patricia tells me about him. He has an honest way of talking."

"What makes you think that?"

"Because it's just a little foolish. She's told me all the silly things he's said at least ten times over. She sees nothing funny in them, James."

"This ends it," he said angrily. "I forbid you to talk to her about him, Mary."

"It's impossible for me to obey you," his wife replied.

He tried to speak, but could not. "Do you mean that?" he managed to say at last.

"Yes."

He jerked open the door and fled, for he was in a panic, and the thing he feared was himself. As he went downstairs, every servant he passed was a blow. He hated their faces, and, to escape them, he fled into the night, down the road, and twisted off onto a bypath until he stood in a place where the evening light filtered softly and coolly about him. There he stood still, and tried to arrange his thoughts.

"Pat!" called a voice. And the sheriff stepped out. "You're losing the old quick eye," the sheriff said. "I made as much noise as a herd of yearlings in stubble, but you never heard me."

"What in the name of the devil are you doing here?"

"I've come down to see the other end of the joke I played on you in Sloan. Seems to have worked out, all right."

"I'll send your man back to you wrapped up in wood before he's a month older," Langley retorted. "I'd have done it long ago, but he refused to fight. Yellow."

"Mostly," said the sheriff, "you lie well. But now you're mad. Going back to that joke..."

"Confound you, Sturgis."

"Now, now," said the sheriff soothingly. "Ain't he a rough talker! I guess Jerry has sort of irritated you, Pat."

"I'll give you two minutes to talk sense and get out."

"That's plenty. I'll tell you, Pat. When I sicced Jerry onto you in Sloan, I sort of thought I was usin' one useless gent to wipe out another. Then I got a letter that made me think maybe I was wastin' a man's life to kill a snake. You bein' the snake. Back in Sloan I thought Jerry was jest a public danger. Now I c'n see he's just young. And all he needed was somethin' to tie to. Can you beat the bad luck that makes him tie to your daughter?"

"Is that bug in your fool head, too?"

"You ain't even got a sense of humor left, have you, Pat?" said the sheriff, wondering. "Funny thing, I figure. When a man's crooked it's a sort of cancer. It starts with a little thing and eats all the good right out of him."

"I can't listen to your chatter any more, Sturgis. Finish and get off the place. I can't waste time on you here."

"So," went on the sheriff calmly, "I figured it this way... I'll go down and see what the boy amounts to now. And I come and what d'you think? Jerry's in love with your kid. Well, Pat, nothin' but a man-size man can be in love with a girl the way he is with her. Now, it wouldn't be right to throw him away to kill a skunk. No, it wouldn't. I seen that. But look at me. You busted me up twenty years ago. I been just driftin' along, mostly no good. And now I see it's my job."

"Ah," said Langley, "I begin to understand. You've come and brought your gun, eh? You really think you can beat me to the draw, Ed?" He smiled almost in friendship on the sheriff.

"No," Sturgis went on. "I know you're faster and straighter. But always before I been figurin' on gettin' in the first shot and then comin' away clean of hurt. Now I see that my one chance to get you, Pat, is to soak up about three of your slugs while I plant one in your innards. Is that straight?"

"So you're going to clean up, Ed?"

"Sure am, Pat."

"When I had that affair with your girl twenty years ago I had an idea that it would end this way... I'd hate to wipe you off the slate. Yet in a way, Ed, I hate to do it, because..."

He had extended his left hand as he spoke, and now he raised his right hand. It came past his waistline carrying a revolver, and the explosion tore off the end of his last word. Flinching from that glint of metal, the sheriff had turned, drawing his own gun. The slug struck him across the chest and the weight of it toppled him to the ground. He would have fallen prone, helpless, had he not struck a tree trunk as he fell, and he slid in a bunch to the ground. He began raising his revolver.

As for Langley, he had paused to observe the effect of his shot, and now he drove in another. It was meant for the forehead of the sheriff, but at that moment he raised his head back with a jerk, and the bullet crashed down through his breast. It sent a quiver through the sheriff, as though he shook with cold. His face seemed already dead, and his mouth was hanging wide, but the muzzle of his revolver, tilted and pointed up, and, as Langley fired for the third time, the sheriff's gun exploded, and the bullet struck Langley squarely between the eyes.

Afterward the sheriff lived long enough to crawl over to the fallen body.

"A good-lookin' man like him," said the sheriff, "had ought to make a good-lookin' stiff."

So he took the arms of Langley and folded them across his breast. And he closed the eyelids, and the open, horrified mouth.

"Now," said the sheriff, "I'll tell a man that was worth doin'. It makes him a picture."

He put his own back against the tree. Presently he felt his right hand growing cold, and, looking down, he saw the revolver that he had never dropped from his fingers.

"Well, well," said the sheriff, "The Voice of La Paloma come in for the last word, after all."

XXV

It was a long time after this.

The United States consul of St. Hilaire sat on the front porch and three Irishmen sat around him. They had been drinking for some time, and there was still liquor before them. They had passed the stage of hilarity; they had reached the stage of solemnity. The consul had just finished a story and he was telling them about it.

"You see that boat?" he said.

A long, low, graceful white launch of comfortable width was sliding up the bay. There happened to be no other boats in the bay except fishing smacks, tilting this way and that as they tacked to port. The wind was coming out from the land, and yet it allowed the murmur of the white boat's engine to come distinctly to the house of the consul.

"That, in fact," said the consul, "is him now."

The three Irishmen did three things. After standing up, one of them raised his hand to his nose, another touched an eye, the third caressed the angle of his jaw. They looked and looked until the yacht was far down the bay.

"That was Jerry standing on the poop," they said in one voice. "And was that his wife?"

"Sure."

"Well, then," said the three Irishmen, and sighed, "Patricia's gone."

"It ought to be a good yarn," they added, turning to the consul.

"It's a good story," he admitted, "but there's a missing link. I still don't know whether he climbed the fence or busted it or mined it."

The three Irishmen made each their peculiar gestures.

"He probably used all the ways," they said. "He could do three things at once fairly well."

THE END

About the Author

Max Brand is the best-known pen name of Frederick Faust, creator of Dr. Kildare, Destry, and many other fictional characters popular with readers and viewers worldwide. Faust wrote for a variety of audiences in many genres. His enormous output, totaling approximately thirty million words or the equivalent of five hundred thirty ordinary books, covered nearly every field: crime, fantasy, historical romance, espionage, Westerns, science fiction, adventure, animal stories, love, war, and fashionable society, big business and big medicine. Eighty motion pictures have been based on his work along with many radio and television programs. For good measure he also published four volumes of poetry. Perhaps no other author has reached more people in more different ways.

Born in Seattle in 1892, orphaned early, Faust grew up in the rural San Joaquin Valley of California. At Berkeley he became a student rebel and one-man literary movement, contributing prodigiously to all campus publications. Denied a degree because of unconventional conduct, he embarked on a series of adventures culminating in New York City where, after a period of near starvation, he received simultaneous recognition as a serious poet and successful author of fiction. Later, he traveled widely, making his home in New York, then in Florence, and finally in Los Angeles.

Once the United States entered the Second World War, Faust abandoned his lucrative writing career and his work as a screenwriter to serve as a war correspondent with the infantry in Italy, despite his fifty-one years and a bad heart. He was killed during a night attack on a hilltop village held by the German army. New books based on magazine serials or unpublished manuscripts or restored versions continue to appear so that, alive or dead, he has averaged a new book every four months for seventy-five years. Beyond this, some work by him is newly reprinted every week of every year in one or another format somewhere in the world. A great deal more about this author and his work can be found in *The Max Brand Companion* (Greenwood Press, 1997) edited by Jon Tuska and Vicki Piekarski. His website is www.MaxBrandOnline.com.